# Dreams

Brittany Glynn

Published by
Cool Titles
439 N. Canon Dr., Suite 200
Beverly Hills, CA 90210
www.cooltitles.com

The Library of Congress Cataloging-in-Publication Data Applied For

Brittany Glynn—
Dreams

p. cm
ISBN 978-1935270034
1. Romance 2. Fiction 3. Christian Fiction I. Title
2010



Printed in the United States of America

1 3 5 7 9 10 8 6 4 2

Book editing and design by Lisa Wysocky, White Horse Enterprises, Inc.

For interviews or information regarding special discounts for bulk purchases,
please contact us at
cindy@cooltitles.com

Distribution to the Trade: Pathway, Book Service,
www.pathwaybook.com, pbs@pathwaybook.com, 1-800-345-6665

## Dedication

To my mom and dad who believed in me at the age of nineteen when I left on a one-way ticket to write this story. And to Kelly, Kristen, Cowboy Church, and the entire community who made Colorado Springs a home to me. This book would not be what it is today without you.

## Dreams

*Human reason says she's crazy—*
*the voice she hears tells otherwise.*

# Prologue

*In the stillness of the moonlit night, a shadow slowly traveled across the impoverished land. Its slender, frail figure passed each shack, never once hesitating until he reached his target.*

*As he drifted by each dwelling, his heart ached from the thought of the inhabitants, most dying from disease and starvation. Oh, why could he not help them all? Some things he would never understand. His flesh desired food and water and shook from fatigue—but a powerful presence pushed him onward.*

*Soon his search would end. He could only pray the one he found would choose the calling he would bestow.*

*He stopped at a hut that looked like all the others, but he knew this was it.*

*Pushing back the covering over the entry, he moved into the cramped space. "Do not fear; the Lord God has sent me here at this hour."*

*His wooden cane creaked as he limped toward a dim light flickering in the corner.*

*"It is too late, she's already dead." Voice shaking, a woman lifted her candle over a lifeless body.*

*"It is not she whom I have come for." He spoke softly.*

*The woman gasped, "But if not her, who?"*

*He turned to the tight, half-lit corner as a baby's sharp cry pierced the silence. The woman went to the infant's side, and the soft candlelight cast shadows over a small bundle on the dirt floor.*

*"It is* she *for whom I have made my journey." Setting aside his cane, he gently picked up the tiny infant. As he did, her cries ceased.*

*"It was her destiny to be born here. She has been brought to Earth to make a difference. I have done all I can, and now this little one will do more. She will do more than I ever could, and God's anointing will stay with her, all the days of her life."*

*"I recognize you now." The lady's eyes grew big and her bottom lip trembled. "You are the prophet who was said to have died."*

*He looked at her tenderly. "I have been kept alive for this moment."*

*Without wasting any more time he pulled from his pocket the only belonging he had carried on his journey, a small vessel of oil. Using two fingers, he placed a drop on the baby's forehead, and then lifted her, blessed her.*

*This child would do great and mighty works in her lifetime. She would heal the sick and find the lost. "Oh child of God, they have been searching all my lifetime, and will continue to search through yours. But you, oh daughter of God, will help them see the truth."*

*The old man looked at the baby one more time, knowing it would be the last, and placed a kiss on her forehead. "The calling on her life is more powerful."*

*Handing her back to the woman, he limped out of the hut where his trembling legs gave out beneath him. His body fell to the cold earth; his eyes would see no more.*

# Chapter One

ALL THE YOUNG WOMAN COULD HEAR was the heavy thumping of her heart. The smell of death surrounded her, which was odd because she'd never smelled death before.

Eyes pressed shut; Emerald McGintay took slow, deep breaths, counting to six to inhale, then six to exhale. But it was no use; her heartbeat drowned out her thoughts.

"Describe to me what you see."

*I see a priest, and a hut.*

Her private darkness gave way to Dr. Sidney Coffman, who relaxed in his Italian leather chair. In his mid thirties, his navy blue Ralph Lauren suit was pressed perfectly, as always. His posture held confidence while his intimidating eyes analyzed her.

Emerald looked at the Rolex watch her father had given him, one more indication that Sidney always got what he wanted, whether it was from a patient or Daddy. Her stomach knotted. She hated the way he always dug for information, as if she were a case study he needed to prove an academic point.

"Emerald, if you don't talk to me, I can't help you." The psychiatrist knew she was holding back. His voice sounded tired, but she knew the man was nowhere near ready to admit defeat.

"I'm trying," she whispered, frustrated that once again tears threatened to flow.

Sidney crossed his legs. "Relax, Emerald. Take a few deep breaths, and try again."

Easy for him to say. He wasn't opening his mind to someone who was looking for reasons to label him insane. Once again she took a deep breath, but nothing could produce the hypnosis Sidney wanted. She couldn't relax, knowing it would unearth the dreams she had worked so hard to bury.

"It's all right, Emerald. We can call it quits for today." Sidney's voice softened, but he had that look in his eye. Perhaps no one else ever caught it, but she saw the irritation that simmered just below the surface.

Her legs trembling, she stood and hurried to the door. She needed to escape his office.

She needed to escape her whole life.

Once she got outside, her father's driver would escort her to the Mercedes for safe transport home. She could demand a stop along the way, but visiting the mall or a coffee shop would not change a thing. The feeling of entrapment would stay.

Sidney's voice followed her from the room. "Emerald, remember you have a choice. You can either let these dreams consume you and take over your life, or you can take control."

∞

The black Mercedes drove through the iron gates and up the drive lined with Leland cypresses. Emerald leaned her face against the rear passenger window as the imposing brick estate came into view. Some found her home dark and gloomy but no one could argue it was an exquisite historical mansion. Millions of dollars had gone into its transformation. As much mystery as the outside hinted to new visitors, the inside held more. With hallways and staircases, each room was masterfully woven together. Old with new. Sometimes Emerald could swear she could hear and feel the stories these walls told.

Molly met her at the door. "Welcome home, Emerald. I hope your appointment went well."

Emerald passed her coat to the older woman. "Lovely weather." She spoke quickly, refusing to address the house manager's questions. They'd only lead to more.

Molly got the hint. "You rushed out earlier without lunch," she said. "I have you a snack."

"I'm not hungry." Emerald ignored Molly's frown and placed her hand on the cool railing that led up an elegant curving staircase that was more than a hundred years old. Daddy was like that. He craved things that were old, one of a kind, and expensive.

She glanced back at the gray haired woman, who was pulling a hanger out of the closet for her coat. "I'm going to nap until dinner." *I'd like to be alone.*

Molly acknowledged Emerald with a tight smile. "Sleep well, dear." Fussing with the latch on the closet door, she muttered under her breath.

As Emerald continued to the landing, a pang of guilt arose. She'd been pulling this spoiled recluse act for about three months now, since her twenty-second birthday. She knew it was rude, but it was far easier than trying to explain her bizarre trances. The house staff had to wonder why she kept herself locked in her room for hours, and sometimes even days.

Somehow Emerald had kept up the front that was necessary for her to survive. Daddy always told her to have a heart of steel so no one could ever break it. But Emerald was beginning to believe it was impossible to control her heart, or her feelings.

∞

When Emerald descended the stairs for dinner that evening, the aroma of pork tenderloin did not entice her. Daddy was supposed to be spending another late night at the office. A formal meal seemed pointless. At the landing, she stopped, surprised to see a light streaming under Daddy's study door.

Molly rounded the corner, ready to call her for dinner.

"Is my father home?" Emerald asked.

Molly hesitated. "I believe so. They had another incident at the clinic."

"Was he there?" Emerald's gaze darted to the light under the closed door.

"No."

No surprise there. Her father had equipped the charity, the Clinic of Hope, to run itself. Emerald had only known him to go there twice in her lifetime—once for a live interview, and once because of a legal problem.

Emerald creaked the study door open. Her father wasn't at his desk, but a light glowed in the sitting area by the fireplace and she could see his sleeve along the arm of his favorite chair. Large boxes surrounded him.

"Daddy?"

Bradford McGintay turned to her, his face pinched. "Emerald. I didn't know you were home already."

"It's after six, and dinner's ready." She paused. "Molly told me there was an incident at the clinic."

Dr. McGintay sighed. "One escapade after the other lately. A woman came in with chest pains. Dr. Laurence treated her for heartburn and sent her home and she had a heart attack two hours later."

She sucked in her breath. "Will you be sued?"

"Probably." He turned back to the boxes.

"What's all this?" Emerald gestured to collection of cardboard. A mess, to say the least. Not something Daddy was accustomed to.

His forehead creased into a frown. "I asked the staff to clear out the storage area and they weren't sure what to do with these things. . . . They were your mother's."

"Mother's?" She studied the boxes, confused. "But I thought you got rid of her things, except of course—" She glanced at the formal portrait of her mother, a young bride, that was centered over the marble fireplace.

He sighed. "I guess, at the time, I couldn't bear tossing these things. But now so much time has passed, I forgot they were there."

Emerald looked down at the boxes, some open. Loose packing material hung out the top of one, as if recently rummaged.

"Daddy, what's this?" Her fingers locked around a gold chain with a cross pendant.

Surprise flickered in his eyes. He huffed, and turned away. "Your mother and her fanatic religious beliefs."

"Religious?" Emerald jolted. She knew very little about her mother, but spiritual was something she would have never expected. "You never told me mother was religious."

He nodded grimly. "She grew up in a traditional church, but then a crazy missionary evangelist twisted her mind—" He grimaced, and then shook his head. "Emerald, this was long ago, before you were even born."

So why did it bother her so much? She watched her father close the box. He refused to believe she was crazy, but called her mother's mind twisted. He scheduled Emerald for therapy, cajoled her to accept medication, and pressured her to get well. This had to be the reason.

His hand reached out to hers.

"Don't worry about these things, Angel; I'm going to have Molly throw them out. Your mother's been gone a long time, and I think it's time to let these things go, too."

She could tell his steely eyes hid a deep pain. It was a pain she would never know as long as he kept that part of his life hidden. It was as if he'd locked it up and lost the key years ago. Maybe this was why he'd warned her never to let others have a place in her heart. His had never healed; no matter what he wanted others to believe.

Emerald tightened her fingers around his hand to give it a

little squeeze, but he pulled away uncomfortably. The action stung, but she was careful not to let her expression show it.

"So, are you eating with me tonight?"

He shook his head as he rose from the chair. "I'd like nothing better than to be graced with your company, but I have to take care of this issue at the clinic before it turns into even more of a fiasco."

There had been a time when he'd been proud of her, happy to be with her. Those days were memories now. As long as she'd been his princess, his prized pianist, she'd had his affection.

"Daddy. . . ."

Having reached the door, he glanced back with eyebrows raised. "Yes?"

She desperately wanted to reach out to him but the truth was in his eyes. The images she there saw ruined more than her mind; they also ruined her spirit.

"The latch on the closet door isn't working again. Can Molly get someone to fix it?"

She waited for him to argue that the door, like everything else in the house, was from a large estate in England and far too delicate for just anyone to touch.

But he sighed wearily. "All right."

He closed the study door behind him, and Emerald sat in silence. The latch had been broken for three years, and finally he agreed it should be fixed.

She slowly released her breath and glanced down at her mother's things. Maybe it was time she learned more about the mother she'd never known. Whoever Alexandra was, she still affected her father after twenty-two years.

∞

Bradford was worried about several things when he left the house, but most of his worry was directed at Emerald. His daughter never wanted to go out or see any of her friends. He could barely stand to look into her distant eyes. He would do anything to connect with her again—as long as her mind was still there to connect with.

He drew in a jagged breath. While he'd already called the clinic's attorney, there wasn't much to do except wait, but he would go to the clinic and flip through the files anyway.

Climbing into his Mercedes, Bradford's BlackBerry phone vibrated in his pocket. Sidney had convinced him he needed one and he barely knew how to operate it. Damn technology. His old fashioned ways left him feeling limited and behind. It must be an e-mail coming in, but he was in no mood to check it. He had more than enough stress without having to be notified the very second a message came through. Maybe he'd go back to his old dinosaur of a phone.

He stared at the picture on the home screen of his phone. It was Emerald, a picture taken at her recital the semester she'd left Julliard. His beautiful pianist. *Emerald what are you thinking these days?* Her beautiful almond eyes smiled back at him. They were so very much her mother's. Her light brown hair was wavy; she'd taken that from him. She'd often complained it was unmanageable and now used some form of straight iron on it. When she was small and it was untamed, she used to cry for him to brush it. He thought of the year they'd gone through a stage, much to the nanny's frustration, where Emerald only wanted Daddy to read to her, brush her hair and even pick out her clothes. He'd never admitted it to anyone but the truth was he'd loved every minute of it.

There had been a time when Alexandra had relied on him, too. Needed him. In the beginning she, too, had been comforted by his extreme order and predictability. It was when he'd become distracted and overworked that she'd sought her comfort in the form of religion.

The reappearance of Alexandra's things had been numbing

and Emerald's obvious fascination had shocked him like an ice-cold wave. Since Emerald had never known her mother, she could not miss her, or have a connection to her things. Specifically those things.

He had to get rid of them. It was the only way to keep Emerald free of the destructive influence of Alexandra's faith. Better she only know the good about Alexandra, what he'd carefully chosen to keep—the portrait, and the charity clinic that he'd founded in her memory.

∞

Emerald could not sleep, so she climbed out of bed, slipped on her blue Christian Dior robe, and made her way down the staircase to her father's study. He was not home yet—maybe wouldn't return until the next day. It was not unusual for him to work several days and nights at a time.

As she flipped on the reading lamp, light showered on the pile of boxes. Emerald bent down to the box where she had found the cross necklace and picked it up. Also inside the box were several picture albums. She lifted the first one out and wiped a thick layer of dust off the cover before carefully opening it. Her heart skipped a beat. Photos of a couple barely out of their teens. Her mother and father, Alexandra and Bradford. They seemed so young, so innocent, wearing jeans and T-shirts. They looked casual, happy, and in love.

Shadowed memories surfaced and she slammed the volume shut, taking a moment to try to make sense of what she was feeling. When she failed she replaced the album in the box, and looked down at the cross in her hand. Her mother had been devout. How strange. Definitely not whom she had envisioned as the love of Daddy's life. So what had attracted him to Alexandra? He was a strong, capable, sensible man. He relied only on himself—not some distant God—and he'd taught her the same. He'd never discussed religion with her, except now to mock it: "Your mother, and her fanatic religious beliefs."

Emerald let the cross slip through her hand and drop back into the box. Perhaps going though her mother's things was a waste of time. But as she turned to leave, a glint of brass caught her eye. Taking another look, she picked her way between the cardboard to a shiny gold box. Curiosity spiked as she opened it. Inside, among other things, was a miniature treasure chest, a simple wooden box with words carved on top: MY MOST PRIZED POSSESSIONS.

Emerald lifted the little chest from the pile. It had a small gold lock that looked easy to pick. With an unwound paper clip from the desk, she drilled into the keyhole. After a moment the lock clicked, and she lifted the lid, revealing two books. One was a Bible, the other a young girl's diary, judging by the light pink cover. A brief disappointment washed over her. What had she expected, gold and jewels?

She set the Bible aside and stared at it for a moment. Her father had said Alexandra had been religious. She took a deep breath, then opened the little pink diary.

FOR THE PART INSIDE OF ME THAT I CAN NEVER TELL,
I WRITE IN THIS BOOK.

Images of a man surfaced from Emerald's memory . . . or had it been a dream? The book burned in her hand, and she let go. She didn't hear it hit the floor.

*A man reached out. "Emerald, I have a message for you from. . . ."*

*The man disappeared. There was her father, furious. She could taste her tears. "I have to find him, Daddy!"*

*"No. They're part of an irrational conspiracy. They destroyed your mother's mind and I won't let them ruin your future!"*

∞

Emerald's eyes shot open. The study looked the same, except for the diary, which lay in a disheveled heap at her feet. She drew a shaky breath. Had she just seen a memory, or the latest evidence that she, too, was losing her mind? Quickly, she returned the Bible and diary to the chest and closed it. She could not get the lock to snap shut, so she put the chest into one of the open boxes, replaced the lid, and left the room.

# Chapter Two

EMERALD SIGHED AS SHE SANK TO the seat of the black grand piano to pass the time before dinner. Her fingers flowed over the keys. She still practiced for hours every day. That was what she had been trained to do. Her father had insisted that she learn music and he attended every recital. It was the one thing she'd ever done that had pleased him.

She stared down at the ivory keys. Did she really enjoy playing the piano, or was it one more thing she did at Daddy's request? Closing the lid sharply she caught a glimpse of Molly, who was in the foyer.

"Emerald, a guest has arrived."

Her father was always home on time for dinner guests. Frowning, she walked to the entrance and froze—Sidney. He was the last person she wanted to spend time with.

"Emerald, it's nice to see you looking more like your old self again."

Daddy must have invited him. Her heart thumped. Daddy was resuming his schemes for dealing with her dreams and visions. She knew Sidney was reading her expression and she turned away, uncomfortable.

"Would you care for a cocktail?" Seating him in the living room, she went to the bar and mixed his favorite martini.

Accepting the drink, he slid over and patted the sofa next to him. His dark oval eyes engulfed her. While he stood an inch shorter than she did, one of her friends from Julliard teased that he was a gorgeous man. But Emerald felt no attraction. She searched for an excuse not to sit there.

"What's wrong, Emerald? You seem anxious."

"I should check with Molly to make sure she doesn't need anything—she always gets stressed with last minute dinner plans. . . ."

Sidney grabbed her hand before she could escape. "I'm not here for dinner." He raised his eyebrows. "Did you forget the benefit tonight?"

"The what?"

"For the Heart Association?"

She froze. That was today? Daddy usually had Molly remind her of these things.

"What time is it?" She glanced at the grandfather clock in the dining room.

"I can give you an hour."

He could give her? "Daddy's going tonight?"

"Yes, of course. But he's going straight from the office, so he asked me to bring you."

For a moment she wanted to tell Sidney she'd changed her mind. But Daddy would be upset; he'd made her promise months ago that she'd attend.

"I won't be long." She hurried upstairs to dress before she could waver.

Less than an hour later she stepped outside to Sidney and his waiting Lexus. She started to open the passenger door but Sidney surprised her by gesturing to the backseat. Riley was exiting a side entrance of the house and headed toward them.

"Here you are, Miss." Daddy's driver opened the back door and she reluctantly slid in, suppressing a groan when Sidney got in the other side next to her. After Riley took his place behind the wheel she knew this had to have been Daddy's idea. It was a big sacrifice for him to go to a benefit without being driven there, which could only confirm one thing: she'd been conveniently placed in the backseat next to Sidney.

Sidney smiled. "You're tense, Emerald. Turn around." He motioned her upper body toward the car door.

She was slow to obey, but did, and his strong hands began to work her shoulders loose.

"It will be good for you to go tonight. Give you something positive to focus on."

Her muscles tensed beneath his hands. Craving political favors, Daddy had always been involved with social and charity events. And Sidney, son of a longtime family friend and top of his class at Harvard, seemed to be her father's younger clone.

"Was this Daddy's idea?"

"Your father and I think it would be good for you to get involved in something again. It would be therapeutic after you've spent all these months cut off from the world." He leaned in closer, until his breath stung the back of her neck. "I'm here to make your transition a little easier."

A chill seized her as she pulled away from him. *This can't be happening again. Daddy promised.*

"I thought my feelings were clear on how my therapy takes place." She meant the words to be firm and confident, but they came out shaky.

His hand slid down her arm. "All I'm asking is that you be more open to possibilities."

She cringed. He didn't just want to treat her; he wanted to date her. She might not have aced Harvard Medical School, but she knew it was unethical and wrong for a doctor to date his patient. Yet the two leading psychiatrists in Philadelphia were sanctioning it—again.

The car pulled up in front of the glitzy hotel holding the event, and the driver opened her door, offering a welcome escape. Shaking off the creepy feeling Sidney's touch had left, she dashed out.

Within seconds, a microphone was in her face and the familiar woman's voice spoke quickly. "And here we have Emerald McGintay, daughter of the famous Dr. McGintay. Emerald, your father has supported this event for almost ten years. Are you following in his footsteps?"

The hand holding the microphone belonged to Anna Lockingdale, the most famous reporter in the area.

Before Emerald could answer, Sidney reached in front of her and gently pushed the microphone out of her face. "Miss McGintay is dedicated to supporting her father's goals in any way she can."

Sidney speaking for her reminded her how rare it was that she ever spoke to reporters. Her father always took front stage with the press, but he and Sidney were careful to protect her from it. While she didn't care anything about giving an interview, having the opportunity to speak for herself would have been nice for once. Maybe she would tell Daddy that.

Her father met them in the lobby with a glass of wine. "Hello, darling." Not noticing her discomfort, he greeted her with a kiss.

She turned a cool cheek, trying to convey how far from fine she was.

Needing to distance herself from both him and Sidney, she wandered into the ballroom where the event was taking place. Within minutes, a crowd of acquaintances and people who knew her through Daddy surrounded her. Emerald sighed and plastered on the fake smile she'd been perfecting her entire life.

Later, she reluctantly sat at the ten-foot grand piano and played one classical piece, to please the small crowd. They encouraged her to play more but instead, she excused herself to the powder room. Once there, she stood over the Egyptian vanity and studied herself in the large mirror as she washed her hands. She'd carried the same glass of champagne around all night and barely sipped it. Yet she felt dizzy.

"Emerald, I don't think we've officially met."

It was Anna Lockingdale. The beautiful, thin blonde was stunning in the dim light as she touched up her makeup.

Emerald held out her hand. "It's nice to meet you."

Anna shook it, then went back to applying her lipstick. "My fiancé, Greg Montgomery, knows your boyfriend."

Emerald shook her head. "Dr. Coffman and I are *not* seeing each other."

Anna's hand went to her neck. "Oh, I'm sorry! Your father believes otherwise."

*Figured.*

A glance at her tiny, delicate, diamond Baume & Mercier watch told Emerald she'd been at the hotel for almost two hours. Long enough. It was time to find Daddy. He could have the driver take her home if he wasn't ready.

She pressed her way through the crowd of people, dodging those who might trap her into conversation for the next half hour. Daddy was nowhere in sight.

An older man approached. Tall, angular face, silver at the temples. Daddy had invited him to dinner before, but his name escaped her. "Hi, Emerald. It's nice to see you again. Are you still at Julliard?"

She gave the man a half smile, just to be polite, but continued to scan the room. "No. I'm looking for my father. Have you seen him?"

"I think he was heading upstairs to the observation lounge earlier. Do you need help finding him?"

"You're kind. Thank you, but no." She darted past him before he could ask more questions. The elevators were just around the corner.

Once in the elevator, she punched the button for floor twenty-two. The mirrored doors whispered open into a wide two-story space that extended to the windows on all four walls. She stepped out onto sumptuous red carpet that silenced her footsteps. At both ends of the room curving staircases swooped up to the second level. A waterfall poured artfully down from the upper level to a pool in the center of the space. It was beautiful, but not many of the hotel's guests had come up to admire the view at this hour of the evening.

Emerald scanned the small knots of men conversing over drinks, but Daddy was nowhere in sight. She then stepped away from the elevator banks to get a better view of the second level gallery.

Sidney.

If he was here, Daddy must also be here.

Chopin's "Nocturne" became discernable in the background as she moved away from the water feature. Could she still play the piece from memory? If she could get Daddy to take her home, maybe she could have a quiet moment to find out. Up to the gallery, then.

A black velvet rope cordoned off the foot of the staircase; clearly, her father and Sidney weren't supposed to be up there. She unfastened it, slipped past, and reattached the elegant barricade. The wall of glass, just past her left shoulder as she mounted the stairs, provided a commanding view of the city lights. Square columns edged the gallery above, with descriptive maps mounted on the marble to inform guests about the details.

Emerald picked her way between the small tables that surrounded a closed bar. The haunting sound of Chopin was replaced by the splash of the waterfall as she reached the midpoint of the room. The lush foliage added to the ambience and shielded her from her father's and Sidney's view.

Her toes were pinching in her Jimmy Choo shoes. She walked carefully across the carpet away from the waterfall, trying to minimize the discomfort. The shoes were spectacular with her outfit, but dreadful to her feet. She stopped to lean against a column and wiggle her toes, seeking some relief. It also gave her a moment to try to locate Daddy. So far she could only see Sidney in a wing chair angled away from her. Another man, not her father, occupied a club chair facing Sidney. Daddy must be up here somewhere. She focused on listening for his voice.

She could only hear Sidney. "It's been two weeks."

"I was having migraines in the middle of the night." A deeper voice she didn't recognize.

"Vicodin can cause headaches. Maybe it's time you change medicine."

"Sidney, I can't. I need the Vicodin. With all the pressure I'm under I can't take a chance of having the pain. Write me a prescription for some Phenergan too, for the headaches."

Sidney was silent, then the man spoke again.

"I'm paying you enough, Sidney. Don't make this an issue."

"I'll take care of it."

"Good."

Emerald took a step back. This probably wasn't a conversation she was meant to overhear.

"Is there still concern Anna might put her nose where it doesn't belong?"

"She's taken care of."

Was that Anna's fiancé, Greg Montgomery? She started to slip away, but froze when the unfamiliar voice spoke her own name.

"You still planning on bringing Emerald into the picture?"

"Yes, but that's more complicated than I'd like it to be."

"Still having hallucinations?"

"Worse than ever."

"She'd never be considered reliable if your business ever leaked."

Emerald's heart thundered. What were they talking about? She wanted to run, but waited to hear Sidney's reply.

"I don't think I have anything to worry about. No one would ever see her as anything but naïve. Maybe sweet and innocent. Not reliable, though, as you say."

"Ha. I should be so lucky. My father thinks Anna is a problem. With her media ties, she could expose everything if she ever got whiff of it. And probably would, in his opinion."

"Well, sometimes you have to take risks."

"No, sometimes you need to eliminate risks."

She might be the one at risk now, if they knew she was listening.

"Send the other one to me and I'll take care of it."

"Gentlemen, good evening. May I break in and take advantage of this quiet spot you've found?"

Daddy's jovial greeting carried over the splashing waterfall to her ears. He must have come up the other staircase. The other men responded in kind.

"Great to see you, Dr. McGintay."

"Hey, Bradford. We were looking for you, and found these comfortable chairs instead. Have a seat."

"I think I will. I really need to take a load off."

"Here, take my chair. If you'll excuse me, I must go check on my lovely fiancé," Greg's deep voice said.

The next voice was her father's. "Did you talk with her?"

Sidney replied. "Yes. She just needs a little time to come around. We'll get her fixed up."

"I know. You've got to get this under control before it's obvious how affected she is."

Emerald froze. They were discussing her. The hurt seized her from deep within. How could Daddy discuss her in public like this? And with a man who wanted her as some type of pawn?

"Well, hello, Beautiful."

Emerald gasped, jumping at the touch on her elbow that accompanied the words. Greg Montgomery stood behind her, eyes narrowed.

"What's a girl like you doing sneaking around the plants in a place like this?"

He couldn't know what she'd heard. She panicked, trying to think what to say. "Trying to get away from the crowds. Since the gallery was closed off, it seemed perfect." She pulled away, eager to escape him—and even more eager to escape Daddy's and Sidney's words. She needed to be "fixed." Of course it was unthinkable that Philadelphia's top psychiatrist would have a psychotic daughter. Just another way she fell short, another reason she didn't deserve her freedom.

Greg reached as if to grab her wrist, but she twisted away and hurried toward the staircase. Her breath became shallow as her pulse pounded in her ears. Must get out of here. She scanned the wide observation floor below.

In her hurry, her spiked heel caught on the stairs' carpeted runner. Hands flailing for a hold, she pitched forward. Her fingers closed on air as she tumbled down the stairs.

"Someone's fallen!"

"Is she okay? Who is it?"

"Emerald, are you all right? Are you hurt?"

She couldn't move. A flurry of voices and bodies surrounded her. Pain, shock, and humiliation sent hot tears to her eyes—but more than the physical hurt from her fall was the slicing pain in her mind. The word "fix" kept ringing in her memory. *I need to be fixed.*

"Are you hurt?"

*Yes*. She shook her head, trying to swallow the tears as she came to a sitting position.

"Do you think you can stand?"

Again she nodded as hands came under her arms and lifted her to shaky legs.

She was missing a shoe. She didn't care. She removed the other and limped to the door.

"Emerald, let me get your father." It was the older gentleman who had stopped her earlier. She still couldn't remember his name.

Anna called to her from the elevator.

Other people shouted behind her, but they were just voices as she stepped past Anna and into the elevator.

Emerald swayed. Images and cries from somewhere far away pressed in her eyes and ears. She exited the elevator and went straight to the main lobby. The images in her mind were becoming more vivid. Losing her hold on reality, she struggled to get it back.

*The familiar man inside of her head spoke. "Emerald, I have a message for you. . . ."*

But this time she could physically hear his voice. "Emerald, wait!"

Whirling around in disbelief she realized he stood right in front of her. He was a petite man with dark hair slicked back, dressed much too casually for a five-star hotel. Stunned, she stood for a moment, voiceless.

He smiled. But his eyes were sad. The first thing that came to her mind was he'd just lost someone he cared deeply for.

She finally asked, "Do I know you?" He was recognizable from somewhere, but she couldn't place him.

"I've waited a long time to find you."

A deep emotion developed inside her. "Why?" she whispered.

His smile broadened, and his eyes engulfed her in a way her father's never had, as if she were the only one in this massive hotel. He reached out to her.

Daddy would be mad. He'd warned her never to talk to strangers, even as an adult. This man was clearly not part of the Heart Association crowd. But she felt compelled to take his hand anyway.

"Emerald!" Her father's voice startled her.

Someone was gripping her arm painfully.

"Daddy, let me go!"

"No." His voice had taken a stern tone now.

"Please—" He didn't understand. This was her chance to find the truth.

She turned back to the man, but he had vanished. "Where is he?"

Frantic, she looked in every direction. The hotel lobby was swarming with people but his face was not among them.

"He's gone, Emerald." Sidney's voice.

"What did you do?" she lashed out at him. This was Sidney's doing. He'd made the man leave.

Daddy glanced around uncomfortably. "We're trying to help you, Sweetheart. You just had a fall."

How could she make him understand? "I have to find him, Daddy!" Her voice was a cry of desperation.

He flinched, and his face paled. And Emerald knew he wasn't going to help her.

∞

Bradford felt the blood drain from his face. He had just sat down to enjoy a drink when Joe had rushed up the stairs with the news of Emerald's fall. His profession had trained him to handle anything. But his daughter having an outbreak here, now, with all these people around was his worst nightmare come true.

He tightened his grip on her arm as he looked at Anna, whose mouth was agape, standing in front of them with Emerald's shoe.

"She lost her shoe up there."

Looking down he realized Emerald was shoeless; she held the other shoe in her hand.

"She'll be fine," he assured Anna.

Anna handed over the shoe. "She hit her head."

He held up his hand to the small crowd forming around them. He had to get Emerald out of here.

"She may be concussed; we should get her to a doctor," Sidney broke in, and Bradford gave him a grateful look. This time Bradford was overwhelmed. Emerald was trembling. Her eyes fluttered as if she'd just seen a ghost, and maybe she had, at least in her head. Why else would she have been talking and grasping at thin air? His pulse quickened. He didn't like to think of the possibilities.

They walked her outside the hotel, where Sidney took over. "Get her in the car. We'll take her to the hospital."

Bradford gently pushed his daughter into the back seat of his Mercedes, then got in beside her. Sidney jumped in front with the driver.

Emerald held her hands together, trying to control her trembling without much success.

Bradford's heart crumbled. This was clear evidence that he should have never attempted to control her treatment. Fatherly instincts impaired his judgment as a psychiatrist. Maybe it was time he left her treatment decisions to Sidney. He had let his heart get in the way of Emerald's health long enough.

He hovered over her as he always did when he was worried about her. "Honey, tell me how you feel?"

Stepping back was going to be harder then he thought. Forcing himself to give her space, he looked at Sidney in the front seat for help. With all his heart, he hoped Sidney could read his silent plea.

∞

Getting hold of herself, Emerald struggled to put together what had just happened.

Sidney reassured her father. "We'll get x-rays, just to be safe."

It dawned on her that they thought she hit her head, but the last thing she needed right now was to go to the hospital. "I'm fine, Daddy."

Neither man believed her. And Daddy was just letting Sidney take over.

Sidney remained calm. "We want to make sure you're okay."

Daddy's mouth twitched. He was upset and trying to hide it. "Did you hit your head going down? Where does it hurt?"

"Nowhere." She crafted a lie. "I just got dizzy. Probably all the people and champagne. That's all."

Daddy turned to Sidney. "We should still take her to the hospital, just to be sure."

Sidney studied her, and she found herself doing something she couldn't have imagined an hour earlier. Her eyes actually pleaded with him. *Please take me home.*

"I think she's probably okay. She's not used to champagne. There are a lot of viruses and that flu bug is going around. No reason to be exposed to all that at the hospital."

The color drained from Daddy's face. Sidney had hit Daddy's weak spot: germs.

"You're right." Bradford nodded. "We were just in a crowd, too. Emerald, do you have that antibacterial hand gel I gave you to carry in your purse?"

"No." Incredible how quickly his concern had shifted.

"Better wash with a good disinfectant when we get home." He sagged back in his seat. She was thankful for the momentary distraction.

When they arrived home, Bradford asked Sidney to join him in his study for a brandy. Emerald went to the kitchen for a glass of water and much-needed aspirin for her throbbing head and arm. As the pain subsided, she thought about what had happened that evening. There had been a man in front of her. She'd felt his warm hand and seen him. But had anyone else?

As she started up the staircase, Sidney's voice stopped her. "Emerald, why don't you come sit down for a minute?"

That was his coaxing tone. Pitched to perfection for a non-threatening sound. But she didn't trust him.

"Come on, Emerald. It's okay."

She hesitated. *I've got enough to think about without Sidney.* The man she saw had been more real than anything she had ever known before.

Though her mind protested, her feet descended the two stairs she'd climbed. Sidney always caught her at her most vulnerable moments.

As he touched her arm to lead her into the living room, Emerald realized he was like a serpent. Slimy, sneaky, and quick to pounce on his prey. Recognizing weakness and fear, he knew just where to put his fangs. Perhaps he had already poisoned her.

A voice deep within her spoke. *He has no power over you. Only I have the keys to death, hell, and the grave.*

A familiar flush spread up her forehead.

"You hear the voice speaking to you now, don't you?"

She met Sidney's eyes. He sat on the sofa next to her with calm patience, as if he had all the time in the world.

*You don't.*

A chill ran down her back, and she jerked when Sidney placed his hand on her bruised shoulder.

His face looked momentarily stricken, but he quickly regained his composure.

They sat in silence for a long moment before he spoke. "You know you can trust me, Emerald. Don't let the voice tell you otherwise. It's lying."

She swallowed hard. "I had a vision again."

"What kind of vision?"

"Cries—children's cries and. . . ."

"And what?"

Dare she continue?

"What is it, Emerald?"

"I saw a man. He was right in front of me. I could touch him."

Sidney leaned forward. "What did he say?"

She shivered. "He said he had a message for me."

"Was that all?"

Unable to remember the message, she closed her eyes. This was so confusing.

Sidney's voice brought her back. "Was there anything else, Emerald?"

"No, Daddy stopped me before I could go with him."

"Hmm. Was there any reason you wanted to leave the hotel?"

She raised her eyebrows. Of course she'd wanted to leave; she never wanted to be there in the first place. But to suggest her vision was an excuse? "I've seen him before. But this time it was more real."

"Do you remember anything significant about him?"

She concentrated. Pressing her eyes closed, she grasped for his image in her head. He had something on his shirt—some kind of embroidery. No, it couldn't be! "A cross."

"A cross?" Puzzlement filled his voice. For once, she'd thrown him. "Why do you think you saw a cross?"

*My mother's cross pendant.* "I don't know." She hesitated. "I'm sorry. I'd like to excuse myself for the night." She stood. The shaking had subsided, but her legs still felt wobbly.

"Don't you think we should talk about this some more?"

"I'm tired."

He frowned, but she left before he could stop her.

∞

Bradford looked from his paperwork as Sidney tapped on the study door. "So how is she?" The strained look on Sidney's face suggested bad news.

"Bradford, I know how you feel about intervention, but I'm afraid it may have come to that point."

Bradford rubbed his hand across his face. Intervention. He'd thought about it before. But considering it for even a second had been troubling enough.

A painful thought of Alexandra stabbed his gut. He had ignored her symptoms. He couldn't do the same with their daughter. Putting Emerald on a treatment program would be accepting defeat, admitting she was ill. Especially with the medications she'd require: strong and addictive, with difficult side effects.

His heart pounded as he thought of her wide-eyed plea that she had to find him. Find whom? He didn't like to think of the possibilities.

Torn between his medical knowledge and his fatherly instincts he asked the question he was most terrified to know. "What did she see?"

"At this time, I still can't discuss that without her permission."

Bradford nodded. Fine time for Sidney to come up with an ethics concern. Still, he had always respected Sidney's ability to care for his daughter. Sidney didn't carry the baggage Bradford had from Alexandra. Emotional ties wouldn't interfere with Sidney's medical decisions on Emerald. That was a comfort.

"Bradford . . . you have never taken Emerald to church?"

The question took him by surprise. "No, I've never exposed her to anything religious, other than a comparative world religion course in her studies." He looked at Sidney. "Why do you ask?"

Sidney sighed. "I don't want you to be alarmed, but I'm afraid her condition might have crossed to another level."

Bradford's body turned to ice as he recalled Alexandra. Religious fanaticism had marked her illness. It couldn't be the same. Emerald wasn't Alexandra. She'd never even known her mother.

"What do you suggest?"

Sidney sat in the chair across from him. "I think I need to talk to her more, do more tests before I can be sure. But if these hallucinations continue. . . ." Sidney's eyes told the rest.

Bradford rose from his desk and placed his hand on Sidney's shoulder. Time to place Emerald's treatment in his partner's hands. "You know best. And I trust your diagnostic judgment."

The pain in his eyes was all too evident.

# Chapter Three

EMERALD STARED OUT THE SITTING ROOM window. Earlier, the gardeners had come, and she liked to watch them work. But for some reason, today they'd left the grass too green and the flowers too bright for her mood.

She left her seat by the window to wander upstairs to her room. She had paced the room almost the entire night, too tired to think but too restless to sleep. The images of the man and the cross were troubling. They had felt so real. Struggling to shake the memories from her mind she wandered her room again until she could no longer stand confinement. She needed to find something—someone. The urgency was real.

Downstairs again, she stepped into her father's study. The boxes were gone; the house staff must have thrown them out. She went to the piano, but after a few listless measures, she turned away, frustrated. Her mother's things kept haunting her. The Bible, the diary, and the cross. Had they triggered the vision? The man?

After another evening alone, she went early to bed. But even in her sleep she was searching—trying to remember, to understand. Were the walls in her house trying to tell her something?

Awaking in a sweat, her heart pounded. *They're in the kitchen by the back door.* She got out of bed. Oblivious to her sweat-soaked nightgown, she opened her door and left her room. *Where am I going?* Down the stairs, through the foyer, then the living room, then the dining room. Moonlight from the tall windows sliced through the darkness. She didn't bother with the light switches. She knew where the furniture was, what areas to avoid. But in the dining room, she stopped.

"Now what?" she whispered.

*The kitchen.*

She went into the kitchen, straight to the back door. By the door were garbage bags and boxes. She rummaged for her mother's "prized possessions" treasure chest. After extricating it from the mess, she located the box with the cross necklace. She reached inside and grasped it. Carrying the cross and the chest, she returned to her room.

As she closed her door, it hit her, what she had just done. In shock, Emerald stared at the chest and necklace. It was unclear how she'd known where they were, and the thought left her trembling. It started in her knees and crept upward. She dropped the necklace and other items; the thick carpet muffled their impact to a dull thud. She clasped her hands over her mouth, and fought back a cry of fear.

Running to her adjoining bathroom, she splashed cold water on her face. After blotting with a towel, she tried to gulp deep breaths of air. It was just all a dream. Surely. . . .

Emerald returned to her room and even before she turned on her lamp, she knew the items were still there. As light flooded the room, sure enough, her mother's things were lying on the pink flowered rug where she had left them. Sleepwalking didn't make sense. She didn't have a history of doing such a thing.

She looked down at the treasure chest that had opened; its contents scattered on the floor. Emerald clutched the towel still in her hand. How had she known where they were?

*They're in the kitchen.*

She felt the trembling coming again. *Down the stairs, through the foyer, then the living room, then the dining room, to the kitchen by the back door.*

Here they were, just as she'd dreamed. Looking closer at the treasure chest turned on its side, open, she noticed the Bible lying next to it. The cross necklace eluded her at first, camouflaged against a red rose in the rug pattern.

After gathering her courage, she sank to the plush carpet. To ensure she wasn't imagining everything, she picked up the Bible. A stroke of its smooth texture satisfied her of its existence. She put it back in the chest. Next, she retrieved the cross.

A fear developed inside her. Would the visions return? She waited a minute and when they didn't, she put the diary and cross on top of the Bible and closed the chest. After staring at the wooden box, unsure what to do next, she carried it to her nightstand. She set the box by the lamp, then ran her fingers over the smooth engraved wood.

Confused, she slid back under the covers and stared at the chest a long time before turning off the lamp. Funny, after the vision of the cross she had been terrified to see it again. Yet now it was so close she almost felt at peace. Maybe it wasn't the walls speaking to her after all. She was only sure about two things: the voice was familiar, and it followed her wherever she went. Surprisingly, with this knowledge, she still drifted into a deep and tranquil sleep.

∞

Sidney's dark brown eyes studied Emerald from behind his office desk, making her feel like a specimen under a microscope. "You haven't had any more visions?"

She hesitated.

"What is it?"

She looked around the room, debating whether she should share last night's experience. It seemed private. Yet it had frightened her. She had spent the entire day trying to understand what had happened, and what it meant.

"I had another dream last night."

"Tell me about it."

Emerald took a deep breath as she caught a glimpse of Sidney's grim face. Agitation? No. But something was bothering him. She thought back to the night at the hotel and the conversation she'd overheard between Greg Montgomery and him. Sidney had secrets. Secrets that possibly involved her. The thought was more than alarming.

"Now, I want you to take your time, Emerald. Just relax, take a few deep, calming breaths. We have plenty of time."

She hesitated, feeling the need to escape. Something was wrong. She studied Sidney. Had she imagined the grimness she had seen a moment before?

He must sense her panic. She sat in silence trying to decide what to do. If she didn't tell him, she may not get her answers. "As weird as this sounds, I had a dream, and then I . . . I did what I dreamed."

"And what was that?" Sidney asked leaning forward.

She couldn't read his expression; he was a master at hiding what he was thinking. *This is a test!* Her stomach twisted, and her chest tightened.

"It's all right, Emerald. Take deep breaths." Sidney came to her side.

But the inevitable shaking came. Violently. Then the cries. Children's cries. She squeezed her eyes shut. Beads of sweat covered her forehead.

"Emerald!"

Sidney's voice faded, and suddenly she was in a different place.

∞

Bradford paced the waiting area, fighting the fear that surged through him. He had never let any of his patients—even the psychotics—faze him. But this wasn't his patient. This was his daughter. His little girl had been admitted to the hospital only a few hours earlier.

He looked up with hope when Sidney entered the room.

Sidney answered the implied question. "She's still not awake." His eyes softened. "I know this is tough, but I think it is time we discuss her illness."

Bradford took a deep breath. *Her illness*. It should have never come to this. When Emerald's dreams began, he hadn't worried much; after all, everyone has nightmares sometimes. But he should have taken a hint when she withdrew from society, when she dropped out of Julliard; but he'd assumed it was adolescent rebellion. He'd been in denial about everything, just as he had been with Alexandra. And he was a psychiatrist!

"Bradford, you can't blame yourself."

How did Sidney always know what he was thinking?

"If anyone is to blame, it's me, for not recognizing the seriousness of her state before now."

Sidney's eyes registered blame, too. This shared hurt bonded them together.

Bradford stiffened. "Okay, tell me what you know."

Sidney nodded with professional curtness. "I have diagnosed what happened today as an acute manic episode. As we already know, she is also suffering from quasi-schizophrenic symptoms. Though I am not sure yet how severe the psychosis is, she is showing indications of hyper-religious ideation."

Bradford's eyes closed for a moment as he sucked in his breath. It was even worse than he thought. He should have known.

*Alexandra.*

He'd always blamed Alexandra's problem on the fools who had brainwashed her. Of course, he'd never know for sure because in his insistence that nothing was mentally wrong with his wife he'd refused to allow a diagnosis. But what if it had been a mental illness, something hereditary that she'd passed on? Then all his efforts to protect Emerald from brainwashing—the immersion in high society, the surveillance, the chaperones—were a waste.

He opened his eyes. "How severe?"

"She is tying together what she sees and hears as a message. The children's cries are calling to her for help." Sidney's gaze met his. "You know we won't know how severe it is until she wakes." He sighed deeply. "She might come back to reality and stay there."

He knew just as well as Sidney how unpredictable her condition could be.

"Is she on Haldol?"

Sidney nodded grimly as he stood to leave.

∞

Sidney stepped inside Emerald's room. She slept peacefully and looked almost like an angel. He cringed as he remembered sedating her through an injection earlier. He touched her hand. Bradford had turned his daughter over to his care; he had trusted his most precious possession to him.

Bradford's feelings had interfered with his professional duty. Sidney thought how hard Bradford had taken Emerald's condition and flinched. It should have never come to this. But he'd make things right. Emerald would become her lovely, high-spirited self again. He had admired Emerald from a distance, even before Bradford introduced them. This was the woman he had grown to love.

He squeezed her hand one last time before leaving the room. Lithium would regulate her mood, and then he'd start her on Risperdal. With luck, the anti-psychotic would block the chemical messenger dopamine that facilitated schizophrenia. When Emerald awoke and settled down, he would talk to Bradford about psychotherapy. It may be difficult for Bradford to send his only daughter away, but at this point he feared it was critical that someone else treat Emerald.

∞

Emerald opened her eyes to the bright light that surrounded her. At first, everything was a blur, and her initial instinct was to close her eyes again. To escape the brightness. But the pounding of her head brought her back to consciousness. Her mouth felt like cotton and her entire body ached.

Where was she? She tried to push herself up, but dizziness overcame her. She looked around. Florescent lights. White bed linens. She was in a hospital room. She tried to swallow, but her mouth was too dry.

Sidney entered the room. He smiled. "Well, I'm glad to see you're awake, sleeping beauty."

She couldn't speak. As if realizing her need for water, Sidney went to a pitcher on the table next to her bed and filled a paper cup.

She took it and drank gratefully until she could move her tongue again.

"My head—" Her voice came out hoarse, and she wondered if Sidney even understood her.

Sidney nodded. "It's normal to experience a headache until the Haldol wears completely off." He reached in his pocket and pulled out a packet of Tylenol. "Take this."

She ignored the Tylenol. "Haldol?" That was a medication for schizophrenics.

Sidney opened the pack himself, then placed one pill at a time in her mouth. After she had swallowed them, he sat next to her.

"Emerald, do you remember what happened?"

She shook her head as confusion swept over her.

Sidney's face was expressionless. "You'll be all right."

She thought back, trying to remember. She had been in Sidney's office, then—

As if recognizing her panic, Sidney rested a hand on her shoulder. "Your condition will be closely watched from now on," he paused, "so this doesn't happen again."

Her condition? She started to ask what he meant when Daddy entered with a large bouquet of flowers.

"Hello, Sweetheart. I'm glad to see you're feeling better."

"Was I sick?" she asked, carefully examining her father's face, then Sidney's.

Emerald could see her father looking to Sidney for guidance, as he always did on her matters. It was funny, she realized for the first time. Her father never had a problem taking charge of anything related to his practice. She always thought of Daddy as a leader, but when it came to her, he surrendered control. Until now, she'd thought her father was the one person she could trust. That had been a mistake. Had he known about the Haldol?

"The good news is your illness can be treated." Sidney's voice was firm. "But I think it would be better if we waited until later to discuss it."

"What illness?" she lashed out. "What are you talking about?"

Sidney turned to Bradford with a telling eye gesture and Bradford sighed, then nodded. "You might as well tell her."

Quiet and contemplative for an ominous moment, Sidney turned back to Emerald.

She felt her throat tighten, and her palms became sweaty.

"You had an episode in my office. We were discussing your dream and then—"

The rest of his explanation began to run together in her ears. Her brain stopped functioning after processing that word. *Episode*. She tried to remember what had happened. She'd started telling Sidney about the dream. She remembered that.

Emerald's heart quickened as her memory returned. She cut into Sidney's long-winded diagnosis. "You drugged me."

The memory of a forced injection cleared her fogged brain. "You were testing me, and you drugged me!" She felt her chest rising and falling at the discovery. Not sure if her sudden anxiety was from anger or fear, she wanted to attack and cry at the same time.

"I know this is all very confusing, but we are going to work through it."

She shifted her gaze from Sidney's set face to Daddy's furrowed brow.

"You knew about this, Daddy?"

Bradford cleared his throat nervously, then moved to her side and took her hand. "I know this is difficult, Emerald, but both Sidney and I are here." A forced smile covered his lips. "We're going to help you through this, Sweetheart." He glanced at Sidney, then back to her. "Why, before long, it will be as if none of this ever happened."

So that was his goal. To make everything go away. What if he couldn't? What if he discovered she was really crazy?

Trying to swallow the lump in her throat she whimpered. "I want to go home, Daddy."

He flinched at her tears, but before he could respond, Sidney took over.

"The best thing you can do right now is rest. Your father and I will be back later to check on you."

She looked at her father, begging for his help to get her out of there and away from Sidney. But all he did was place a kiss on her cheek. He was on Sidney's side. He had betrayed her. Again.

# Chapter Four

EMERALD SAT BY HER WINDOW WITH a cup of green tea. She had been hospitalized for eight days and brought home the day before. She had survived all the tests and procedures, which Sidney assured her, were routine. Her sessions with Sidney would now occur every day. Looking down at the now-melting pill she clutched in her hand, she wished the whole gooey capsule would dissolve away. She thought of the fear she'd seen in Daddy's eyes over the last week and swallowed it down.

Her *illness* had to be serious if Sidney and her father refused to discuss it. She didn't know what was worse. Not knowing what was wrong with her, or knowing they didn't want her to know. At least she had experienced no more dreams or visions since her hospital stay, but this offered no relief. She knew they'd return.

"That's a good girl." Molly's hand patted hers. Emerald handed her the empty cup of tea, ignoring the affection. The household staff was treating her like Daddy was: sick, helpless, and in need of constant surveillance.

Wearing an olive green suit with a khaki colored shirt and tie, Sidney entered the room and sat beside her. "How are you feeling today?"

She was tired of that question. Even when her father and Sidney were not around, Molly hovered over her every moment. The house was a prison.

"Emerald?"

"I'm fine." She lowered her eyes.

"Are you?" His question hung in the air. "I can't imagine how hard it must be to stay in this house all the time."

Her head shot up. No way would she let him ask her out again.

"I like it here," she whispered quickly. A definite lie.

Sidney took her hand, and she fought the urge to snatch it away.

"It's perfectly normal for a person to feel the need to seclude herself during a time like this." He squeezed her hand and his eyes deepened. "But you must realize the danger in doing so."

Her defenses rose until she realized he might retaliate by diagnosing her with something even worse.

"I'm sorry, Sidney. I know how you and Daddy feel about me going out, but—"

"What if it was easier than that, Emerald?"

"What do you mean?"

"You feel the need to stay in the same place, but I want you to get out." He released her hand. "So why don't we compromise?"

She drew in her breath, reluctant to hear Sidney's idea of compromise.

"There's a small resort in Tampa, Florida where a lot of people vacation. After a while, they come back feeling like a completely different person." He smiled. "You can get away for a while."

"What kind of resort?" Emerald braced herself for more gut twisting.

His smile did not falter. "It's normal to feel anxious about leaving home. But I promise once you get there and get to know the people there, everything will get better."

She jumped to her feet. "If you think I am going anywhere, then you're mistaken." The nerve he had!

"This is your decision, of course. It's a place where you can relax and get the help you need."

*The help I need?*

"All I ask is that you think about it," he added. "And remember, you have a choice Emerald, you always have a choice." Then he turned and left the room.

Emerald knew she didn't have a choice. She hadn't chosen to see Sidney in the first place, or to take the medication. She sank back in the seat, her legs trembling. *It will be okay. Daddy would not go along with such a thing.*

*But she couldn't help but wonder . . . would he?*

∞

Emerald sat across from her father at dinner. She knew he had been working on a very difficult case. He must be taking a break, which was unlike him. That fact left her feeling uneasy.

"I heard Sidney stopped by today." He pretended to be casual, but he watched her intently.

"Daddy, he wants me to go away." A sob caught in her throat.

She studied his face. A smile was the last thing she expected. "Emerald, you act as if you'd be gone forever."

She stared at her father in shock. So he did know. And he approved. She tried to swallow her astonishment. "And you act like it's some kind of vacation! It's a hospital, Daddy!"

She felt the tears come, and his face softened.

"It's not a hospital, Sweetheart, it's a clinic. And a good one. I've done a lot of research, and they have a very impressive reputation."

*You did research?*

She looked at him, her jaw set. She was twenty-two years old, and he couldn't force her to do this. "I'm not going."

He picked up his fork. "I knew you 'd say that. That's why

I scheduled a trip for us to go together, this weekend. We leave Saturday. But don't worry, Sidney will accompany us, and I'm sure once you see the place you'll feel differently."

She squelched a faint stirring of panic. No. Not now. She could not let herself be vulnerable at a time like this, when she needed to be able to stand up to her father, not prove him right. Quickly, she stood and left the table.

∞

Her eyes opened, her heart was thundering. She lay there afraid to move a muscle. Silence. Emerald sat up and looked around her dimly lit bedroom. The sleeping pill Molly had given her must have hit her fast. She had no idea how long she'd been asleep but she was still wearing her clothes.

She stood up with a moan and glanced at the clock. It was after midnight. The feeling of entrapment was suffocating and she knew she must have had another nightmare. Cracking open her bedroom door she headed for the staircase. She'd left her laptop in the library earlier.

When she entered the room, which was lined with bookshelves, the light from the hallway was enough for her to find her way to the large armchair. She'd left her computer there. She quietly sat in the chair and began sifting through the fifty-seven unopened e-mails. She was in the middle of replying to an old friend from Julliard, who she hadn't talked to in six months, when she heard a voice down the hall.

On instinct, she closed her laptop. It was a strange action, considering this was her home and she was past the age of curfew. Daddy had left shortly after their confrontation at the dinner table. She knew this from Molly, who had told her when she'd come up to check on her and brought her the sleeping pill.

The voice was so muffled she couldn't tell if it belonged to any of the household staff or not. As quietly as possible, she shifted her computer to her chair and stood. Her socked feet slid silently across the floor as she reached the wall and pressed her back against it. As she got closer to the door, she froze.

It was Daddy's voice!

"She's sleeping. I found it on her nightstand."

Curiosity getting the best of her she slowly peaked around the corner. Daddy, still dressed in his dress clothes from dinner, was on the hallway telephone standing with his back to her.

"I don't know when she got it. It bothers me, Sidney. This isn't good."

It was then that her eyes caught a glimpse of her mother's treasure chest sitting on the table next to the phone. Daddy, or Molly, must have taken it while she was sleeping.

After a moment Daddy hung up the phone and carried the chest down the hallway. She waited until she was sure he was gone, then rushed back up the stairs. Half an hour later she stepped out of the shower and dried herself with a large fluffy towel before slipping into her pajamas. The warm, pulsating water had revived her physically, but it couldn't wash away the feeling that her father considered her a problem. Someone had sneaked into her room and taken her mother's chest, and Daddy considered it an issue that she had it. His solution was to send her away.

Emerald wondered what her mother would have done if she were alive. Would she be as anxious to get rid of her daughter as Daddy was?

She opened her top nightstand drawer, where she'd left the cross necklace that morning. On impulse, she slipped it around her neck. As she cradled the cross in her hand she felt a strange sensation surge through her. It represented something she had never known . . . never believed. She thought hard for a moment, trying to unlock some memory from long ago. It hovered on the edge of her mind, and then slipped away.

The treasure chest Daddy or Molly had taken only had the

Bible in it. She removed the small pink book, her mother's diary from the drawer. No longer feeling she was invading privacy, she yielded to an irresistible urge to open the book. Perhaps it was the chance to learn about the woman she had never known; perhaps it was something else.

> *Dear Diary,*
>
> *For the part of me that cannot be known, I write in this book.*

Emerald turned to the next page. It was dated August 24, a year before Emerald was born. She looked past the date and noticed something different. Something very important. Instead of *Dear Diary*, it was now addressed, *Dear God.*

> *Dear God,*
>
> *I originally intended this book to be a diary of my secret thoughts, in which I never seemed to have time to write. I guess you knew it needed saving for something bigger. My life has changed dramatically, and I know I am not the person I used to be. Though Bradford does not understand yet, I pray that one day he may see what you have done in my life. And so, this book is no longer a diary, but a journal in which I will write words that you give me. That I may always remember our conversations, and never forget the things you tell me.*

Emerald stared at the page in dismay. A letter to God? Her life had changed dramatically? Confusion swept over her as she read and re-read the letter. But each reading only puzzled her more.

What did Alexandra mean by that last line? Had she really talked to God?

Any other time Emerald would have laughed. But this was not a joke to her now. It was real. A pool of memories, dreams, and images swam in her subconscious—only she couldn't grasp any of them. She closed her eyes. She had always recognized the voice but couldn't place it. Maybe the voice belonged to the man she'd seen, but no, his voice had been different.

Sometime later in the night she lay in her bed, staring into the dark. She could hear the beating of her heart and feel the hard, cold surface of the cross against her chest. Her mother had talked to God. That was preposterous, talking to someone who did not exist. No wonder her father had not gone along. Dr. Bradford McGintay relied only on himself.

Emerald forced her eyes shut. All she needed was darkness. She didn't want to think about her father, or Sidney, or their plan to send her away. She didn't want to think about her problem, or fear, or her mother's confusing possessions.

*Emerald.*

The voice was clear but gentle.

She looked around in the darkness.

*You're not alone.*

"Who's there?" She saw no one.

*I have been here all along.*

Sudden anger surged. "You are the one who has been causing the dreams!"

*You have a calling, Emerald.*

"Who are you?" she demanded, but he was gone. The presence she had felt was gone.

And suddenly the cries came. Only this time they were not just cries, but something more.

*Emerald!*

Cold chills ran down her, and her throat tightened. They were calling her name.

*Emerald, help us!*

Children's cries, but now the cries of men and women joined the children's. They were so close. She could feel their pain. Not physically, no, this pain was far more powerful, more intense. It was the worst pain she had ever felt. Tears of agony came, and she clenched her fists and her entire body trembled.

"Make it go away. Make them go away," she cried helplessly. "Please, whoever you are. I can't take it anymore. I'll do anything, just make them go away."

*Will you follow me*? the voice asked.

"Yes," she whispered.

Suddenly the pain was gone, and the crying ceased. It was only she—and a hand that reached out to her. Then the voice.

*Follow me.*

At first Emerald hesitated, but then it was as if she had known the voice all along. Not taking this hand wasn't an option. When she placed her hand in his, something changed. She felt something she had never experienced before. From what source it came, she couldn't be sure. All she knew was that it was very powerful.

# Chapter Five

A RUSH OF PEOPLE PUSHED PAST as Emerald stepped off the train at New York City's Penn Station. It was two A.M. What were so many people doing awake and traveling this time of night?

Emerald clutched her Louie Vuitton tote tightly as she walked. Her pace was quick. She knew Penn Station well, as she'd traveled the Philly-to-New York route many times for Julliard, and for Manhattan shopping trips. Of course she'd always had chaperones before. Now she was alone. This was the first time she had ever traveled alone. She should be afraid, hesitant, but an unknown force propelled her to move. No time to think, to reconsider, to fear or rejoice.

Leaving the station, Emerald stepped off the curb to hail a cab, then jumped at a man's shout behind her.

"Fire and brimstone! You're going to burn!"

Her heart thumping loudly, she turned to see what the commotion was about. But one man stood alone wearing a worn, collared suit. He was holding a Bible.

A street preacher.

Seeing he had her attention, the preacher shook his Bible her way and reminded her of a half-starved animal. Hungry for something. "Are you saved by the blood of Jesus, young lady?"

Her breath caught in her throat. Her father had told her these people were like dogs; sometimes they just liked to hear themselves bark. She relaxed, but then the man took a step closer to her. His deep blue eyes penetrated through her to a place in her soul so unfamiliar that it frightened her.

"If you don't know Jesus, you're risking eternal damnation!"

She tried to run but couldn't will her legs to move.

A policeman stepped between them. "Keep it down."

Emerald took a breath of relief and rushed down the street, waving for a cab.

She was resisting Daddy's control. Would she resist his beliefs, too? He had taught her there was no God. It was possible that Daddy didn't know everything. That thought left her with something to ponder. But it would have to be later. Right now she couldn't afford distractions.

A cab pulled up next to her, and she leapt in. "Take me to JFK."

The Indian cab driver stared at her before obeying. Did he know she was running away? That was ridiculous. What did he care?

Taking a deep breath, she steadied her heart. Her entire plan played out in her head: the money, the flight, the schedule. Her move every turn of the way. She watched the buildings pass. The city was still alive, even at this hour. So much different from Philadelphia. But it wasn't the nightlife that drew her. It was the freedom.

Here she was with no chaperones, no permission, just five hundred dollars out of her savings, withdrawn from the ATM nearest to her home in Philadelphia. She would have taken every last cent, but was stuck with the maximum amount she could withdraw daily. She had cab fare to Philly's 30th Street Station and a one-way ticket to New York City she'd purchased on her credit card. At the moment, five hundred dollars would be enough.

∞

When the cab stopped at the curb of the airport, Emerald hesitated before counting out the fare. This paying with cash was new to her. Daddy's credit cards and chaperones had always taken care of her before.

She moved quickly inside the airport, going directly to the ticket counter. After showing her identification and receiving the ticket she'd reserved by cell phone, she found her terminal.

A tall woman with blonde hair and dark sunglasses pushed past her, dropping her luggage where Emerald wanted to sit. The woman was no movie star, but her clothing screamed designer. Emerald wondered if she was visiting L.A. or if she lived there. Would she stay off Rodeo Drive or make it her first stop?

She shook the thought from her mind. No distractions. She focused her attention on a row of pay phones about fifty yards away. When she reached the first phone she stopped, hoping someone else would get to it first. She needed to call; it was the next step and a vital move in the plan.

Emerald clasped the phone in her hand and quickly keyed Sidney's office number before she lost her nerve. It was only four forty-five. He wouldn't be at the office yet.

Unless he'd spent the night there.

Sidney's voicemail picked up and Emerald sighed in relief.

"Hello, Sidney, it's me. I've decided to take a little trip, get away for a while. Please tell Daddy I'm fine, and not to worry."

She hung up. It was perfect. In the course of her therapy she noticed Sidney never returned calls before seven.

They would trace the call, Emerald was sure of that. But by then she would be gone.

The plane called for her zone to board, and she swung her tote over her shoulder.

"Hello, Ma'am, been to L.A. before?" The ticket agent flashed a friendly smile as he took her ticket. Now, of all times, someone chose to talk to her. She knew it was nothing more than a courtesy, but the fewer people who noticed her, the better.

"No." Emerald boarded the plane, and the flight attendants all welcomed her. She had an aisle seat in the middle of the plane. It was a large plane, though, with only a few other passengers. She wanted to blend in. That's why she had chosen L.A. Someone could disappear there.

Perhaps no one would notice her absence. No one was sitting beside her to report her missing. She glanced at the man sitting across the aisle, already snoozing. The sound of babies crying filled the plane and she looked back to see a large-framed woman with a toddler on her hip and a baby carrier with a newborn—both of them wailing. A diaper bag lay on the floor, spilling its contents into the aisle. The stewardess rushed to assist the woman and Emerald seized the moment. Now was her chance.

She stood up and maneuvered to the front of the airplane, as if heading to the bathroom. Then she took a sharp turn and exited the plane. She walked quickly through the tunnel, waiting for someone to follow her or yell after her. But no one did. Sneaking past the busy ticket agent, whose back was to her as he talked to a last minute passenger who was attempting to carry on too much luggage, she left JFK and hailed a cab.

"Penn Station."

Emerald glanced at her watch. It was now six-thirty. She would catch a Metroliner to D.C. and arrive at Union Station around eleven-thirty A.M. By then, her father and Sidney would have discovered the plane ticket to L.A. on her credit card. They would search L.A. and think she'd disappeared into the city. Here on in, she'd pay cash.

∞

Emerald awoke from an unsatisfying sleep. Her back ached from the long ride against the stiff seat. In her lap, she held the tote that she had hurriedly packed. She pushed her matted hair back from her face, wishing she had the hairbrush she'd stuffed somewhere in her bag. If she had remembered to pack it.

Her stomach muscles clenched. She'd had no food since that poor imitation of a turkey club sandwich she'd grabbed from the bus station in St. Louis. Sustenance hadn't been a real priority during the last few days of bus travel.

She peered out the window into daylight. Colorado. The bus climbed the wall of a canyon whose tall rock structures left her breathless. They were soon in the center of a large bowl of mountain faces and peaks that stretched into the sky. Some disappeared into the low lingering clouds. Others' sharp edges cut vividly into the brilliant blue sky. Still others' smooth, rounded summits blended into the rocky desert, almost as if painted by an Impressionist artist.

Emerald slumped back into her seat. What had made her flee West—and in a ratty old Greyhound? She wasn't sure. When she'd arrived at Dulles Airport, she could have flown anywhere. But something had drawn her to this westbound bus, and she'd been riding it ever since.

With each passing mile she found herself asking the same question that followed her everywhere. Was she crazy? Nothing she had done in the past even came close to this. All she knew was she had never felt surer about anything in her life. She hadn't been able to decide yet if it had been a dream, a vision, or her imagination. Whatever it was, it gave her the courage to leave. And despite her confusion and fear, she'd never felt better.

"Next stop, Tussle Springs," the driver's voice blared over the intercom and Emerald's pulse raced as she repeated the question she had faced at each stop. Should she get off here?

They approached a sign that read, WELCOME TO CANYON RIDGE MOUNTAIN. She watched in amazement as they entered a small town; it looked like something out of a Western. Marveling at the dusty old shops with names like Martha's Home Cooking, Hank's Drug Store, Blackberry Bakery and Rocky Mountain

Trading Post, Emerald straightened up in her seat. The Greyhound had almost become a time machine.

A horse tied up to a post outside Hank's Drug Store startled her. She watched in curiosity as a boy who looked about fourteen left the drugstore with a paper bag. After untying the horse, he jumped on. The horse trotted through town as if he did it on a daily basis. A smile tugged at her lips.

"This is it, isn't it?" she whispered.

A voice inside her said, *Yes, Emerald, this is it.*

She jumped from her seat and rushed to the front of the bus past surprised glares. "Stop. I need to get off here."

The bus driver glanced back. "Our next stop is Tussle Springs."

She bit her bottom lip as she watched the shops and small town fade into the distance. Her entire being told her Canyon Ridge, not Tussle Springs.

"I need something to eat, I have low blood sugar."

The man frowned. "We'll be in Tussle Springs in less than half an hour."

"I need to get off the bus now!"

The bus rocked to a halt. "You realize, Miss, that you will have to travel to the next town for the closest station."

"Thank you." Emerald swung her bag over her shoulder as she exited. She walked half a mile before reaching the main street of the small town. People gawked at her, but they seemed friendly enough. She noticed everything, from the old building structures to the style of clothing—mostly jeans, cowboy boots and hats.

Emerald took a deep breath. Where to first?

She would need a place to stay; in a few hours it would be dark. She scanned the main drag, and Hank's Drug Store caught her attention, probably because of the horse.

She entered the shop, and looked around in wonder. Old wooden shelves lined the walls. Behind a counter just long enough for three red bar stools hung a hand-painted sign: SODA FOUNTAIN.

"Can I help you?"

She jumped at the voice from behind her and turned to see an older man with gray hair, cowboy boots, and a white stained apron. Before she could respond, he scrunched his eyebrows together. "You ain't from around here, are ya?"

She shook her head. "No. I was wondering if you knew of anyone who takes boarders?"

The man shook his head. "Sorry, Ma'am, the only people looking for boarders around these parts are dude ranches looking for workers."

"Thank you."

She walked to the door and stepped back outside the shop. Dude ranches? This really was cowboy country. She thought of her childhood fascination with the West. And the image of a man wearing jeans, cowboy boots, and a collared shirt burned in her brain.

*He lives out West, Daddy! I just know he does!*

She surveyed the street again and focused on Martha's Home Cooking. Her low-blood-sugar gambit with the bus driver actually had some truth; maybe after a good meal she could think more clearly. She entered the semi-crowded restaurant, and the aroma of barbeque filled her nostrils. A wooden sign read: HAVE A SEAT WHEREVER YOU'D LIKE. Emerald hesitated, then her stomach took over. She slipped into the nearest empty booth and picked up a menu.

"What can I get ya, honey?" The woman was probably in her fifties. She blew at a piece of hair that had escaped her bun and fallen into her face.

Emerald glanced back at the menu. "I'll have a burger and a club soda."

"They'll be right up." The women scribbled on her pad then hurried off.

Emerald's eyes drifted across the restaurant and stopped at the cowboy sitting in the booth facing her. Was he staring at her? She couldn't tell. His hat dipped low over his eyes, so perhaps he was sleeping.

The waitress set a barbeque sandwich and a Pepsi in front of him, and he mumbled something Emerald couldn't hear. The waitress laughed. Suddenly he removed the hat and set it on the table. His eyes met hers briefly and her heart caught in her throat. He had dark hair, curling up from where his hat had been, and dark eyes.

He lowered his head and closed his eyes. What was he doing? Napping over his lunch? When his head rose, his eyes met hers again briefly. She quickly looked away this time, her face flushing. Twice he'd caught her staring.

When the waitress set her food before her, she placed the paper napkin in her lap and diverted her attention to her meal. She had better things to worry about right now than a cowboy.

She took the last bite of her hamburger. The waitress returned with a bill, and Emerald handed her the money. "What are my options for places to stay around here?"

The women frowned before stuffing the money into her pocket. "If you're here for the tour, it's the next town over. Tussle Springs."

Emerald shook her head. "I'm not looking for a tour."

The women tucked a strand of hair behind her ear. "Well, Miss, this isn't really a vacation town."

"I'm not vacationing."

The women clicked her tongue. "There is no hotel here."

"Is there any place around here that takes boarders?" Emerald felt stares from the other patrons. She remembered what the man had said at the drugstore. "Money isn't an issue," she added.

The woman looked at her slightly surprised, then sighed. "Sorry, Miss, I think you've come to the wrong place.

The wrong place? She had been so sure this was it. Who was

this waitress to question the first thing she had been certain of in a long time?

Emerald walked slowly out of the restaurant, and looked around helplessly. She would need transportation to Tussle Springs. She searched the street for an answer, but none seemed apparent. She waited on the narrow sidewalk, hoping for some sort of revelation. There was something about this small town.

*Was it possible I was mistaken?*

She forced her legs to move, unsure where she was going but certain she didn't want to leave. As she turned around, her eyes widened at the view of the canyon. It had been there all along, but she'd been too focused on the town. The crags and mountain peaks—impressive even from the bus's confinement––now spread around her for miles.

*One thing's for sure; I don't feel like a prisoner here.*

Emerald had seen many beautiful scenes on her trip, but there was something about the Rockies in front of her that captivated her more than anything else. She needed to reach them, be surrounded by their beauty. Without another thought, Emerald threw her Louie Vuitton tote over her shoulder and began her journey across the plains.

She soon discovered that her high heeled boots were not the best choice for hiking. Her feet ached and blisters rubbed, but the splendor surrounding her drew her onward. As the prairie succumbed to rolling hills, the dying grass and dirt gave way to rocks. Exhaustion threatened to overtake her. Emerald dropped her tote and sank to the ground. If she could just catch her breath.

She thought back to the burger. She should have eaten more.

Emerald rested until she felt control over her lungs, then she rose and threw her luggage over her shoulder. No longer intoxicated by the lure of the mountains, she faced reality.

*Where am I going?*

The question haunted her but she didn't have time to wait for an answer. The sun was fading fast behind the mountains.

Emerald looked around in desperation. Scanning the hills in front of her, she noticed a small structure to the west. A home. Struggling for a deep breath, she forced her legs to move toward it. The journey up the ridge was excruciating. Reaching the top, she collapsed, gulping air and seeing only blackness. It was strange that she was having breathing problems. She'd never had a history of asthma.

After a moment, haze replaced the darkness then finally cleared, revealing what looked like a ranch. The cabin reminded her of the ones she'd seen in Vermont at a ski lodge. Built of timber, it was cozy, and inviting. Mountains surrounding at every angle made this place seem like a postcard. A rich thicket of trees dotted behind the home against the foothills. On the other side the land was mostly clear of trees and seemed to go on forever.

The sky had turned an astonishing palate of pink, purple, and blue. Emerald looked in awe at the way light played over the peaks, forming shadows and beams of radiance. It seemed evidence of the existence of something greater than she. As she opened her mind to this thought, an issue more important than her next breath seared her brain. She only considered it for a split second, but that was enough for her to question her sanity.

*How can such magnificent beauty exist if God doesn't?*

# Chapter Six

AS SHE HALF-WALKED, HALF-LIMPED toward the house; Emerald felt warmth, security, and a sense of belonging—like she was home.

"Can I help you?"

The voice from behind snapped her back into reality. She jumped and turned to see a cowboy dressed in jeans and a work shirt, boots, and a cowboy hat dismounting from his horse. He looked to be in his thirties. She gasped as familiar dark eyes met hers from beneath the hat.

She stumbled for words. "Yes, I would like to speak with the owner."

"Jack Evens," he said with a slight nod.

He must not recognize her.

"I'm looking for a place to stay. I . . . I was wondering if you would be open to taking in a boarder?"

It hit her that she'd just asked a complete stranger for a home. But she was running out of options.

The man stared at her and a look of confusion crossed his face. Then he shook his head and pulled a work glove off his hand. "Someone must have directed you wrong. This is a working ranch."

Her heart fell. She didn't care what kind of ranch it was. It had been her hope, her salvation. She wasn't sure which thought was more awful, making the long journey back over all the hills to town, or leaving this haven of beauty.

"So you don't have a room for rent? Or somewhere where I could stay until I find another place?" Her voice was desperate. Emerald felt ashamed for begging, but at this point, it seemed her best alternative.

The man studied her with a strange expression. "Sorry," he said, "the only space outside the house is for people who work here."

"Oh."

She stood before him in silence, unsure what else to say, but unable to walk away. She searched his eyes, dreading what he was thinking.

To her surprise, though, his gaze was soft and curious. "Did you come here all the way from town?"

She licked her dry lips and nodded. His brows raised and she waited for him to question her further. Instead, he took a step toward her.

A man shouted from behind him. "Jack!"

He turned. "I'll be right there!"

"I need to go," he said to Emerald. His eyes dropped to the tote bag at her feet. "I'll be back in a few minutes and give you a ride back to town. It'll be dark soon, and it's too long a hike."

Unsure how to respond, she watched him walk to the man who was waiting for him across the pasture. Go back to the bus station, to seek a new destination? Maybe she could find another town like this one. Tussle Springs was where everyone kept directing her. There had to be other places that were just as breathtaking; she'd passed many on her bus ride. Yet something had impelled her to get off the bus here, in the middle of nowhere.

She made up her mind, and took a deep breath. This ranch offered her more than a place to hide. It offered life. That was it. Something about this town restored the lively feeling she had lived so long without.

Emerald watched Jack Evens cross the pasture and calm a horse another man was riding.

She threw her tote bag over her shoulder. She didn't care that this was a working ranch, or that all the tourists went to Tussle Springs, or that this town shunned newcomers. Feeling she had no other choice, she headed away from the house and toward the forest. The unknown. Just like her whole journey. She had already determined that she was not going to go back the way she had come. The hill might be a lot easier going down than up, but it still haunted her.

By now the sky had faded to a solid gray splotched with darker shadows. In a short time it would be dark. She felt pressure on her chest, and for a moment could scarcely breathe. The heaviness on her torso increased. Lightheadedness overtook her and she stumbled, pitching forward. Blackness overtook her.

The rustling sound could not wake her from her slumber. She felt herself being lifted from the ground. Moaning slightly, she opened her eyes to a blurry figure.

"You'll be all right." The voice was familiar, but without a face she couldn't place it.

*I can't . . . breathe.* But the words wouldn't come.

"Just take it easy, you'll be fine." The voice spoke with warm assurance, but she felt apprehensive.

She tried to respond again, but he hushed her. "Don't try to speak, just breathe."

Easy for him to say.

Emerald struggled to obey as once again the world began to spin, and then turned to darkness.

∞

Emerald woke with something cold and hard pressed against her lips.

"You have to drink." The voice was stern, and though her first instinct had been to turn her head away, she forced her mouth open as cold water from a glass hit her lips and slid past her throat. Something behind her back was propping her up. The glass again tipped and she struggled to swallow faster.

"I know it's hard, but you have to keep drinking."

Emerald choked and turned her head away.

"Please. . . ." she whispered.

"Just a little more."

She opened her mouth enough to take one more sip.

He set the glass down beside the bed and removed his arm from behind her. She lay back in relief, looking at the man in front of her. Jack Evens.

He wore the same jeans and work shirt that she had seen on him earlier. Only now, he was without his hat. His dark brown hair was tussled, and sweat dotted his forehead. Confused, she studied the room. She was lying on a bed. The furniture was masculine and was made out of logs. Her eyes shifted quickly to Jack, still standing over her. His mouth was set in a firm line.

"What happened?" Her voice came out in a hoarse whisper.

"You fainted. I found you near the house." His face pinched. Was it the fainting part or her venture on his ranch that bothered him? Maybe both.

His gaze settled on her. "Not from around these parts, are ya?"

She shook her head, unable to answer.

He wiped the sweat from his brow. "Ever been up this high in the mountains?"

She shook her head again.

"Air's thin up here." He picked up the glass of water on the nightstand. "The best thing for altitude sickness is this. So the more you can drink, the better."

Before she could respond his arm was once again sliding around her, lifting her upright. She drank until she could drink no more, then he gently helped her lie back down.

"So, you have a name?"

"Emerald McGintay."

She mentally kicked herself. She shouldn't have used her real name. What if he'd heard of her father? But Jack showed no signs of recognition and she let out a breath of relief.

He picked up the pitcher of water on the nightstand and refilled her glass. "Well, Emerald, it's not every day I find a city girl wandering around my ranch, passing out from the altitude."

He stuffed his hands in his pockets and headed toward the door. "I had my ranchman, Milt, bring in your bag." He nodded to the tote sitting by the door. "You'll want to stay in bed and keep drinking water until you've adjusted to the oxygen level. I'm going to go start dinner; holler if you need anything." He pulled the door ajar, then left.

∞

Emerald's eyes fluttered open sometime later to a dull throbbing in her head. The room was dark except for a small lamp on the nightstand. Disoriented, she pushed herself to a sitting position, searching the dim light. The anxiety left as she began to remember what had happened. She felt a strong sense of comfort and warmth, which was odd because she was in a stranger's house, a working ranch in a town in Colorado that she knew nothing about. She ought to be terrified, but for some reason, the thought brought peace.

She pushed back the blue quilt and glanced at the empty water glass and pitcher beside her. She urgently needed to get up. Carefully, she grasped the nightstand and hoisted herself to her feet. Her knees felt weak and almost buckled beneath her. She took a deep breath and made her way to the door, grabbing furniture along the way for support.

Emerald hesitated to leave the room. She couldn't remember Jack bringing her into the house. How in the world was she going to know where the bathroom was? Gathering all her courage, she opened the door. Darkness greeted her, and she stood in silence until her eyes adjusted. The increasing pressure on her bladder prodded her to move. She ventured out cautiously, looking to the left and right.

To the right was darkness; to the left, a hallway. This was her best chance. When she made it there she realized all the doors were closed. Feeling her anxiety rising she tried to think fast. How was she to know which was the bathroom? She didn't want to wander into someone's bedroom. But she had to do something soon; every moment on her feet made that quite clear. Somewhat lightheaded, the hallway began to close in on her.

Her hands stretched out, feeling for the wall to catch her. They were met by thin air. Instead of going forward, her legs gave away beneath her, and she felt herself falling backwards. But before she hit the ground, strong arms grasped her and she fell against a hard torso.

"I told you to stay in bed." Jack's voice was low and soft.

"I have to go to the bathroom."

In an instant, he lifted her into his arms and carried her a short distance. Pushing open a door, a light flicked on and he gently set her back on her feet. Though it took a moment for her eyes to adjust to the brightness, she knew where she was.

"Take it slow and easy." He loosened his grip on her.

*Let me take it from here.*

As if he could read her mind, he released her. "Be careful," he said.

He closed the door firmly when he left.

∞

When Emerald stepped back into the hall, she half expected to find Jack standing outside. She was relieved when she instead saw the glow of a lamp coming from the main room. Feeling much better, she shuffled down the hallway and when she didn't spot him in the large den, was tempted to return to her room.

"Feel better?"

He was standing in the corner leaning against the wall.

Her cheeks burned with embarrassment. "Yes, thank you."

"Hungry?" He took a step toward her. The light caught the soft expression on his face.

Something fluttered inside her. She shook her head. "No."

He nodded. "All right. I put some tea on while you were in the bathroom. Maybe you can drink it easier than the water."

She thought she had drunk the water just fine.

"Why don't you sit before you fall down again?"

She looked away, unable to meet his face. Overcome with awkwardness, she realized he had already rescued her twice. She sank weakly into an armchair.

Jack left the room, then returned with two mugs of steaming liquid.

He sat in the armchair across from her. "So where did you say you were from again?"

She hadn't. She took a sip of tea while composing her answer. Not green tea. Something dark and spicy. The smell revived her. "From up north."

"I knew that." He sat his cup down on the end table beside him.

"My accent gave it away?" She smiled at her humor attempt.

"And your heels."

She laughed. "I'll remember not to wear them next time I decide to hike a mountain."

"You took the road up here?"

She shook her head. "Guess that would have been the easier route?"

Jack's eyebrows rose in disbelief. "I couldn't believe it when I thought you took the road all the way here from town. If you came here from the prairie it's a wonder you're not dead."

She laughed, louder this time. "Well, next time I'll know about altitude sickness."

Jack leaned forward in his chair and his face turned serious. "I'm just glad I found you. You could have been in serious trouble."

Humbled at that thought, she forced herself to her feet. "Well, I think I'm going to lie back down now."

He rose also. "When was the last time you drank before hiking up here today?"

"I had a little club soda a few hours ago."

"No wonder it hit you so hard. You were probably near dehydration, anyway. Up here you have to drink twice as much as normal."

"I'll keep drinking," she promised. She glanced down the hallway to make note of where the bathroom was. She hoped that next time she wouldn't need any help getting there.

# Chapter Seven

THE NEXT MORNING EMERALD AWOKE TO a room filled with sunshine. For the first time, she was able to fully examine where she was. The bed had white linens and a blue quilt. The walls were timber, and the remaining furniture consisted of a simple, masculine dresser and a nightstand.

Emerald carefully got to her feet. Though she still felt a little weak, she was doing much better. Basking in the sunshine, she crossed to a window dressed in simple, white cotton curtains. She pulled one back and peered out at the prairie stretched out before her to the distant mountains. Closer to the window, horses grazed.

With a smile, she let the drapes fall back in place. The view from outside would be even better. She shuffled through her bag and her hand landed on the leather cover of her mother's Bible. She looked at it for a moment then put it back inside the treasure box it had fallen out of. She'd taken great risk to get this book back. For what reason she still did not know.

Her hand went to the shiny gold cross necklace that still hung underneath her shirt. She hadn't taken it off since the night she'd left home. The thought occurred to her that maybe she shouldn't be wearing it. She certainly wasn't a believer.

Instead of unfastening it she went to the mirror and studied her appearance. Her face was devoid of makeup, her clothes wrinkled beyond recognition, and her light brown hair, ordinarily wavy, was matted into a nest of tangles. Emerald knew she couldn't leave her room looking like this. She glanced at her tote, lifted it onto the bed and examined the hurriedly thrown-in contents. Eventually, she settled on couture jeans, a pink top, and her most comfortable pair of shoes: soft brown leather Prada sandals. After dressing she worked on her hair with the brush, found a rubber band, and pulled her hair into a simple ponytail. She only glanced at the small makeup bag. Maybe later.

Sneaking to the bathroom to brush her teeth and wash her face, Emerald went back to the main room and looked around. The entire house had a rustic feel to it with two brown, distressed leather sofas and two large matching armchairs in the main room. The floor was a Spanish tile, pinkish brown with black flecks of granite. On each side of the large stone fireplace, timber bookshelves stretched to the ceiling. Almost everything, from the frame to the furniture, seemed built from the very trees she had attempted to venture though the night before.

The door opened, interrupting her thoughts. A gray-headed man in blue jeans supported by a wide brown leather belt walked in, stomping his boots on the rug. When he saw Emerald, a warm smile crossed his face. "So you must be the city girl suffering from the thin air?"

She forced an embarrassed smile as the man extended his hand. "Tony Evens."

"Emerald McGintay," she said softly.

The man seemed forthcoming and friendly.

"Why don't we go on in the kitchen?" He extended his hand toward the area where Jack had brought her tea the night before. "Jack puts together great breakfasts, but since he's running a little late this morning I guess I'll have to start."

The kitchen was large and open—though nothing like her Daddy's in Philadelphia—and lined with late-model stainless steel appliances. Nevertheless, the basic wood countertops and cabinets were warm and inviting.

Tony motioned to a simple rectangular wooden table that sat in front of a large bay window. "You just sit down and tell me how you like your eggs."

Emerald sat down on one of the straight-backed chairs. "I'm really not hungry this morning, maybe just a glass of orange juice, if you have it."

"Ah." Tony pulled out a glass, then brought a carton out of the fridge. He poured her juice, then filled a mug with coffee. He sat down beside her and sighed. "It's been a long morning already."

He laughed, and Emerald smiled. Something about him put her at ease—maybe the warmth in his eyes or the lightness in his voice. Maybe it was the old, yet vibrant, blue eyes and the snowy white hair. Or, the aged skin from years in the sun and the cowboy boots. She wasn't sure and didn't care.

"So where you from?"

The sound of the door opening and closing saved her from the question. Jack entered the kitchen with a cheery, "Good morning." He gave her a slight nod and turned to Tony. "I thought you were going to start breakfast?"

Tony pushed back his chair with a little laugh. "I was, but Emerald isn't hungry so I thought I'd wait and let you have the honors. We both know you're the better cook."

Jack took a carton of eggs from the fridge. "Ever had a Colorado omelet, Emerald?"

"You mean a Texas omelet!" Tony turned to Emerald. "I'm originally from Dallas. Jack's mother and I moved out here when she was pregnant with him. I may not be much of a cook, but the one thing I learned to do right was a Texas omelet."

"Like steak?" Jack asked impatiently.

"Yes," she answered hesitantly.

"Jack, don't make the poor girl eat if she isn't hungry," said Tony.

She sighed in relief. *Thanks for speaking up for me.*

Jack glanced at Tony. "She may not want to eat, but if she wants her strength back she needs to."

"Son, it may have been thirty years since I moved out here, but that doesn't mean I've forgotten how the air affected me. I didn't have an appetite for days."

Jack cracked an egg into the skillet. "She won't have to worry about that. She'll be leaving soon."

Tony opened his mouth, but then turned away. "Guess I'd better get started with the mare."

"You're not going to stay for breakfast?" Jack asked.

Tony shook his head. "Nope, got a lot of work to get done." He turned to Emerald with his unfaltering smile. "It was nice meeting you, Emerald. May God bless your day."

She stammered out a thank-you.

She'd never had anyone wish God to bless anything in her life. Though she usually dismissed anything to do with God, the statement touched her in a way she couldn't explain.

Jack glanced at her as Tony left the kitchen. "There's some cereal and fruit if you want something lighter."

"Thank you."

Emerald felt a sudden awkwardness alone with Jack in the kitchen. She took a banana from the fruit bowl and peeled it. The last time she had eaten had been the day before at lunchtime. The kitchen soon filled with the aroma of steak and eggs. Under different circumstances, she might have found the smell appetizing.

Finally, with an omelet that almost took up his whole plate, Jack joined her at the table. He folded a napkin in his lap then bowed his head and closed his eyes. "Dear heavenly Father, thank you for this new day and this breakfast, Amen."

Jack glanced up at her, and she wondered if she should have closed her eyes, but he didn't say a word. After seeing his large breakfast, she had assumed he must be ravenous, and watched now as he chewed slowly. What did he think of her? He'd had to carry her to the bathroom the night before. The memory made sitting across from him all the more awkward.

He broke the silence. "I take it you're feeling a little better?"

"Yes, thank you."

He nodded. "I didn't hear anything else last night so I take it you slept okay?"

She looked away as her cheeks flushed.

"Don't worry about it. The important thing is that you're okay. And you'll start feeling a lot better once we get you back down to a lower altitude." He took another bite. "It looks like you've already dressed, but if you need to use the shower or anything, help yourself."

"Thank you."

"I have a couple of things I have to get done this morning but I got a good early start. So, I'll probably be ready in the next hour to take you back to town."

He seemed to be watching her closely, and she wondered if it was because she had fled the last time he offered to drive her down. He clearly wanted to get rid of her. And she'd secretly been hoping otherwise.

Emerald swallowed the last bite of banana then washed it down with the rest of her orange juice. She didn't want to be someone's charity case.

Jack picked up his empty plate and carried it to the sink. "I'll be back shortly." Then without another word, he left.

∞

Once outside, Jack felt the crisp morning air cool his warm face. She didn't want to go back to town; that was obvious. What was a young city girl doing at Canyon Ridge Mountain anyway? Why had she left yesterday when he had offered to drive her back to town? Last night he'd been partly relieved to learn her wandering was a bathroom run and not another escape attempt. Had he lived as a bachelor for so long that it had come to this?

He found Tony working with Missy, their new mare, and thought of his father's theory on breaking horses. Horses were like people, Tony said. They responded to love and kindness before forcefulness or discipline.

The mare snorted, pawed, and shook her black head. His father spoke some soothing words then gave her a break, heading to the side of the fence where Jack stood watching.

"I told you she was going to take some time, Dad." He watched the mare trot circles in the round pen.

Tony shook his head. "She does have a mind of her own. But then again, they all do."

Jack sensed Tony was talking about more than horses, but dismissed the notion. "Can you handle things while I take Emerald back into town?"

Tony nodded and led the horse out of the corral. "Find out where she's from?"

"It doesn't matter."

But for some reason it did.

After he finished his feed chores, Jack went back to the house. Heading to the bathroom to wash up, he passed by Emerald's room. He stopped. Pushing the door open, he confirmed his suspicions. The bed was neatly made, and her things were gone.

"Emerald?" He dashed down the hallway and found the bathroom empty. Next, he checked the kitchen, though he knew what he wouldn't find.

She had left so completely it was as if she had never been there.

# Chapter Eight

EMERALD SAT ON A LARGE ROCK, amazed at how the altitude constricted her breathing. How far would she get before Jack realized she'd left? He might not bother looking for her this time. Regardless, she wasn't leaving this beautiful area. With the ranch out of sight, she sat atop a small hill. In the distance she saw only mountains and crags, no sign of habitation. Yet her spirit was calmed, insisting she would survive.

She breathed in the crisp air, feeling a presence, something invisible yet powerful. She closed her eyes as the wind gently blew through her hair and touched her face. The presence increased.

"Who are you?" she finally asked.

The voice in her head was so intimate, so close.

*You already know who I am, Emerald.*

The voice couldn't be real . . . could it? And if it were, why would it speak to her? She gulped from the water bottle she had packed, then stood, strength returning to her legs. Firming her resolve, Emerald looked at the mountains in front of her, and continued toward them.

∞

"I'm not leaving until I find my daughter."

Bradford hung up his hotel phone. His eyes ached, which

indicated a migraine could be creeping up, but his day was far from over. He and Sidney, along with one of the best PI's in the country, had spent the last three days in L.A. searching for any sign of Emerald. She'd just disappeared. The last trace they had was her withdrawing money, then getting on the airplane at JFK. After arriving at the airport they had not one lead or trace to her.

How could she disappear into thin air?

A knock on the door shook him out of his thought and he crossed the hotel's plush carpet to answer it. The Beverly Wilshire's Four Seasons hotel had excellent service, and he'd been shocked that Emerald wasn't there when they arrived. It was the only place she'd ever stayed with him when visiting L.A. to shop on Rodeo Drive.

"May I come in?"

It was Sidney. "I can't leave yet, Sidney."

Sidney nodded. "Don't lose hope. They'll find her."

Bradford went to the bar in his room and pulled out two airport bottles of Grand Marnier. He handed one to Sidney, then drank his own.

"They searched every five star hotel in L.A., Malibu and Newport Beach."

Bradford crossed the room and shut the drapes, closing out the view of the pool below. The room darkened with only the tiny stream of light peeping between the crack he'd left.

"My head's starting to kill me," he explained.

"Have you taken something?"

"No."

"I have some Phenergan if you need it. It's good for migraines."

Bradford looked up in surprise from where he had laid down on the sofa. "What are you doing with Phenergan?"

Sidney cleared his throat. "Emergencies. It's the season for stomach bugs."

Bradford moaned. The airplane, with its stale air, could birth germs. And with this stupid airport security he was restricted to how much hand sanitizer he could carry on board. A three ounce bottle? He'd used most of his entire bottle during the flight!

"Do you need some?"

His mind whirled for a moment on all the germs he must have been exposed to. And Emerald. What if she was sick somewhere? Breaking a sweat he nodded at Sidney, then hesitated.

"I've been drinking."

Sidney shrugged as he reached into his pocket and popped open a bottle. "It won't kill you."

"That's encouraging." He stared at the pill for a second then reluctantly took it from Sidney.

"Did you check San Diego?"

"Yes."

"I took her to the zoo there once." They were grasping at straws.

"Don't beat yourself up, Bradford."

"How does a father lose his daughter?"

"She isn't a child anymore. Unfortunately, she has free will."

"Well of course she does. She always has." Why was he snapping at his colleague? He was feeling edgier by the moment. The thought of Emerald being out there somewhere, and not in a five star hotel, disturbed him greatly.

"They're checking all hotels and motels now."

"Motels?" He raised his head up from his pillow in shock.

Sidney nodded. "She only had a few hundred dollars, Bradford."

That was true. The thought of her lying in a nasty motel room made him nauseated. Good thing he took the medicine, his stomach was going to need it. She wouldn't have been able to afford more than a night or two at the Four Seasons, and that was if she got one of the lower rate rooms without a view. Of course she had a credit card, an unlimited one he'd provided for her five years ago. Why wouldn't she use it?

There was only one reason. Because she didn't want them to find her.

Why would she go to such great risk to hide? He shuddered to think of the conditions his little girl was enduring, and the reason why.

∞

Hours later, Emerald shivered as what had been a gentle, refreshing breeze turned into a cold harsh wind that cut into her unprotected flesh. She peered into the darkening sky, a sky dominated by one large angry gray cloud. The distant mountains had vanished. The temperature dropped and large drops of rain fell, soaking her clothing.

Emerald sank to the ground in soggy defeat, wrapping her arms around herself. Lightning split the sky, followed by an earthshaking roar of thunder. She looked around in fear. No trees. If lightning struck the tallest point, she was in danger. The rain intensified and a hard pellet struck her cheek. Hail, the size of a quarter, pounded the ground. Emerald forced herself to her feet; she had to do something.

A flash of something moved in front of her. It wasn't lightening. A hand reached out from the shadows and rain. It was the same hand she had taken the night she left Philadelphia.

*I'm here. You can trust me.*

Daddy would think she was mad. God help her if he was right. That was, if God existed.

*Follow me.*

She grasped the strong hand as it pulled her forward.

∞

Emerald walked blindly through the storm and at some point realized she was no longer holding the hand. Stopping, she looked around and a crude building came into view. She fought her way to it and leaned against the wooden wall, feeling around the structure for an opening. Stumbling through a large door on the wind-sheltered side, she steadied herself, her heart pounding. With lightning flashing through the windows, through a brief illumination Emerald saw plain wood panels and a hay-strewn floor. A barn?

Her teeth chattered as a chill wracked her body. She didn't know where her bag was. Maybe she'd lost it. She had no strength to fumble for it in the dark. Her breathing was ragged from the altitude, the cold, or maybe both. She rolled herself in a ball, hugging her legs to her chest.

*I am with you always.*

She didn't know whether to be grateful or terrified.

∞

Emerald woke to darkness and calm, and a strange reassurance that she was safe. As her eyes adjusted to the darkness, the sliver of moonlight creeping through the windows confirmed her earlier suspicion. She was in a barn.

Her clothes were still wet, but she no longer shook from cold. She groped for her bag and found it just a few feet away. Relieved, she unzipped it, then searched inside until she found a sweater and her car keys. She pulled on her sweater, and turned on the small flashlight attached to her keychain.

Though the light was dim, it helped her find her mother's treasure chest. She opened it and pulled out the Bible. Her heart raced as the thin pages fluttered lightly against her thumb. The pages fell open to the book of Matthew and she put her finger on Chapter 28:20. *And surely, I am with you always, to the very end of time.*

Emerald's heart caught in her throat. *How could these words be the same words that were spoken to her?* She leaned back against the hard, rough wall. *What is this? And more importantly, what does it mean?*

∞

Early morning sunlight poured through the windows, casting streams of light into the barn. Thankful for the warmth, Emerald curled up in a corner on the hay that had served as her bed.

A shuffling noise jerked her to a sitting position, and she looked around.

"I've got a lot of stacking I've got to get done today." A woman's puffing voice. And quite nearby.

A gruff man spoke. "I got to pick up that bull today, but maybe I can help you tomorrow."

The voices drew closer and Emerald snatched her unzipped tote, spilling half its contents. Her mother's treasure box tumbled to the floor. She glanced to the half-wall that separated her from the strangers. In seconds they'd find her. Would they call the police?

Emerald thought of the yard men back home who had discovered a broken window in the guesthouse one Christmas. Someone had been living there, and Daddy had been outraged. She shivered at the fate the homeless man had found. With her heart pounding, she jumped to her feet, grabbing for her belongings. She froze when the voices continued behind her.

"Kati, I really don't think it's a good idea."

Whirling around, she found a man and woman in their fifties staring back at her.

"Ma'am?" The man took a step towards her.

She wanted to answer, to explain, but she couldn't breathe. The walls spun around her.

"Grab her, Pete. Can't you see she's going to faint?"

A hand grasped her arm, and Emerald tried to speak but couldn't.

The woman assumed control. "Let's take her to my house."

The altitude kicked in and Emerald fought to breathe as they carried her outside the barn.

The man's voice gained new urgency. "I'll take her in my truck, it'll be faster."

He hoisted her up into a large green pickup, and as the truck rocked into motion, Emerald once again drifted from consciousness.

∞

Her eyes fluttered open. Something wet was across her forehead. Touching it, she knew it was a cold cloth. Her other hand went to the soft cushion; she was lying on a sofa.

"Reckon we ought'ta call the doctor?" The man's voice came from a distance.

"No, not yet."

"She looks like a city girl in that pink, don't she?" the man said. "Though Lord knows how she got up here."

"Now, Pete, that doesn't matter right now."

The woman entered the room and offered her a glass of water. "Darling, do you think you might be able to drink some?"

Nodding, Emerald tried to push herself to a sitting position.

The man gripped her arms to help her. Her fingers wrapped around the water glass and with shaky hands she managed to gulp it down.

"That's a girl."

The woman smiled warmly. Not the greeting she was expecting for a trespasser.

"What's your name, honey?"

She glanced from her to the puzzled man. He was tall and lean, and fit Canyon Ridge's apparent dress code of blue jeans, flannel shirt, and cowboy boots. His hair was silvery.

The woman also wore blue jeans with cowboy boots, but

had a white button-up shirt with horses on the collar. A ponytail held her dark brownish-gray shoulder-length hair. She was youthful and full of energy, and her blue eyes looked familiar, but Emerald was too disoriented to know for sure.

The woman was waiting for her name and her answer came hoarsely. "Emerald." *Please don't call the police.*

"I'm Kati, and this is Pete. If you don't mind me asking, honey, do you know what altitude sickness is?"

Emerald smiled. Boy, did she. "I've heard of it."

Kati nodded. "Well darling, I think you've been affected by it."

Kati glanced at the man. "Pete and I found you in our storage barn. Do you know where you are?"

Emerald shook her head, and once again the man and woman exchanged a glance. If they had called the police, Daddy might be her only recourse. The thought made her sick.

"So, Emerald, tell us how you got up here." Pete sat in the worn armchair across from her.

She hadn't the strength for fabrication. "I hiked."

"Hiked?" Pete leaned forward as if he wasn't sure he had heard right.

"Yes, I started the day before yesterday. Last night I got caught in the storm, and I found your barn. I went in for shelter, that's all. I wasn't stealing anything"

Kati wore a surprised expression, and Pete's jaw dropped.

"No wonder you're so fatigued. And what a terrible storm to be caught in." Kati reached out and patted her on the knee.

"You hiked in those?" Pete nodded to her open-toe Prada sandals.

Kati dismissed his question. "You must be starved to death, Darling. I'll get some breakfast started right away. Pete, I know you've got to go pick up that bull. If you see Karen, please tell her I said hello."

Pete rose, looking one last time at Emerald, and removed the cowboy hat from the rack by the door. "I'll give you a holler later on." Hesitating, he left.

Kati turned to her from the kitchen doorway. "Now you stay seated right there and I'll whip something up in just a jiffy."

Emerald leaned against the soft back of the couch and looked around. The living room was simple, like Jack's, yet with a different style, more like a farmhouse. Family photos and sculptures of horses dominated the décor. The faded flowered couch and hunter green armchairs bore the evidence of much use.

After a few minutes, Kati carried a tray from the kitchen. "I'm embarrassed to say that we're a cattle ranch, since I seem to be out of steak." She laid the tray, holding poached eggs, toast, and milk, in Emerald's lap. "I hope this will do."

"Thank you." Though Emerald knew she needed to eat, she still had no appetite.

Kati sat beside her. "So, what are your plans now that you've made it into the mountains?"

Emerald took a bite of her toast and chewed, surprised by the warmth in Kati's eyes. "I was hoping I could find a place that would accept a boarder."

"Umm." Was all Kati said and Emerald braced for the usual go-to-Tussle-Springs. But instead Kati added, "Well, honey, I've got to get to work. Got some stacking to get done today. You just make yourself at home, and if you need anything, I'll be where we just came from."

Emerald had no idea where that was but she swallowed her toast in surprise at Kati's willingness to open her house to a stranger. At home they had the most sophisticated alarm system made, and an arrangement with the police to patrol the house several times during the day—and even more often at night. Her entire life had been ruled by protection. How could this town be so careless?

"You'll need to spend the day mostly lying around. I'm afraid I don't have a television or anything, but I have a lot of reading material." She waved to the bookshelves in the corner. "I'll be back in around lunch time."

Pondering the woman's hospitality, Emerald leaned weakly against the couch. Back home, hospitality came from household staff directed at people Daddy wanted to impress or needed something from. Not strangers without a place to stay. This place and the ways of these people were completely foreign to her. Yet, it was exactly this foreign laid-back-ness that she was relying on right now.

Maybe she'd discovered far more than the beauty of the mountains.

# Chapter Nine

EMERALD TOOK A BITE OF THE white bean chili that Kati had prepared for dinner. It was warm with a spicy zing. She sat back in the breakfast nook of the petite yet comfortable kitchen. Glass doors framed a gorgeous view of the mountains.

"Have you seen a Colorado sunset yet?" Kati asked with a smile.

Emerald shook her head. Storms and altitude sickness had ruined her first two chances at the opportunity.

Kati took a sip of her coffee. "It's going to be a clear night tonight. When you're finished we'll just have to go sit outside."

Emerald marveled at the kindness Kati had shown. The woman had treated her as a welcomed guest, never broaching the subject of leaving. To Emerald's surprise, she had spent most of the day sleeping, managing to flip through a book, *Pioneer Woman,* before succumbing to exhaustion.

Sipping her milk it took her a minute to swallow it. Its rich creaminess was something she wasn't used to.

"You all right?"

Emerald nodded. "I just haven't drunk this since I was about eight."

"You haven't had milk since you were eight?"

Emerald shook her head. "Oh no. I've had milk. Soy milk."

Kati's eyebrows raised, but she didn't reply.

Emerald broke the silence. "I guess Pete hasn't gotten home

from picking up the bull?" She knew nothing about bulls, or transporting them, but she could imagine it was quite a job.

Kati glanced at her watch. "Pete should be home by now. He lives about a mile from here. His wife died of cancer six years ago. He came to work for us not long afterward, and my brother subdivided a few acres of his own land to build a home for him. Pete's been a great addition and a big help on the ranch. In fact, I'm not sure what we'd do without him."

"So your brother lives with you?"

Kati had throughout the day repeatedly referred to a "we" that apparently didn't include Pete.

Kati shook her head. "Not with me, I live here alone. Our father left us this land, about twelve sections altogether. We tried to split it up evenly; my brother and his wife have a home that way." She pointed east. "Then their son has his part south of me. We gave Pete some to the southeast and my son, Caleb, has his home to the west of here. He, however, decided he didn't want to be a cattle rancher, so he gave a lot of his land to his cousin." She smiled. "We all work together though. Pete helps all of us take care of the cattle and check the fences and scout stock auctions and a million other things, too.

Kati stood to clear the table and Emerald realized she should offer to help. She'd never washed dishes in her life but there was no reason for Kati to know that. When she reached the kitchen sink Kati waved her off. "You go on and sit outside. I've seen many Colorado sunsets."

Emerald hesitated, but Kati insisted. Sliding open the door she stepped outside to the small concrete patio with a worn picnic table, benches, and two lawn chairs. The crisp mountain air met her, and she sank into one of the chairs. As she peered into the sky, Emerald marveled at its brilliance of soft colors that trumped any painting. Streams of pastels blended together, outlining the clouds with color. She sighed at the beauty before her. Something inside her knew she was supposed to be here.

"It's lovely, isn't it?" Kati sat down on the chair beside her.

Emerald could only nod. Words could not describe how she felt.

They sat in silence until slowly the streams of light lowered, and the sky had changed to gray.

Kati stood and stretched. "Well, honey, I don't know about you, but I think I'm going to hit the hay."

Emerald pondered the remark with heaviness in her heart. Katie had invited her to stay the night but she couldn't keep wandering from one home to the next expecting hospitality.

"Thank you Kati, for everything." Hours of contemplating where she'd go and how long she'd last without Daddy were now replaced with humble appreciation. At least she'd survive one more night without her father. Right now, that was enough.

Kati opened the sliding door and stepped inside. "The quilt on your bed isn't very thick. I don't know what kind of weather you're used to, but if you want, I can get you some extra covers."

Half an hour later, Emerald lay in the bed that Kati had drowned with blankets. Pulling one of the faded quilts over her face, the smell of cedar filled her nostrils. She'd never considered the fact that she'd missed having a mom before. So why she was thinking of it now she didn't know.

The only motherly figure with any significance in her life was Molly. Daddy had hired her as a nanny when Emerald was three, after having fired her first one. Over the years, as Emerald outgrew her, Molly had worked her way up to household manager. With two maids, a chef, the gardeners, and Daddy's driver to manage, Molly still managed to look after Emerald. Since she'd returned from school, though, it was more in the form of doling out pills and monitoring her behavior to report back to Daddy.

Kati was different. A warm tingly feeling Emerald had never known radiated her body. She dare not allow herself to hope that she'd found her home. No, she couldn't take that chance yet. Maybe Kati, out of a tender heart, was just giving her a place to rest until she was over the altitude. Emerald would not allow herself to be one of those "leeches" Daddy described when talking about the neglected children at the clinic who grew into clingy, needy adults.

She closed her eyes inhaling the cedar scent. For now, she would bask in this new feeling. Just for now.

∞

"What do you mean she took the disk?" Sidney was stunned by Greg's suggestion. "That's ridiculous, Greg."

"She was there, Sidney."

"But that doesn't mean she took the disk." Just because Greg had spotted Emerald possibly eavesdropping on Bradford and him at the hotel didn't mean she'd taken the disk.

"Then why did she run?"

" Greg, I'm not at liberty to discuss her condition."

"Since when?"

Sidney looked around his apartment. While Bradford craved things old and expensive, he craved things new and even more expensive. He flopped down on the four-figure couch and took a moment to admire the one exception to new: the Picasso hanging over his mantle. All the other exquisite original art was from newer artists, but this one demanded to be center of attention.

Greg sat down across from him on a funky yellow wing chair shaped like a doughnut.

"It's going to be all right, Greg. Even if she did have the disk, the chances she'd know what she was looking at are slim."

He was much more concerned about the bartender or someone else picking it up. He was living in the belief that it was likely the cleaning crew had disposed of it. He'd already called the hotel multiple times, and no one had turned anything in.

"If it wasn't for the damn bartender, we'd never have this issue."

Greg had requested that a bartender come up to make them drinks, even though the area was closed. It had been when Sidney and Greg were at the bar having their martinis made that the bartender had a spill and Sidney's jacket was soaked. He'd left the coat hanging on the stool to dry when they went into the lounge to sit by the fire.

The disk had been in his pocket then, because he'd pulled it out to assure himself it hadn't been damaged. He'd gone over the possibility a million times that perhaps he hadn't replaced it back in his pocket afterwards. He knew, though, that he had.

"If someone finds that disk it puts me at great, risk," Greg said, wiping the sweat from his brow. He'd been obsessed by this possibility ever since Sidney had broken the news to him this morning. Sidney's career would be in just as much jeopardy, but there was no need to speak of that fact. Normally Greg would have handled this much better. The growing intensity of his paranoia and anxiety was apparent.

"Let me write you a prescription for some Zanax."

Greg nodded. "All right."

∞

Emerald woke to a pounding in her ears. Her breath was fast; beads of sweat poked out on her forehead and seeped through her clothes. In one quick move, she pushed the covers back and leapt out of bed. She opened the window shade and stared out into the night.

The suspense was real—too real—and she rested her hand over her thumping heart. *Am I crazy or not? I have to know.*

∞

Emerald had been awake for hours. As the sun rose, she heard humming from the kitchen and stepped into the hallway.

Kati was up, dressed, and brewing coffee. Its rich aroma tempted Emerald, but she didn't drink coffee.

Kati smiled. "Good morning."

Emerald interrupted. "Could I please use your phone?"

Kati paused for a moment. "You could, if I had one. Is everything okay?"

*No. Everything was far from okay. The furthest it had ever been. And wait a minute. Did she just say "if she had one?"*

Feeling self-conscious from her anxiety, Emerald tugged at the wrinkled blouse she'd slept in. She'd left her cell phone sitting at home on her nightstand. It had GPS on it and Daddy could locate her through it. "Do you know where the nearest phone is?"

"Both my son and nephew have telephones. I think Caleb might have done away with his landline when he got a mobile so he could be more reachable." She glanced at her watch. "He's probably gone for the day already but my nephew has a landline."

"Okay."

"My nephew's house is close. Want to go there?"

Emerald nodded, knowing the request left her open to questions, but Kati only asked, "How soon?"

*As soon as possible!* Emerald forced herself to relax. Panicking wouldn't get her anywhere. She could wait. "At your earliest convenience."

"All right." Kati nodded. "Let me finish breakfast, then I have a couple of chores. I'll take you after that."

∞

Hot water beat down on Emerald's tense shoulders. She shampooed her hair with Kati's Suave and recalled that her bag––with all her clean clothes—was in the barn. So that she'd be ready when Kati finished with her work, she resolved to stick with yesterday's attire.

Sitting on the top step of the front porch, the sun stood high and bathed her with radiance. A cool breeze ran through her wet hair—a perfect complement to the sun's warmth.

To the west she saw the barn, shaded by two large pines. To the east there were pastures with cattle grazing, along with a few horses. Behind all was a backdrop of mountains that stretched to the horizon.

Emerald had traveled Europe with her father to experience the Eiffel Tower, the Cathedral of Notre Dame, and Michelangelo's Sistine Chapel. She'd vacationed on the lushest isles of the Caribbean. Yet somehow the Rockies outshone every other place she'd been.

The strange sensation fluttered within her and as the warmth grew, she knew she could doubt no longer that it was real. She got up as she spotted Kati heading toward her, wiping the sweat off her brow with her sleeve.

"Ready?" Kati slapped the dust from her jeans.

Emerald nodded. But was she? Did she have any idea what she was doing?

∞

The green Dodge truck moved at a comfortable pace down the dirt road. Any other time she would have enjoyed the drive and the scenery. Now, only questions consumed her. What was the truth? She had to know. She clenched her fists and squirmed.

Kati glanced at her from the driver's seat. "Honey, is everything all right?"

Emerald forced a smile. "Yes. Thank you for taking me, I really appreciate it."

Kati returned her smile. "Oh, I always like a reason to drive a truck that's not mine." She slapped the steering wheel and laughed.

"This is Pete's truck?" she asked.

Kati nodded. "My old Chevy broke down about a month ago. Until the income comes in to have it repaired, I have Pete's. Between Pete and my son, I have transportation when I need it."

So had Emerald, back in Philadelphia, thanks to drivers and chaperones and a little BMW she'd barely driven yet had the keys to in her bag back in the barn. Of course it wasn't the keys she'd needed for the trip but the flashlight Daddy had given her. It seemed like a good idea to bring them all.

This was the first time Emerald had ever lived free of protection and surveillance.

"That's his ranch around the corner." Kati nodded toward the house they approached.

Emerald strained her eyes and realized the ranch was familiar. When she saw the timber log walls, she felt her breath catch in her throat.

*Kati's nephew is Jack!*

While Kati parked under a large pine, Emerald's heart pounded. She hesitated before opening the truck door. Would he expose her? Force her to go back to town?

"Coming honey?" Halfway to the door, Kati looked back with a hand that shaded her eyes from the sun.

Emerald had to force her legs to move. Kati couldn't deliberately be bringing her to Jack's to dispose of her. Emerald herself had asked for a phone. Kati had to be ignorant.

When they reached the front of the home, Kati skipped two stairs at a time to the large front porch. She was remarkably fit for her age, moving with more energy than Emerald herself felt most of the time.

Without knocking, Kati opened the door. "I doubt he's here this time of day. My nephew's probably out in the pastures." She turned back to her. "But lunch time is soon." She winked.

Yeah, that's what Emerald was afraid of. She'd just have to be quick. Stepping inside the too-familiar home, she was afraid to enjoy its rustic coziness. She knew she should run—before Jack arrived to pry her once again from the place she knew she belonged. Forcing these thoughts from her head, she reminded herself she was there for a reason. Not even the fear of her unknown future could keep her from finding out. Emerald lifted her head in determination. She had to know, no matter what the cost.

Kati led her to the kitchen and pointed to a white phone on the wall. "I'm going to go check on their stacking progress." She winked again. "I know they have more hands than me, but I always finish before they do."

Emerald watched as Kati left the kitchen. When she heard the front door close she glanced at the phone, knowing it was traceable. Her need to have an answer was enough to push her to take the chance. She had to know. Emerald forced her shaky fingers to key the number before she lost her nerve. The line rang, and she clutched the receiver. She would soon know the truth.

∞

Jack slowed his horse to a steady pace. He had been riding fences all morning, encountering more needed repairs than he'd expected. As he neared the house, a dull green truck came into view—Kati. He had planned to visit Kati after work, now he wouldn't have to wait to see her. He scanned the land and spotted his aunt's familiar figure entering the barn.

The inside of the barn was cool; he removed his hat, thankful to be out of the sun.

Kati examined the remaining bales of hay. "Meet your standards, Auntie?" He placed a quick kiss on her cheek.

She laughed. "Well, I have to say you're making better progress than you usually do."

"I tell you every time that it isn't a competition. If you would just let me finish once before you, then I could help you."

She shook her head. "I told you I don't need any help. Besides, I have Pete."

His voice turned serious. "You could have Caleb, too, if he wasn't so busy with—"

"Now Jack, let's not start that."

When he met her eyes, his face softened. He was tired of thinking about Caleb. He cleared his throat to discuss something of more importance. "Kati, last night I brought a truck load of feed to store in the barn."

Kati nodded. "I saw it this morning. You're worried about the feed this summer aren't you?"

He sighed. "Couple nights ago was the first good rainfall we've had in months."

They both knew that rainfall determined everything.

"We just have to pray for the good Lord to provide," she said as if her answer concluded the conversation.

But his thoughts had already moved to the question that had been haunting him all day.

"When I was in the barn last night I found this." He lifted the Louie Vuitton tote from one of the wide shelves. He'd looked up the print online a few nights ago to confirm it was indeed an expensive designer bag. He'd known she wasn't from around here from her northern accent and ignorance of the land. Now that he knew she'd come from money, it made her seeking to board on a ranch even more suspicious.

Kati frowned. "I think I know who it belongs to."

His eyes widened and he felt a strange pulse in his throat. "So you've seen her?"

Kati raised her eyebrows, but at the moment he didn't care how he sounded. For the past two days, he had been worried about that strange girl, tormented by thoughts of her helpless and alone in the wilderness. That greenhorn wouldn't last a day on her own.

"Pete and I found a girl in the barn yesterday morning. She was in terrible shape, had been caught in that storm, and she was suffering from the thin air."

It was Emerald all right. But as relieved as he was to hear that the land had not devoured her, he sensed something from the look on Kati's face.

"Is she all right?"

Kati hesitated. "Well, she seems to be doing better physically, but I get the feeling that something is wrong. She hasn't said a thing about where she's from. I wonder if she is running away from something." Kati looked deep in thought. "This morning she was panic-stricken. She was adamant about needing to use a phone."

"Did she?"

Kati sighed. "That's why I'm here. She's using yours right now."

Emerald was here. In his house. Using his phone. Jack headed for the barn door and broke into a run toward the house. He could hear Kati yelling after him, but he didn't listen. Skipping three stairs at a time, he climbed to the porch and burst through the door.

He stopped short at the look on Emerald's face. She was pale, and she looked at him as if he were a ghost.

He struggled to catch his breath, then realized it wasn't his breath but his heart he needed to steady. As he searched for the right words, Emerald brushed past him and went out the door. Jack gripped the door as he watched her flee across the pasture. Then he clenched his jaw. Was he just going to stand there and watch her escape from him again? Anger growing, he took off after her.

∞

Emerald ran until her breathing became ragged and her body trembled with exhaustion. She would not admit defeat, however, even as a strong body tackled her to the ground.

"Get off me," she screamed. "Let me go!"

He obeyed, slowly rolling over to the side and panting to catch his breath. He gripped her by the shoulders and turned her to face him.

"Don't you know the open range is no place for a girl alone?"

He turned away, and she wrapped her arms around herself, as if it might soothe her mind as well.

"I didn't want to leave," she said hoarsely. "I've never found somewhere so beautiful, I just couldn't leave. Please try to understand."

"Emerald. . . ." He paused and spoke again. "This isn't a theme park. This is wide-open range. Forty degrees at night, even in June, with bears, coyotes, mountain lions, and all kinds of wildlife." He shook his head. "Not to mention the weather. Storms, lightning, hail. . . ."

Her chest tightened. "I know that already. From the other night." She lifted her chin proudly. "And I survived it. Bring on the bears and the mountain lions."

He threw up his hands. "Is this all some kind of joke to you?"

*If he only knew. It was the farthest thing from a joke.*

"You survived the other night because you found my aunt's barn. But what if you hadn't? If you'd chosen another direction, you might be dead by now."

She knew she could never justify risking her life to him. She had known all the risks, and yet somehow she survived on only a feeling that she would. She couldn't explain to him, as it was something she herself didn't understand.

Jack wiped the sweat from his face, then stood. "Are you going to come back to the house with me, or play *Survivor* again?"

So, television did exist at this altitude.

"I'm done with that. Though I don't think I did half bad." She cracked a smile despite the serious look on Jack's face.

"Are you coming or not?" His voice was short.

"I'm going to stay out here a little while and think. I won't run away again." She watched his face.

He shrugged. "If you do, I'm not coming after you this time."

She looked at him curiously. "You came after me the first time?"

"Yes. And the second time my father and I searched for you, and the third," he held up his hands, "I'm here." Then he picked up his hat and headed toward the house.

Emerald watched him until his lean, strong figure disappeared. She scanned the land before her. The smell of cow manure filled the air, and she realized that the fence she had jumped put her in a pasture. She placed her hands behind her, leaned back, and closed her eyes.

Maybe Jack would be back to grab her and drag her back to town. Not much she could do to resist, except she could find another place to live. In the meantime, she needed to process what had happened before Jack interrupted her.

∞

*Sidney's voice came over the cell phone.*

*Emerald, where in God's name are you?' He wasn't his usual calm and cool.*

*'Did you get my message?'*

*'You mean the message you left at four-thirty in the morning saying you were taking a trip?'*

*Somehow this didn't sound like concern for her well-being.*

*He cleared his throat as if re-thinking his reaction. When he spoke again his voice sounded more like the Sidney she had always known. 'Emerald, I'm sorry. The important thing is that you're okay. Now tell me where you are so I can come get you.'*

*So he could come get her? She tried to control the shaking that was overcoming her entire body. She had to stand up to him. She had called to find out the truth, not to surrender control again.*

*'I'm not coming back. I need some time.' How easily the words came out. Yes, she could do this.*

*'Now Emerald, I need you to listen to me. I hate to tell you this over the phone, but you leave me no choice. Right now, you are in a very dangerous and serious state. If you want time alone, I can get you that, but not this way. You need to be somewhere safe, someplace where your father and I can see to your needs. Please, Emerald. Tell me where you are and you won't have to worry about anything else.'*

*No, I suppose not. Least of all making my own decisions. Least of all the real world.*

*'I'm not coming home, Sidney. I feel more stable and in control than ever in my life. And. . . .' She hesitated but knew she had to tell him. 'I'm really close to finding the truth.'*

*Sidney was silent and Emerald knew he was trying to figure out how to manipulate her. 'Is it your dreams and visions that are telling you to do this?'*

*She licked her dry lips. 'No, not exactly. I can't explain it. I just feel this presence, it's as if I'm not alone. Like something else exists, and it's trying to show me something.'*

*Now the voice on the other end became urgent, even desperate. 'Emerald, have you been taking your medication?'*

*She didn't answer. She hadn't brought any meds with her but that didn't have anything to do with this . . . or did it?*

*'Emerald, listen to me. You have to control this. You have a choice. If you do not control it, it will control you.'*

*She leaned against the wall behind her. 'No, Sidney. I think you're wrong. It's not here to control me, only to show me. And yes, I do have a choice. I'm choosing to find and know this presence whatever it is.'*

*Sidney was quiet. When he spoke his voice was soft. 'Emerald, we're not trying to hinder you from this path you have chosen. You are on an important search, but you don't have to be on it alone.'*

*She knew he was upset. '*

*'Tell me the nearest pharmacy and I'll call in your prescriptions.'*

*She pushed a strand of hair out of her face. 'I'm a legal adult, Sidney. You and Daddy have to respect my choice.' She hesitated. 'I have access to the tabloids.' Not exactly true, but the lie was crucial to assuring her safety. 'I'm ready to give an exclusive interview about everything that's gone on in secret concerning my illness and treatment—including us seeing each other outside of sessions.'*

*'Emerald, you don't mean that. You would never do that to your father.'*

*So he was playing the father card. She closed her eyes for a moment as she thought how hurt Bradford would be. A threat like that would ruin Daddy—publicly and legally.*

*'If you attempt to find me the headlines and national news will give the truth.' Emerald ended the call—a movement that demonstrated she was in control.*

It was over. She knew the truth. Sidney's words had matched precisely what she'd heard from him before—last night, when she had dreamed every moment and every detail of the telephone conversation.

∞

Emerald opened her eyes to the meadows and rolling hills. She was ready to accept and to discover the presence that was with her. She was not naive to the possibility she could be crazy. But now things were different. Could her dreams and visions really predict the future?

The thought was terrifying.

"I want to know you, whoever you are."

# Chapter Ten

JACK FILLED A GLASS WITH WATER from the kitchen sink. Why had he tackled Emerald and shouted at her? It hadn't exactly been his plan. He just wanted her to understand how hard it would be for her to stay here. The memory of his rashness left him with a sick feeling in his gut.

He downed the water quickly and looked out the front bay window. He could see his aunt coming out of the barn. Did Aunt Kati know what Emerald was getting herself into? He sat down in a large armchair.

The front door opened and Kati entered. When she spotted him in the chair, she studied him closely. "I saw you chasing her in the pasture. I take that it didn't go very well."

Jack sighed. "I overreacted."

"No. You?"

"You don't know the situation."

She sank in the chair next to him. "No, I guess I don't. Care to fill me in?"

He stood and paced to the window and back. No Emerald, but he wasn't surprised.

"She showed up here the day before yesterday. Must have hiked the whole way."

Kati nodded. "She did."

"She was looking for a place to stay. To board, is what she said. I told her no and offered to drive her to town and she left."

A smile crossed his aunt's face. "Well, she wanted to stay up here."

Jack scowled. "This is only the second time I've seen her, but the third time I have run after her. It's funny how I don't know anything about her except that she is stubborn and fast!"

Kati laughed. "The girl definitely has her wits about her. After all, she survived a night in the mountains."

Jack stretched his hand out in a gesture of agreement. "Exactly. What kind of girl would be so desperate to spend the night in the wild?"

"People camp up here all the time, Jack."

He thought of his aunt's words in the barn. "You're right. She must be running away from something."

Kati shrugged. "Could be. But I think, no matter what the reason, she has come to the right place."

"Are you saying you're going to let her stay?"

"I'm saying that maybe she was led here for a reason."

Jack opened his mouth, but she cut him off. "Whatever her circumstances, a girl can always use a few good friends."

He watched as his aunt headed for the door. "I need to get back, got a lot of work before dark. Do you think you could drive her back?"

Kati was gone before he could respond. He watched out the window as his aunt jumped into the old truck. He sighed. He had work to get done, too.

∞

Emerald carefully climbed over the barbed wire fence. It hadn't been this hard going over the first time, but she had crossed over a less dangerous part. The sun was beginning to sink into the Rockies, and the temperature felt twenty degrees lower than in the last hour. As she neared the house, she realized that Kati's truck was gone. With a feeling of dread, she stopped.

Kati had left her with Jack, who wanted only to get rid of her.

She pondered a moment, and then started toward the house with her head high. As she neared the large front porch, the door opened to Jack leaning against the frame. She silently passed him to enter the house.

"You missed lunch, so I made an early dinner." He hesitated. "Kati had some work that she had to get back to, so I can drive you back after we eat." His tone had changed. His voice was gentler, more uncertain.

He led the way to the kitchen while Emerald tried to process what he'd just said. "Kati is going to let me stay with her?"

A slow grin crept over his face. "I warned her about your running away habit, but she seems to think I'm the only one that has that problem with you."

Emerald liked Jack's smile. It was non-threatening and she felt her guard lowering.

"So. You hungry?" He turned away quickly.

She nodded. "Starved. In fact, I think this is the first time I've had an appetite since I've been here."

"You seemed to eat good in town the other day."

She touched the wood countertop and looked up at him in surprise. So he had been watching her at the restaurant.

His eyes locked with hers. "Well, then, we'd best eat."

Emerald watched as he went to the stove and uncovered a large platter that held two sizzling hunks of meat. "Do you like steak?"

She nodded as her mouth watered. She sat at the table and waited while he brought the platter, then carried a bowl of corn, a basket of biscuits, and a smaller bowl of applesauce.

Emerald reached for the closest thing, the corn. She stopped as she noticed him staring at her. He bowed his head.

"Dear heavenly Father, we thank You for this day that You have given to us, as well as this meal. Amen."

He looked up, then reached for her plate and piled it with

food. Too much, it seemed at first, but she cleared her plate easily. Food at home was always healthy. Meats were organic and vegetables were almost always left crunchy. Molly said when they became limp they were dead. And the biscuits would have never been on the table unless they were whole-wheat and served plain or drizzled with olive oil, never butter.

Emerald realized she hadn't given meals a thought since she'd left home. One would have thought her daddy's warnings of clogged arteries would be plaguing her, but they didn't, not in the least.

She sagged back into her chair. "I think I just ate enough for two of me."

Jack laughed. "You'll learn to eat if you stay up here. We cowboys have to eat good; our hard work depends on it."

She studied him carefully. If she stayed? It was up to her? That was progress over his insisting he drive her back to town.

Jack stood and began clearing the dishes. Emerald began helping; she'd watched enough TV to know it was polite. He shook his head. "I'm just going to put them in the sink for now. I'll wash them later." He looked at Emerald. "Do you like key lime pie?"

She laughed. "Yes, but I'm not sure I could fit any in right now!"

He went to the refrigerator and pulled out a covered pie pan. "Oh, you'll be able to fit my mom's in."

Emerald watched as Jack lit the fireplace then carried two helpings of pie and coffee into the living room. She sat in the chair nearest the fire, thankful for the warmth.

"Nights here do drop." He studied her for a moment.

She wrapped her arms around herself. "Yes, it probably doesn't help wearing this thin shirt either."

Jack set his plate and coffee down. "You probably would like to change, wouldn't you?"

Confused, she watched as he opened the front door and

stepped into the night. She took a bite of the creamy pie and savored its tartness. A few minutes later, Jack returned with something under his arm.

"My bag?"

He handed it to her. "I found it in Kati's barn last night."

She clasped it gratefully.

He motioned down the hall. "Feel free."

Relief washed over her. Ten minutes later she stepped out of the bathroom feeling like a new woman in black leggings, a black cotton skirt, and a red top.

It was casual attire back home, comfy and cute, but Jack's expression suggested something different. He sat on the sofa, his eyes engulfing her. He motioned to the seat next to him; apparently he'd moved her dessert to the coffee table in front of him.

"Thank you." She hesitantly sat down beside him. His pie was already gone. He picked up his coffee mug and leaned back, watching her as she ate. Maybe she shouldn't have sat with him, but moving would make her discomfort obvious.

She peeked at Jack again, who was still watching her. She set her fork down on the plate and turned to him. "So did you have a hard day's work?"

He shrugged. "Moved the cattle to another pasture, checked fences."

"Oh." Her eyebrows scrunched together in thought.

"Tell me about ranch work."

"What would you like to know?"

She hesitated. "What do you check fences for?" How silly the question must have sounded to him.

But Jack leaned back with no hint of impatience. "Checking fences is a critical job for a rancher. Damaged fences are one of ranchers' greatest concerns because it can lead to loss of cattle, or injury." His eyes met hers. "We ride the fences as much as we can. There is no average of how often; it depends on a lot of circumstances such as the cattle, weather, and season."

She leaned forward. "So how do these things affect the fences?"

"Well, if there is a storm, a tree could fall and knock down a fence. Or, if the rain is hard enough, in certain parts it can actually wash the fence away. And sometimes bulls from different pastures get into a fight and charge right through them."

Her eyes widened. "What do you do when that happens?"

"It depends. You repair the fence, of course, but you also have to check to make sure your cattle are all right. If any have escaped then you herd them back in."

She bit her bottom lip in thought.

Jack propped his feet on the coffee table and stretched. "It's a tough job. Milt's house is half a mile from here. He helps me out a lot, but even then, sometimes it's not enough."

The phone rang in the kitchen, and he stood. "I'll be right back."

Emerald settled back against the leather couch as Jack disappeared. The fireplace brought irresistible warmth to the room, and Jack's manner had put her at ease.

What was it about this rustic room and the crackling fire that brought such contentment? Had someone told her a year ago that she would be happy on this ranch, she would have laughed. Yet something about this foreign world brought a gratification she had never known.

Could she really stay here? She knew nothing about cattle ranching. She could only imagine what Sidney and her father would say if they knew her thoughts. To them, it would be confirmation that she was going insane. Maybe she was, but she could learn about ranching in the process. She had to. If that was what it would take to stay here, so be it. A smile crept over her lips.

Jack walked in from the kitchen and leaned against the wall with an odd expression. She was about to ask what was wrong when his face changed. He straightened and walked to the armchair across from her.

"Would you care for any more coffee?"

"No, thank you." She shifted closer to the edge of the couch.

His face grew quizzical; maybe he knew what she was about to ask.

She took a deep breath. Now or never. "Earlier you said that Milt works with you, but sometimes his help isn't enough."

Jack stretched back into his chair and frowned. "Sometimes, but we also get done what needs to be done. Sometimes that means everyone working together."

She leaned forward. "You mean your father, Pete, Kati, and her son?"

Jack scowled. "I mean the true ranchers who are willing to work hard twenty-four hours a day seven days a week. My father, Pete, Kati, Milt, and myself."

He had not included Kati's son. "But your father and Kati each have their own ranches," she said slowly, "their own responsibilities. That must make it hard when you need help."

"What are you getting at?"

Emerald hesitated. "I can help you."

"Emerald—"

"I can ride, and I'm a quick leaner." It made perfect sense to her. Jack stood though, and moved away from her.

"I never said I needed extra help." He picked up the coffee mugs and headed toward the kitchen.

She waited for him to return but heard the water run and dishes began to clatter. That had been his answer and she wasn't at all pleased by it.

She jumped up and dashed to the kitchen. Maybe he had misunderstood her intentions. "Jack, I don't have to be paid. I could work for my keep."

Jack glanced over his shoulder from the sink. "You're staying with Kati, not me. If you're interested in working for your keep, talk to her."

Emerald's mouth opened then closed, and Jack winced.

She returned to the living room and heard the hiss of the sink go silent.

She stood by the fireplace and didn't look up when Jack entered. He went to the closet and grabbed his jacket. "It's getting late, and we have church tomorrow. I'll drive you to Kati's."

∞

When Jack returned home, the house was cold. The fire had burnt out, and the Colorado night air had crept its way inside. Instead of starting another fire, he lay on the couch. His father's call had put him on edge. Kati must have called Tony and told him that Emerald was with him. His father had called to remind him that Emerald needed to be shown some decent hospitality. He was beginning to sound like Caleb. Out of all the things his father would call to tell him.

He should start another fire. No, he should go to bed. He had to get up early to ride the pastures before church. Jack turned off the lamp and headed to the bathroom for a hot shower. The bathroom filled with steam, and he began peeling his clothes off. When he dropped his jeans a small piece of paper fluttered across the bathroom tile. It was a business card and must have fallen out of Emerald's bag.

Jack frowned as he picked it up. The logo side said DR. SIDNEY COFFMAN, M.D. P.A., GREATER PHILADELPHIA BEHAVIORAL HEALTH EXPERTS. He flipped the card over. YOUR NEXT APPOINTMENT IS, followed by a handwritten date and time.

As he stared at the card his breath caught. Emerald was seeing a psychiatrist. He felt a sudden chill, but not from cold. He was being paranoid. Lots of people saw shrinks. And besides, it was none of his business. Should he give her the card? No, the appointment was old. He'd only make her uncomfortable.

Jack placed the card on the bathroom counter, stepped into the shower, and let the hot water soothe his tired muscles before he grabbed a bar of soap. He lathered his body then rinsed.

He would just throw the card away and forget he'd ever seen it. But what if her psychiatric problem was serious?

He turned the water off, then grabbed a towel. Why did it even matter to him? He left the bathroom and went to his bedroom where he plopped onto the bed without bothering to pull down the covers. Not something he usually did, except for nights he was really tired. This wasn't one of those nights; Emerald haunted his thoughts and kept him awake. Okay, it was cold. Maybe he should put something on. He went to his wardrobe and pulled out some old sweats. He looked back at his rumpled bed.

Yes, it was his business; she was staying with his aunt.

Jack went back to the bathroom and snatched the card from the counter. He flipped on the lights in the main room and looked at it. Across the bottom he saw a URL for the Greater Philadelphia Behavioral Health Experts web site.

He turned his computer on, opened his browser and typed in the URL. A picture of a fiftyish man appeared. Dr. Coffman? No. Dr. Bradford McGintay.

McGintay? Emerald McGintay. Bradford McGintay. The resemblance was not obvious, but it was there. He wore a suit, a distant expression, and his hair was balding on top; but he had the same nose, the same jaw line.

He took a deep breath. Was Bradford McGintay Emerald's father? Or perhaps they were related otherwise? He scrolled to the picture below Dr. McGintay's. It was a thirtyish man. Something about him looked too . . . perfect. He smiled broadly. The name under his picture was Dr. Sidney Coffman.

Jack returned to the top menu and looked at the options: About Us, FAQs, Our Staff, Patient Login, Contact Us. Jack clicked on Our Staff.

*Dr. McGintay graduated from Duke University. He moved to Philadelphia at age twenty-nine to work as a psychiatrist. By age thirty he owned his own practice. He specializes in treating people with extreme anxiety disorders, OCD, and ADD. Dr. McGintay at age thirty-one founded Clinic of Hope, the nation's largest non-profit family practice.*

Jack stared at the man's picture again. He was obviously very successful. Did Emerald have a close relationship with him? Did he know she was here?

Jack scrolled down to Dr. Coffman's credentials.

*Dr. Coffman graduated from Harvard. He has owned his own practice, and his primary focus is manic depression, bipolarism, and schizophrenia.*

No, Emerald couldn't have one of these disorders; maybe she was odd, but she wasn't insane. He read on.

*Dr. Coffman is known as Philadelphia's number one psychiatrist specializing in these disorders and forms of psychosis.*

Jack then went to an Internet search engine and typed in *psychosis.* The first result came from a web site called "Mental Health Answers."

*Psychosis can be a clinical condition or an emotional illness; a state that causes very serious disorganized thinking and loss of reality.*

He read on.

*One psychotic disorder is schizophrenia. Psychosis is generally a temporary condition that can be treated by medications or eventually overcome by therapy, depending on the severity of the case.*

Jack twirled his chair away from the computer. Psychotic. Not Emerald. At least not severely. Apart from running away, she seemed normal. He stood and looked again at the appointment on the card. November fourteenth. Over five months ago. Maybe her treatment had ended. He allowed himself to relax. He would give Emerald a chance.

# Chapter Eleven

CHURCH. SHE DIDN'T KNOW IF SHE was ready for this.

Emerald glanced at Kati, who was behind the wheel in a Western hat. Emerald wore a pair of Citizens of Humanity jeans and a Juicy Couture top. Not exactly cowboy attire, but it would have to do. Kati said that was all she'd need. Jeans to church. That was different from what she'd imagined. Not that she'd ever even been inside a church; it wasn't what her life was about.

They turned down a winding dirt road into the foothills and neared a large wooden sign. It held bold, hand-carved letters: WELCOME TO COWBOY CHURCH. Was that some kind of a joke? The small timber chapel sat atop a grassy hill. Old pickups scattered the scraggly grass near the building, and a few horses stood moored at hitching posts.

Kati parked the truck, and Emerald stepped out. A few people lingered outside the entrance talking and greeting others who ambled inside. All wore Wrangler jeans; button up shirts, cowboy boots, and of course, cowboy hats. To the left of the building a few children played on a set of tire swings. One little boy straddled a log she guessed was supposed to be a horse.

She didn't belong here.

Kati motioned her to come, and reluctantly, she followed. At this point there was no other choice but sit in the truck and wait for two hours. When they reached the crowd gathered in front of the church, the people greeted her with warm smiles.

Kati touched her shoulder. "This is Emerald; she's staying with me for a while."

"Howdy." A man tipped his hat.

A younger woman clasped her hand. "I'm Cheryl; it's so good to have you here at Cowboy Church."

It really was called Cowboy Church. Emerald wondered if her surprise and uncertainty showed. Kati took her arm and led her up the stairs to the entrance.

The church had wooden plank floors and walls, and folding chairs formed two rows leaving a middle aisle. The small platform in front held one folding chair and a projector. The children's excited shouts drifted in through the open windows.

"Guess you've never been to a cowboy church before?"

Emerald turned to see Jack behind her. Kati had drifted away, and Emerald wondered how long she'd been standing there alone.

Jack touched her shoulder lightly. "What's wrong?"

She swallowed hard. "I've never been to *any* church before."

"Never?"

"Never."

He took her arm and pulled her toward the front of the church. "Come on, I'll introduce you to the pastor."

She resisted, but he only tugged harder.

Jack led her to a group of three people. "Caleb, I have someone for you to meet."

A man about six-two with Jack's build turned with a large smile. "I'm Pastor Caleb, welcome to Cowboy Church."

Bright blue eyes met hers with warmth from beneath a wide-brimmed hat and slowed Emerald's speeding heart. This was the pastor?

"You must be Emerald." He threw a quick glance at Jack.

Jack touched her shoulder. "I've got someone I need to talk to." He was gone in an instant, leaving her with a stranger. But Emerald had to admit Caleb seemed pretty harmless, even if he was a pastor, someone Daddy had definitely warned her never to get close to.

Caleb didn't notice her discomfort. "My mom told me you're going to be staying with her for a while."

"You're Kati's son?"

"Yep. She's quite a woman isn't she?"

"Don't tell me I'm living in your teenage years again." Kati's voice boomed behind Emerald. Emerald turned, and Kati winked. "I'm only 'quite a woman' when he wants something."

Caleb laughed, then nudged Emerald. "Or when I'm trying to impress a pretty girl."

"Yeah, yeah. Come on, Emerald, we'd best go find a seat. One thing I can warn you about cowboys is when they are out to impress, they often do a good job of sticking their foot in their mouth."

Caleb shot back, "Hey, I heard that!"

Emerald sat down and looked around self-consciously. She wished she could sneak to the back and hide. Kati reached over and patted her knee, as if noticing her insecurity.

Emerald glanced back at the exit and jumped when a voice inside her head voice told her to leave.

*You don't belong here.*

But she couldn't move.

*I want to know you, whoever you are,* Emerald said silently.

Emerald's breathing quickened. These were the words she had called into the wind. Why was she remembering them now? She was getting closer. The frightening question was to what, or who?

She watched cowboys fill the seats of the small church. Laughter and howdys filled the space. One cowboy drank from a tipped-up milk carton. Any other time, Emerald would probably have laughed. Now she didn't. While her mind told her she was in the wrong place, something else told her she had never been closer to the right place.

Jack mounted the stage with a guitar, took the chair and propped the instrument on his legs. Immediately the commotion inside the church quieted and Emerald stood with the congregation. The strum of the guitar filled the air as Jack's strong voice rang out. Though others joined in, as he sang the rest of the church faded away. Her Julliard training might prompt her to think otherwise, but the music was beautiful.

The song ended. Jack removed the strap from his neck and set the guitar down, and Caleb stepped onto the stage. Caleb's professional voice startled Emerald. In person he was warm and friendly, but behind the lectern he radiated strength and enthusiasm. Emerald wanted to understand this whole church thing, but it was just too overwhelming.

Before she realized what was happening, the service ended and Emerald felt an arm slip around her—Kati's. The arm brought comfort, and Kati further surprised her with a large hug as she waved toward her son. "Caleb just opened a therapeutic riding center here at the church. If you're interested in working there, you should talk to him."

Emerald glanced at Caleb, who was surrounded by congregants eager to shake his hand or hug him. Caleb caught her stare. He quickly dismissed the couple before him, and they waved goodbye as he approached her.

"I hope you enjoyed the service."

Her heart beat strangely. "I did."

He nodded. "My mom told me you might be interested in working at our therapeutic riding center."

"Yes, I. . . ."

"She already has a job."

Emerald whirled to see Jack standing behind her.

"I need some extra help on the ranch and she has already offered to work." His jaw was set, and his eyes were narrow. "You start tomorrow. And I suggest you start learning how to dress like a cowgirl if you want to play the part."

Emerald opened her mouth in shock. Jack was already leaving and he stopped briefly to tip his hat to two elderly women at the door.

She turned back to Caleb, who was also watching Jack. He offered a smile. "Well, good luck with your new job."

"So you're going to be working at the riding center, then?" Kati approached, trying to get caught up on the conversation.

Caleb laughed. "It looks like Jack beat me to offering her a job."

"Jack?" Kati looked from Caleb to Emerald in surprise.

Emerald nodded with uncertainty.

Jack. A cowboy. And she was going to become a cowgirl.

# Chapter Twelve

"SIDNEY I'M LEAVING FOR D.C. IN the morning and I hoped we'd have this thing wrapped up."

"I did too," Sidney sighed. But he had to admit his attention had been diverted since Emerald's phone call yesterday.

"Still no trace of her?"

Greg had read his thoughts. "No."

"Sidney, I hate to be the one to break this to you but I received a phone call this morning and we have a witness who says she saw Emerald take the disk."

"What?" He paused in the middle of pouring his coffee, stunned. "What witness?"

"An Hispanic woman from the maintenance crew. From our understanding she'd just ridden up the back maintenance elevator to work on a clogged toilet in the women's bathroom and saw Emerald at the bar going through your jacket."

Sidney's head was spinning. "Wait a minute, what do you mean "from our understanding?"

Greg tapped his BlackBerry. "I sent one of my men into interview some of the staff to see if they had any leads."

Heart racing, Sidney took a step forward. "Greg, we didn't discuss this."

"What does it matter? I got information that needed to be gotten. It was Emerald, so now you know."

Sidney's mind was racing. "Emerald called yesterday."

"Well? Did you trace the call?"

"Yes. She's in Colorado. Some small town off the map. Bradford doesn't know yet."

"Good." Greg sighed in relief. "Just get the disk back and if she knows anything, Bradford will just think she's crazy."

"I don't know if it's going to be that easy."

"What do you mean?"

"She threatened to go to the press and expose any secrets if we came after her."

"Dear God."

"I'll take care of it," said Sidney.

"How?"

"I don't know yet."

∞

"Good luck."

Emerald hesitated after Kati parked the truck in front of Jack's ranch. Lifting her head high, she opened the door and stepped out. But once Kati drove away, she wavered again. Emerald looked at the pastures with cattle grazing and the horse corral. Cowgirl. How hard could it be? At least she'd have a beautiful first day. Warm sun and zero clouds, with a light breeze fluttering the aspens.

Clad in the same jeans and shirt from the day before, she knocked on the front door of the house, but got no answer. She hadn't seen Jack in the fields. Where was he? Then she detected movement to the east—a horse with two Border collies by its side. She stepped down from the front porch and waited as they came closer.

In one swift move Jack slid off his horse, who was a beautiful dark gold with light brown zebra-like stripes. "Morning."

"Good morning." She felt a thrill of excitement.

Jack eyed her and frowned.

Realizing he'd been serious about that dress-like-a-cowgirl directive at church, Emerald said, "Kati and I aren't the same size. She'll take me into town to buy what I need." She motioned to her inadequate garb. "For now, this is all I have."

The Border collies approached to sniff her, their tales wagging happily to see a newcomer. Though her daddy hated any animal, and she'd given up early on asking for a puppy, she'd secretly played with the neighbor's dogs often.

"Hey girl," she bent down to pet one of the smiling dogs.

"Don't touch my dog."

Emerald jerked her hand back at the tone in Jack's voice. The dog looked harmless. She was friendly—hadn't been about to bite.

"She isn't a pet. She's a working dog." Without more of an explanation he held the reins of his horse out to her. "I'll show you around, but first, take Houdini to the stables."

She hesitated as the reins fell into her hand. "What do you want me to do with him?"

"Un-tack him; I'm not going to ride him anymore today."

"I . . . uh . . . I don't know how."

Jack turned to her, and their eyes met. She had told him she could ride. She waited for him to call her bluff but he just adjusted his hat.

"Well then, it's time you learned."

She watched as he walked toward the barn, leaving her and Houdini behind. He glanced over his shoulder. "You coming?"

She pulled on Houdini's reins, but he would not move. She glanced at Jack, now far ahead. She tugged harder, and slowly Houdini decided to follow her.

Jack's stables weren't like where she'd taken riding lessons when she was younger—this was much smaller with fewer horses. Different horses, too. She'd always ridden tall, elegant Thoroughbreds. Jack's horses were heavier, shorter, and bulkier.

The smell of leather, manure, and hay filled her nostrils. It would take some getting used to, but it wasn't anything her love of horses and her determination to learn could not overcome.

Jack opened a door. "This is the tack room. If you're going to be working here, then you'll learn to know this room like the back of your hand."

Emerald peeked inside a room lined with shelves and pegs holding various riding equipment and tools.

Jack pointed to shelves of towels, blankets, curry combs, and a selection of jugs and bottles. "Grooming materials." He then walked to a row of racks lined with saddles. Above them hung bridles, halters, and ropes. "Quick lesson on riding gear."

He picked up two rings with two sturdy metal rods that linked them together. "There are lots of different kinds of bits. Snaffles, curbs, pelhams, kimberwick . . . and the list goes on. The one you need to be the most familiar with is the snaffle."

He finished explaining about the equipment, then showed her how to tie Houdini.

"Ready to un-tack?"

Emerald nodded.

She watched as he unsaddled the horse then removed the leather piece on his head.

"Bridle?" she asked as she struggled to remember what little she'd learned from her riding lessons.

He nodded. "The bit is always attached to the bridle."

She watched as he undid first the back, and then the front cinch. Then he re-tightened them and said, "Your turn."

She looked at him, surprised. He helped her re-saddle the horse, then left her to remove everything, this time on her own.

∞

Jack leaned against a corner post as Emerald struggled to carry the saddle to its rack. She turned around in time to catch him trying to hide a grin.

"Ready?"

Emerald lifted her chin. "Yes." She would show him.

She left Houdini in his stall, then followed Jack.

"This is the generator room." He opened a door to a small cramped area that held a large fridge. Odd place for it.

"This is where we keep vaccines and antibodies for the cattle."

He stepped back outside and closed the door. "So, have any questions yet?"

Emerald nodded. "Yes. These horses look different from the ones I've ridden before."

"That would be because they're Quarter Horses. Not made for jumping or competing—at least not the kind of competing you're used to. Quarter Horses are built for strength, endurance, and most importantly, for cutting cattle."

He adjusted his hat. "Anything else?"

She shook her head and watched as he stopped at a stall to pat a black gelding.

Emerald smiled. "He's beautiful."

The horse's head bobbed at Jack's touch. "Name's Denver. He's three years old and just green broke."

"Green broke?"

"Means he can't handle much past the saddle."

"Oh."

She reached out to rub his neck and immediately felt the strong, toned muscles. "He's built well."

"He's also stubborn." The young gelding snorted, as if to confirm.

Something nudged the back of Emerald's arm, and she turned, then shrieked, as Houdini stood in the aisle behind her.

Jack glanced at the horse with a grin. "He has that name for a reason."

She looked at Jack, confused. "Didn't I just put him away?"

Jack reached around her and firmly smacked the horse's fanny. "Get on."

Houdini returned to his stall, walking calmly through the open door.

Jack followed, closed the stall, and pulled up a chain and lock she hadn't noticed before. "We named Houdini for his skills. The horse can pretty much figure out how to get out of any stall. That's why we lock it."

"But why didn't you tell me—?"

He shrugged. "Knew sooner or later you'd forget to do it, thought it best to learn the lesson right off."

She frowned, but he didn't seem to notice. He looked past her to the opening outside. "I'll show you the barn."

Emerald tried to keep up with his quick pace as they crossed a meadow to a tall, dark brown building. It was much larger than Kati's.

Hay and barrels of feed filled the barn, but Jack first led her to a corner with shelves and cabinets. "This is the workshop."

Machinery consumed most of this space. A tractor blade and pitchfork sat in the corner. She wouldn't be working any of this equipment, would she?

Emerald turned to Jack. "Now please show me the cattle."

"Don't need to see them."

"I thought—"

"I said I was going to give you a job. I didn't say it was going to have anything to do with cattle."

Emerald was relieved. Maybe this job wouldn't be so tough. Just simple ranch chores. She smiled. All that scary machinery was nothing to worry about.

Jack opened the metal cabinet and searched. "Here ya go." He handed her two metal hooks with handles on them and a pair of wire cutters.

What were these for?

He nodded toward the bales of hay. "Use the hooks to stack all but two of the bales over in the corner there, and take those two to the stables. That's where you'll need to cut the cord."

"All of them?" She must be misunderstanding. They would reach the ceiling when she was finished! She wasn't even that tall!

"Yep. I'll be out in the pastures this morning but you can come to the house at noon for lunch." He left without a backward glance.

Emerald sized up the bales of hay and mentally counted them. Two, four, six, eight, ten, twelve. Dare she continue? The number didn't matter. She had to stack them all.

Studying a bale that came up just a few inches below her knees she bent down, grasped at the cord with one of the metal hooks, missed and fell backwards. Tossing the hooks aside, she grabbed the cord with her hands and pulled. With perspiration dotting her forehead, she tugged from different angles. It didn't budge. She looked at all the bales awaiting her. The task seemed impossible. How was she going to transport them all if she couldn't even lift one?

Had Jack really thought she could do this? Or had he given her the toughest possible job to make her want to quit? The thought sent anger surging through her. With determination she gripped the cord and summoned all her strength. She half carried and half dragged the bale to the corner Jack had indicated.

Emerald threw all her weight into the exertion. The bale's only handgrip—two thin cords, cut—into her fingers, but she kept pulling.

Twelve bales later, she sank weakly to the nearest stack. Her whole body ached, but her worst dread was her bloody hands, now staining her jeans. She couldn't go on like this. Maybe she could get to the house and find something to wrap her wounds in before Jack returned.

The heat of the sun met her outside the barn. As she passed the corral and neared the house, she saw a white Dodge Ram parked out front. Caleb stepped down from the front porch and waved at her. "How's your first day at the ranch?"

Despite her despair, Emerald smiled. "What are you doing here?"

"I needed to talk to Jack about the mares that I'm getting from him for the riding center. I thought I might catch him at lunchtime." He looked at her hands, and his expression changed. "Emerald. . . ."

"Stacking hay." She offered a weary smile.

"Weren't you wearing gloves?"

Gloves? "I guess that would have been a good idea."

Caleb reached out and touched her arm. "Let's go in the house. We need to get you cleaned up."

She followed Caleb into the kitchen where he reached into the cabinets above the stove. "I think this is where Jack keeps his . . . ah, here it is." He pulled down a small metal box and pointed Emerald to the sink. He took her hands.

"I can do it."

Ignoring her protest, he pulled out a bottle of peroxide and directed her over the basin. "This is going to sting." Holding one hand in his, he used his free hand to pour the antiseptic over her injuries then repeated it on the second hand.

Emerald bit her tongue and tensed. It felt like needles on her already raw skin.

"How much hay did you stack anyway?"

Emerald blinked hard against tears. "Only twelve bales."

"Almost half a ton. A lot for someone who's never stacked and isn't wearing gloves."

"It didn't even put a dent into what I have left."

Caleb applied antibiotic ointment and then wrapped a bandage around her wound, cutting the end of the fabric with scissors. "It might hurt to finish it, but even with the bandage I'd still wear gloves. That will give you some protection."

Emerald sagged against the cabinet. "Thanks, Caleb."

He stowed the supplies. "Why don't you go sit down, and I'll make lunch."

Unable to deny her fatigue, she sat down at the table while Caleb went to the fridge and pulled out luncheon meat. She tried to ignore the pain in her hands as she watched him set his cowboy hat aside and make sandwiches.

The front door opened, and Jack entered the kitchen. "Making lunch?"

"Turkey sandwiches okay?"

"Sounds great." Jack grabbed a glass, then filled it at the sink.

After he downed it, he looked at Emerald. "How is your day going so far?"

"I've got twelve bales done."

Caleb looked up from spreading mayonnaise but didn't mention the gloves.

Jack filled his glass again. "There's still a lot of day left."

Emerald cringed at the thought of how much hay remained. Yes, there was a lot of day left. But how much flesh on her hands?

During lunch, Jack and Caleb discussed the horses that Cowboy Church would be getting from Jack for their therapeutic riding center. Emerald was mostly quiet, and took advantage of this time to sit.

She reached for her glass of water, and Jack stopped midsentence. "What's wrong with your hand, Emerald?"

Knowing Jack would call her a wimp, she sighed weakly. "The cords."

A look of realization passed over his face. "Emerald, I'm sorry. I should have given you gloves. I'm so used to working without them, I didn't even think—"

"Maybe next time you will." Caleb stood from the table with his plate and carried it to the sink. "They're pretty deep cuts, Jack."

Jack got up and followed Caleb. "I'll call you tomorrow about what day you can pick up the horses." Was Jack telling Caleb to leave?

Caleb looked at Emerald, then grabbed his hat off the counter. "Don't be too hard on her."

Emerald carried her own dish to the sink, feeling awkward. She sensed issues between the two cousins. Was Jack angry that Caleb was telling him what to do?

Jack left the kitchen but Emerald did not hear the front door open. Maybe he was rethinking her position on his ranch. And he might be right; she wasn't working out so far. Maybe she wasn't cut out for this kind of work.

When Jack returned to the kitchen, though, he brought a pair of gloves. "These should help."

When he left to work with a horse, Emerald went back to the hay. The gloves and bandage helped, but her hands still hurt. The only distraction from the burn was the growing ache in her back and fatigue in her legs and arms.

By now she could only drag the hay, and as the stacks grew higher she could scarcely get the bales to the top. One slipped, and she caught it on her knee.

Strong arms reached around her and took the hay from her grip. She watched as Jack placed the hay on the top stack. He turned back to her. "I think you've done enough for one day."

*Thank God.* She tried to hide her relief. Her willpower and determination had run out, and her entire body trembled.

Jack grabbed a bale of hay and headed toward the door. "Let me take what's needed to the horses, then we can be on our way."

While grateful to be finished working, she was disappointed to leave so soon.

Jack returned for another bale; then she walked with him to the truck. The red pickup pulled onto the dirt road, then turned right, toward town, instead of left, toward Kati's.

"Where are we going?"

Jack smoothed his hair back and then replaced his hat. "There are some things you're going to need if you're going to work on the ranch." He glanced at her. "What you wore suited you fine today, but for the other work; you're going to need real ranch clothes."

She studied his face. Was this guilt? He did look sorry when he saw her hands—just before he sent her right back to work. She concluded that Jack was just being practical. She asked for this job, and work needed to be done. But wait, hadn't they been over this already? Kati had promised to take Emerald shopping. Didn't Jack trust her to. . . .? The thought of Kati reminded her that all her cash was at her house.

"Jack, I don't have any money on me."

"I'm covering it. Consider it part of your wages." A quick glance warned her not to argue.

After a few miles, Jack parked the truck in front of a store called "Western Wear."

Inside he nodded toward the women's section. "Find a couple pair of jeans and shirts you can work in." He held up a solid blue button-up shirt made out of a thick, stiff denim material. "Something like this for the shirts."

Emerald brushed past old panel walls lined with wooden shelves and unsteady racks piled high with clothes. Amid the menagerie of hats, boots, and ropes she saw a couple of leather purses that seemed knockoffs of Brighton. Closer examination of the stitching and price tag, though, proved them to be a top-quality designer brand she'd never heard of. Amazing what she was discovering here.

"Howdy, Jack!"

The store owner greeted Jack and inquired about the cattle, apparently the only topic of conversation in these parts. The two men seemed to know each other well; they'd probably be talking for a while.

Good. She needed time to look around.

The shirt Jack had chosen happened to be her size, so she held onto it and chose another like it in a lighter blue. Next she chose two pair of Wranglers and slipped into the only dressing room—a small alcove in the back corner with a sheet for a door.

Though she knew the shirts would fit, she wondered about the jeans, never having worn Wranglers before. A little loose in the waist, but comfy everywhere else. She would keep them. She might need a little extra room in the waist to tuck her shirts in anyway.

When she reached the front, Jack addressed the owner. "Can you fit her for boots?"

The man nodded and led them to the back. "Any particular kind?"

"Good working ones."

"I think I know just the pair."

The man went to the storeroom, then returned with a pair of brown and black leather boots in her size. She tried walking in them. They felt odd, but she could get used to them. After Jack's examination and approval, the man carried her items to the checkout counter at the front of the store.

"That'll be two-sixty."

Emerald was amazed. That would barely buy a single shirt back home.

But still, this bill wasn't going to Daddy. How would Jack handle it?

Without a change of expression, he pulled out his wallet and paid the man in cash.

In the truck, Emerald realized how comfortable she felt with Jack assuming a traditional male role and taking care of her. The feeling infuriated her. If she was going to take care of herself she couldn't let Jack replace Daddy. "I'll pay you back."

Jack shook his head. "Your work will pay it off."

She looked at him as they headed back up into the foothills. He trusted her, even though she hadn't given him a reason to. He didn't know she wouldn't run away again, so he was taking a big chance. This was the first time anyone had trusted her to do anything on her own. What she was feeling at the moment could only be described as pride. And not the kind you feel when you're wearing the best designer gown at the party.

She leaned back against the bench seat of the truck and glanced at the profile of Jack's handsome face.

She wouldn't let him down.

∞

By the time Emerald arrived at Kati's that night, Kati had already prepared dinner. The pot roast and steaming vegetables smelled wonderful, especially with the appetite she'd worked up.

"That's the most I've seen you eat since you've been here," Kati said as Emerald helped her clear the table. Emerald reached for the empty potato bowl, but her arm muscles seemed to stall on her.

As if sensing her pain, Kati took the bowl. "Why don't we get you into a bath with Epsom salts? It's the best thing to work out that soreness. If you want any hope of being able to move tomorrow, I highly suggest you soak for a while."

Kati was right. An hour and a half later Emerald felt much looser and more relaxed as she slipped into the old, oversized cotton T-shirt that Kati loaned her to sleep in. She hadn't thought of pajamas when she'd crammed necessities into her duffle bag.

Before crawling under the covers, Emerald pulled her tote bag from under the bed—hardly a secure place, but better than out in the open. She wasn't worried about Kati snooping anyway. She opened the treasure box and removed her mother's diary. She knew her envelope full of cash was under the Bible—again, the safest of the unsafe places.

She sat on the bed and opened her mother's diary. The next entry was marked September 30, a little over a month since her mother's first writing.

*Dear God,*

*Thank you for leading me to the Church of Eternal Blessing. I joined today and as the congregation greeted me, I knew for the first time in my life, I was where You wanted me to be. I write this letter knowing the path I am choosing to follow won't be easy. While I am completely aware of the hard stones I must cross on my new journey, I pray with each new step, You will lead me.*

*Resting in Your Love,*
*Alexandra*

Emerald sat in stunned silence. What path had her mother chosen that seemed so right? And was it truly right? Or was Daddy right when he insisted Alexandra was crazy? Her mother had trusted God to lead her. Did He?

Emerald read on. The date on the next page was November 3.

*Thank You for Your unfailing Love! When I feel the world is against me, when the enemy attacks, You are always there to deliver me and set my soul at rest! In the midst of darkness, my eyes have been opened to the many wonders of Your beauty. My soul longs to sing praises, just as David!*

*Praise the Lord, O my soul; all my inmost being, praise his holy name. Praise the Lord O my soul, and forget not all his benefits who forgive all your sins and heals all your diseases, who redeems your life from the pit and crowns you with love and compassion, who satisfies your desires with good things so that your youth is renewed like the eagle's.—Psalm 103:1-5.*

Emerald stared at the page, her breathing shallow and her body trembling. Alexandra—her mother—had believed these words. Had Alexandra been deceived? Blindly led astray to believe foolishness? What had Daddy thought? She closed her eyes as a familiar scene flashed before her.

A man was beside her. He had something important to tell her.

*"Emerald, I have a message for you. . . ."*

The man vanished.

*"Get out of my house!"*

*"Daddy, no!"*

*"Amelia, you are relieved of your nanny duties, effective immediately. How could you let that man in?"*

*"He didn't harm the child!"*

*"I have to find him, Daddy!"*

Emerald opened her eyes. The wavering images didn't make sense. She must be going crazy. Must be. She looked again at her mother's journal. Bradford hadn't shared her mother's beliefs. Alexandra had hoped one day he would, but he never had. Daddy liked to know he had control. Maybe it was easier for him to believe that there was no God than to admit otherwise. Or maybe he was right and there was no God.

Emerald read the verse again: *"who forgives all your sins and heals all your diseases, who redeems your life from the pit. . . ."*

Had her mother's life been redeemed from the pit? And what about healing diseases? How could that be possible? Had her mother believed that, too? Emerald had never known such confusion, or such despair.

∞

Bradford sat alone in his office. He hadn't eaten a complete meal in days, was washing his hands more than ever and had cut down significantly on his patient load. He had focused nearly all his attention and strength on finding his daughter. One of the best PI's had turned into a team of them . . . and still, nothing.

Removing his reading glasses he laid down the patient files he'd been examining. How much longer could he last this way? Not like he had a choice.

He picked up his office phone and paged Molly. "Did they find anything on her computer?"

"I'm afraid not, Dr. McGintay."

He tapped his glasses on his desk. *Shoot.* Between e-mails to friends and research history he'd been positive they'd come up with something. Wherever she had gone she hadn't studied the place or asked a single person about it. Her impulsion was troubling, to say the least.

"Call Dr. Coffman and ask if he can take over a few more of my patients."

"Yes, sir."

He hung up the phone before she could ask if he needed anything. He resisted the impulse to go to the bathroom and wash his hands. His OCD was kicking in big time. It always did in desperate times when he lost control. He was going to have to treat it better. He'd up his dose of medication.

Opening his drawer to pull out a bottle of his pills he caught a glimpse of an open closet door at the other end of the room. Earlier, he'd told Molly to scour his office with disinfectant, including every nook and cranny. He realized his need to keep germs away was also increasing.

Bradford crossed the room to close the door and glanced down at the safe before he did. Before she'd left, Emerald had taken Alexandra's chest with the Bible. He'd given her the safe's code years ago when he went over every possible way of escaping if an intruder ever came in, along with what she'd need to do if he himself ever died. He closed the closet door and pulled his key from his pocket to deadbolt it. Emerald had the only other key and had left it sitting on top of his desk before she left. That action alone disturbed him, as well as the fact that he had a hundred grand in cash sitting in there in case of emergency. Yet, she'd chosen the Bible and left the money. Now what kind of sensible choice was that?

Emerald wasn't using her credit card, because she didn't want to be found, but she also hadn't taken any of his money nor made a single ATM withdrawal since the night she fled. How could she have survived this long on a few hundred dollars? Was it even possible that she had?

He was breaking into a sweat. He pushed the bookshelves back in front of the door. She'd even managed to move the shelves completely on her own the night she'd gotten into his safe. He himself had taught her the trick of using her weight and sliding them.

Rubbing his hands together in a quick friction that killed germs, he took a deep breath and began replacing all of the books, one at a time, in alphabetical order. After he was finished he spent another half hour making sure each one was perfectly straight. Then he went to the bathroom to wash his hands.

∞

Emerald slipped between the covers and turned off her bedside lamp. But her sleep turned restless as voices and images took over her dreams. She awoke sitting up in a sweaty, heart-thumping panic. The dream. The pleas of the crying children were terrifying. And all the hands grasping at her, reaching out. What did they want? Did it even mean anything? The dreams had stopped when she was on her meds. She had to face the possibility that Daddy and Sidney were right. She, like her mother before her, was psychotic.

She closed her eyes again, desperate to hold onto the dream, to find any answers that might be out there.

*I want to know you, whoever you are.*

Emerald choked. She had called the words out to the wind, to endless miles of land and mountains, and then again in church. Was anyone there to hear?

# Chapter Thirteen

JACK LEFT THE CATTLE AUCTION EMPTY-handed; he'd passed on the few good deals. He climbed into the red Dodge with his Border collies and drove to his parents' house. His mom, Libby, had returned from her visit home to Texas and invited him to dinner; he anticipated Blue Bell for dessert. No doubt Libby had once again toted back an ice chest full of the beloved ice cream from her childhood.

When Jack pulled into the driveway, Tony stomped the dirt from his shoes as Jack held the car door open long enough for the dogs to jump out.

"You're here earlier than I expected. How'd the auction go?"

Jack shook his head. "I didn't buy any."

"The heifers you interested in go too high?"

Jack glanced toward the house and adjusted his hat. "No, I just changed my mind."

Tony was quiet for a minute. "Well, I need to go feed. I think your mom is finishing dinner."

Knowing Tony wanted more information, Jack followed his dad. "I'll help you."

They took hay from the barn to the corral and fed in silence. Tony pulled off his work gloves. "I heard you're going to donate two mares to the church for the therapeutic riding center." He looked into his son's eyes with approval. "Sure is a nice thing to do, Son."

Jack stroked a white and brown colt. "I have more horses than I need right now." He knew the implication. Why didn't he sell the mares for a comfortable sum to spend at the auction?

But Tony didn't reply, instead he just leaned against the fence. "Kati told me you gave Emerald a job at the ranch. How's that going?"

Jack stiffened and wiped the sweat from his brow. "She needed a job, Dad, and I could use the extra help." It was that simple, but he knew Tony read more into it.

"I'm glad you did it. I just hope it wasn't for the wrong reason."

"What do you mean?"

"You know I like the girl, Jack. I wanted you to help her from the beginning."

"I know, so why—?"

Tony took a step forward and rested a hand on Jack's shoulder. "I know how you feel about Caleb. But he's no less family just because he gave up most of his land." He smiled. "Besides, where would this town be without his initiative? Still just talking about building an actual church!" He lowered his voice. "I don't want you at odds with your cousin."

Jack turned away from Tony. He knew it looked as if he'd only hired Emerald so Caleb couldn't. But Emerald had asked him first, and she'd shown a real interest in ranching. She wouldn't have enjoyed spending all her time in a riding arena.

Jack took the feed buckets back to the barn. Okay, maybe the old rivalry influenced the hiring a little. But there was something else. If Emerald had been seeing this Dr. Coffman, she could have some kind of problem. If she did, he needed to watch her. And if she didn't, he needed to know. After all, Emerald had run away for a reason, and he had sensed her fear more than once.

∞

Emerald lifted the last bale of hay, then stood back, hands resting on her hips, and smiled. She studied her work with renewed satisfaction. Sweat soaked through her new work clothes and dampened her hair. Her hands burned despite the bandages and gloves, and her whole body ached. That didn't matter. She had finished a job—the first real job of her life. And it was work that required her entire body and determination.

She wanted to leap for joy, but since she could barely walk, she settled for the ecstasy that bubbled inside. Had her father or Sidney ever sweat like this?

Jack's collies ran into the barn with tails wagging. That must mean Jack was back from the pastures. She smiled as she bent to pet each of the dogs. She had to be sneaky and show them affection when Jack wasn't around. He had made his rules clear. "They're not pets, they're herding dogs."

Emerald limped out of the barn into the heat of the day—her third on the job. Surprised she could still move, she pulled her gloves off as she spotted Jack in the arena with a filly. Though his schedule was erratic, he usually fed in the early morning, then worked with the filly until lunchtime. After that, he hit the pastures, sometimes alone, other times with Milt.

He rested his hand against the horse's neck and talked to her soothingly. When Emerald approached, he looked at her with a smile. "Taking a break?"

Emerald shook her head with a proud smile. "Nope, I'm finished."

Jack turned back to the horse. "Knew you could do it."

Not quite the enthusiasm she had expected.

She watched him with the horse. She'd heard him tell Caleb that a wire fence had injured the filly's leg a month ago. Now that it was healed, Jack had been working with her to get the leg stronger again.

She pushed the damp hair from her face. "Want me to make lunch?"

"Hungry already?"

She nodded. "You're right. Hard work does work up an appetite." Would he consider her work hard?

"Okay, you go ahead. I'll put this one away and come in."

Emerald made roast beef sandwiches, then set a bowl of fresh fruit in the middle of the table. Jack came in, washed up in the sink, then sat.

This time Emerald waited for him to say the blessing before eating. If she could get used to hard work, maybe she'd eventually get used to prayers.

Jack looked at her from across the table. "So, how does it feel to have accomplished your first ranch chore?"

Ranch chore? Was that how he saw all that effort? A chore?

She shrugged and smiled. "You didn't think I could do it, did you?"

Jack took a strawberry from the bowl and popped it into his mouth. "I never doubted you. I only hoped that you wouldn't either."

She had doubted herself, at least a hundred times. Nevertheless, she had done it. She lifted her chin, and her eyes filled with excitement. Here was her chance.

"Now I want the opportunity to do some *real* ranch work."

"Real ranch work?"

"You know, like riding and working cattle."

Jack carried his plate to the sink. "Emerald let's not get ahead of yourself. Stacking hay doesn't qualify you to work cattle."

Okay, maybe that was fair. After all, she had never done anything like this before. Still, couldn't he at least give her hope?

Jack eyed her from the sink. "Besides, there are lots of other things that I need done while I'm riding the pastures."

Emerald checked herself. Yes, she wanted to learn, but he had hired her to help. Had she ever really helped anyone in her life?

"So what's one of these things you need done?" She stood from the table, sensing stiffness settling in from too much sitting.

Jack grabbed his hat from the counter. "Cleaning stalls, for one."

∞

Emerald replaced the pitchfork on it's hook, then went to feed the horses. Her arms ached, and defied all efforts to lift them. Finished in the stables, she limped out into the late afternoon. Her work week was over. But while her muscles rejoiced at the rest, she felt sadness. The hard work made her whole.

A white Dodge truck sat near the house. Caleb's. She smiled. She wasn't sure why, but the idea of church no longer scared her, and something about Caleb enticed her. As she passed the truck, she spotted three men riding from one of the higher pastures. Jack, Milt, and Caleb. She waited as they neared.

"Good afternoon, Cowgirl!" Caleb swung down from his horse, a nice gelding named Roper.

"Were you out with the cattle?"

He laughed, and she suddenly realized how it had sounded. She hadn't meant it that way. She glanced at Jack who was also hiding a smile. Hadn't he said Caleb wasn't a rancher?

"I was helping Jack check the heifers."

"Is something wrong?"

Jack swung down from his horse. "Calving season."

She limped to Caleb's horse, who looked similar to the black gelding she'd admired in Jack's stable. Would Jack ever let her ride him?

Caleb dismounted. "Jack told me you helped him change trenches today?"

She nodded. "The mosquitoes were awful." She showed off the bites on her neck. Insects were rare on Jack's ranch except around the muck of the irrigation trenches.

Caleb nodded. "They can be. You have to watch out for West Nile. We had a few people infected with it last summer."

She raised her eyebrows. "Really? Jack never mentioned it."

Jack broke his conversation with Milt. "No, but I gave you that repellent and told you to make sure you wore a long-sleeved shirt today."

That awful, foul-smelling repellent. Could the men still smell it on her, or were their noses desensitized?

She followed the men as they unsaddled their horses. Her pain and stiffness made it difficult to keep up.

Jack glanced at her with his eyebrows scrunched together. "Emerald, it'll take you a while to get used to this kind of work, but I hope you aren't letting it discourage you."

She shook her head. "I'm just a little sore, that's all."

"Learning what its like to be a cowgirl, huh?" Caleb said.

"She'll be all right. She's a hard worker."

The praise from Jack surprised her. That one compliment made up for a week's worth of scolding.

Emerald walked Caleb back to the truck, leaving Jack and Milt in the stable with the horses.

Caleb stopped halfway and pointed up to a craggy peak. "See that? Elk."

Emerald looked in time to catch two creatures moving swiftly into the forest. "Sure is a lot of wildlife around here." She pushed several strings of damp hair back from her face, straining to see in the darkness of the woods. "Do you ever see white horned sheep?" She'd read about them in one of the books at Kati's house.

"Sometimes, but not too often at this elevation. They're higher up. Have you had much of a chance to see the country?"

She shook her head.

"If you'd like, I'd be happy to take you on a hike into the mountains. There's a lot of wildlife up there, and of course, the scenery isn't bad either."

The mountains? Too good to be true! "I'd like that."

"Okay."

His eyes turned serious, damping Emerald's excitement. "I would also love to share with you about Cowboy Church and what we believe. That is, if it's okay with you?"

His words brought a sudden panic. What was he getting at?

As if sensing her anxiety, Caleb rested a hand on her arm. "No pressure. Just to share."

Her mind said no. Meeting with a pastor seemed too personal—too dangerous.

"What are you afraid of, Emerald?"

Her jaw dropped. He'd read her mind.

*Do not be afraid. I am with you.*

She looked into Caleb's face, and unexpectedly her eyes met his. Not in a threatening way. As he said, he just wanted to share.

"All right."

He smiled. "How about tomorrow?"

Saturday. Her day off. "Okay."

Emerald watched him drive away. Where had the voice come from and why had she decided to go? Was it something about Caleb? Her eyes went to the mountaintops. Something was waiting to be found. Maybe it was up there.

# Chapter Fourteen

JACK HIT THE GROUND HARD FOR the second time. Pushing himself back to his feet, he stared at Denver, the stubborn black gelding Emerald had admired. Why hadn't she asked to ride him yet?

And Caleb. Jack had seen how impressed Emerald was when Caleb was on the back of a horse. He frowned. Or was it the horse she'd been impressed with? He'd watched her leave the stables and walk Caleb to his truck.

He forced his attention back to the young gelding. Denver was fine with the saddle but went ballistic at Jack's efforts to ride him. What was wrong? Jack relaxed, mounted again, and soon Denver, too, relaxed. Jack rode around a few times, then unsaddled the youngster.

Though his stomach wanted lunch, he resisted and went to the barn. Amid the current drought, broken only by one hard rain last week, the water trenches he and Emerald had set were critical. He needed the four-wheeler to check them.

Inside the barn, he stopped at the bales of hay stacked neatly against the wall. Emerald had moved at least half of them; he'd sneaked the rest over when she wasn't around. No need to embarrass her.

He jumped on the four-wheeler and put it in reverse. As he rode out to the pastures, he thought how this ranch and everything about it energized Emerald. She pelted him with questions such as: how often cows gave birth, or if a bull had ever charged him. She thrilled at whatever the day's routine involved—clinging to him when he floored the four-wheeler over a rocky edge, laughing when he almost fell face first into mud, or begging to pet one of the goats Aunt Kati had given him last year. How could anything be mentally wrong with Emerald? He'd done more research and learned that psychotics had trouble carrying on simple conversations. Other than avoiding discussions about where she came from, Emerald seemed perfectly capable of communicating.

Emerald? Psychotic? Jack almost laughed at the thought. Maybe if he could get her to trust him, he could find out the truth.

∞

Emerald sat on a rock to catch her breath. Caleb handed her a water bottle. "I told you it was a long way up."

He hadn't been kidding. She took a few deep breaths, then sipped the water.

Caleb stood in front of her. No cowboy hat and boots today. He wore loose jeans with hiking boots and a T-shirt that hinted at rippling muscles underneath. Evidence of hard work like Jack's? Or weight training?

She stood, glad he was carrying the picnic lunch in his backpack. "Do you hike often?"

Caleb reached out to help her up the rocky cliff. "As often as I can."

The morning had started off chilly. Now, outside the shade of the trees, the sun beat down, bringing perspiration to her face. "Either you've done this a lot, or I'm out of shape."

Caleb laughed. "You can't be that out of shape or you wouldn't have lasted with Jack."

Nothing in the gym that Daddy built for her had prepared her for ranch work. "Then maybe my Pilates and yoga accounted for something." Though she doubted it.

Madame Jawarhu, her private instructor, had come to her house three times a week to train her not in strengthening and toning but in relaxation and discovering the energy within. Might have been some brainwashing in there, too. After all, Daddy and Sidney had hired her.

The two reached the top of the slope and found a meadow of wildflowers. Caleb removed the backpack and took out a blanket. He spread it in the shade of a row of aspens. From the bag he removed a feast of sandwiches, grapes and apples, and chocolate chip cookies that Kati had baked for them the night before.

Caleb bowed his head. "Dear Father, we thank You for this beautiful day and for this food. Let each thing we discover on our adventure today be a reminder of You. Amen."

Emerald pondered Caleb's words. His blessing had been different from any she had yet heard. Then she recalled her mother's words: *opening my eyes to the many wonders of your beauty.*

Was God a mystery to be solved? If so, then it made sense why her father never chose to believe. After all, her father knew how to manipulate, control. That's why he had gotten along so well with Sidney.

Caleb opened a bottle of water as he followed Emerald's stare to the mountain peaks. "If you're up to it after lunch, there's a view up there you have to see."

Looking around the meadow she touched one of the many yellow flowers dancing in the wind. "Black-eyed daisies?"

Caleb nodded. "Wait until we get further up. Close to the waterfall there are all kinds of wildflowers."

"Waterfall?" Now, that would be something.

Emerald finished her lunch quickly, then headed up the rocky cliff.

"Hang on!" Caleb hurriedly stuffed everything back into his pack.

An hour and a half later, the roar of rushing water grew steadily louder, interrupting the quiet of the forest as they drew nearer. Every step led upward, and Emerald could see they were nearing the crest of the ridge, but the water remained hidden from view. They rounded a bend, and Emerald gasped at the sight of a massive cascade rushing over the boulders beside the path and tumbling hundreds of feet down the mountainside below her. She'd never seen a waterfall from so close to the top.

Emerald grabbed Caleb's arm, her eyes glimmering. "I want to get closer!"

He dropped the backpack on a boulder, flailing after Emerald as she darted over the rock formations toward the water. "Hang on—be careful!"

When they stopped a few feet from the cliff she felt the cool spray on her skin.

"I'm not close enough. I want to feel the water more." She ventured forward.

"Wait, Emerald." He grabbed her arm. "The rocks are slippery."

But instead of pulling her back, he stepped forward with a secure hold. Together they made it to an aspen on the edge.

"Hold onto me." Emerald removed one hand from the tree and took Caleb's hand. She leaned over the edge, tilted her head forward, and laughed.

"All right, I think that's enough." He tugged her back, her hair soaked and face spotted with beads of mist.

Emerald smiled. "Now your turn."

"Oh no, I don't think so."

"Come on, why not?"

Caleb frowned. "Because I might slip."

Emerald laughed as they picked their way back over the rocks. "I've never done anything like that before. Daddy wouldn't even let me run track in elementary school. Imagine if he'd seen me here!"

Emerald blanched. She'd slipped and mentioned Daddy. Hoping Caleb hadn't noticed, she resolved to be more careful.

Caleb looked up the trail. "So do you still want to go to the top, or are you ready to start heading back down?"

She shook her head. "We've made it this far."

"Okay, then. The waterfall was just an appetizer."

∞

Emerald perched on a boulder beside Caleb looking at the valley below. In one direction she saw miles of ranch land; in the other, the small town.

Caleb pointed. "Canyon Ridge Mountain, and over there you can see Tussle Springs. About a hundred miles that way is Denver."

"I've never seen anything like it."

"Just look around you. We are surrounded by God's creation."

Caleb's words rolled over in her head. She glanced at him. He sat with eyes closed and head tilted up. He took a deep breath, and his face seemed to radiate.

"God is with us always," said Caleb, "but there is something about being up here that I feel closest to the Divine. I like to come up here and talk to God."

The wind had picked up as they climbed, so she wrapped her arms around her thin body. Despite the beauty of the view, she felt cold, lost, broken—desperate for something more. Searching for. . . .

"Surrender."

Emerald turned to Caleb, surprised. "What?"

He was looking at her as if he knew, but that was impossible. How could he know how she felt? Their eyes locked and though she wanted to look away his soft expression held her.

Finally he turned to the mountains. "I don't know what you're going through Emerald, what you're searching for. But I don't have to know, because He does."

"He?" she whispered.

"God. His presence is here." He faced her. "You feel it, don't you?"

Emerald looked away as something stirred within her, and the feeling grew until she felt deep warmth. Her imagination. Had to be. Or maybe Daddy and Sidney were right and she was going crazy. Caleb had somehow triggered it. But she had felt it before he said anything—the same presence that led her to her mother's diary and Bible. It had brought her West to the Rockies, to Jack's ranch, to Kati's barn.

"Don't fight it, Emerald. Just surrender."

She closed her eyes and felt beauty. She felt power, strength, and peace. It was . . . divine. Her past, everything she had been taught by her father, by Sidney, urged her to resist. She could. But she didn't want to. The wind blew through her hair, but instead of chilling her, it touched her. She remembered that exhilarating moment when she stood near the top of the waterfall. She had felt the power of the water, the trembling of the earth, the mist of the spray. In that moment she knew that such a powerful creation must have a creator. There was only one thing she could do. But did she have the strength to do it?

# Chapter Fifteen

CALEB SAT READY TO MOUNT THE podium after Jack finished the song that began Sunday morning worship. He had stayed up the entire night before preparing his sermon. He always did that ahead of time—Wednesday at the latest. But last night he was guided toward a different message.

Caleb wanted to peek at Emerald, but knew it was foolish. Not when he was supposed to be praying. He took a deep breath. Nerves? He'd never been nervous before preaching. He stood as Jack said, "Amen."

"Each of us," said Caleb, "is chosen by God. We may think we are here on our own, but we are not here by chance. God has chosen us, has given us a promise that He has called us to His purpose.

"I'll never forget my father. He was a man of great faith. When I was a small boy one summer it hadn't rained and we were about to lose everything." He glanced at his mom, who nodded. "Dad prayed for rain. I'll never forget going outside and hearing my father praying. He looked at me after he finished and said, 'Son, run and tell your mother not to worry. It's going to rain soon.'

"I remember looking up at the scorching afternoon sun with no clouds in the sky and thinking there was no chance it would rain. But you know what? Later on that day it poured, and that rain saved our ranch. Just as it took faith in my father's words that God could save the ranch by making it rain, it also takes faith to believe at all. My father had been praying for rain for weeks, perhaps even months. So why was it that day that it rained? What did he do differently? He believed, by speaking God's promises into existence.

"What did it take for my father to do that? When I looked at the sky I saw no chance of rain, so what did my dad see that was different?" Caleb paused. "Believe it or not, it took me years to answer this question. We have our human eye, in which we see the physical." He smiled. "And then we have our spiritual eye, which is where faith comes in.

"Reason says it isn't possible. Reason doesn't understand. But our hearts know the answer. That is the Way, the Truth and the Life."

∞

Emerald followed Kati outside and then waited while Kati spoke with a group of friends. She spotted Jack, who was finishing a conversation with two cowboys. They waved goodbye, and Emerald approached him.

She touched his shoulder. "Jack, I need to talk to you."

"Sure."

"I was wondering if you'd teach me how to ride."

"You don't know how?"

Emerald flushed. "Well, I did some, when I was younger. But—"

"That was rich girl riding, round and round a little ring, probably English style."

How did he know that? Emerald ignored his tone. "I'd like to learn how to ride on the ranch."

"We've already talked about this."

Caleb broke into the conversation. "Come on Jack, she just wants to ride." He stepped beside them with a wink at Emerald.

Jack balked. "Then why don't *you* teach her?"

Caleb smiled. "All right, Emerald, what do you say?" He paused. "Of course, I realize I'm not a real cowboy like, Jack."

"All right." Emerald glanced at Jack then back at Caleb. "So, when do we start?"

"How about right now?"

∞

Emerald struggled to calm her uneasiness with deep breathing.

"Nervous?" Caleb's warm hand gripped hers as he hoisted her into the saddle.

"It's been almost thirteen years since I've ridden." She worked her right boot into the stirrup, then gripped the saddle horn.

"You'll be fine, just relax." He handed her the reins then mounted his gelding, Roper.

She glanced at Jack, who was leading one of the therapy horses out of the corral. "Is he going to ride with us?"

Caleb nudged his horse forward. "No, he's going to work with the mare. We used her with a new client the other day and she got a little tense with a young lady with Down syndrome who got frustrated halfway through the session and began shouting."

Emerald steadied her pace behind Caleb. Caleb had chosen her horse because of his gentle personality, assuring her she'd be safe. Sandy brown with a white nose, the gelding was pretty—but lacked the vibrancy of Jack's black gelding, Denver.

"We'll ride around the corral first; then when you're ready, we'll take 'em out." He nodded toward a pasture to the east where a little stream ran by the mountainside.

As she followed Caleb around the corral Emerald tried to follow his instructions about keeping her legs underneath her,

her heels down, and her hands off the saddle so she could steer. She was doing fine until she noticed Jack watching. Emerald forced her concentration to the horse beneath her. Why was she nervous, anyway? Hadn't she wanted to get back to this for thirteen years? They circled the corral, Jack's gaze still following her. He was making her nervous, which was ridiculous.

"You're doing great Emerald. Just loosen up. The horse can tell when you're uptight."

Was it that obvious? She forced herself to unwind. Soon she relaxed, and her body joined the rhythm of the horse's steps.

"Good," Caleb spoke as he asked his horse to stop. "Are you ready to take them out?"

Emerald nodded and Caleb slid from his horse to open the gate. After they left the corral he moved Roper to ride alongside her. It was a cloudy day, a bit chilly; but Kati had loaned Emerald a jacket that morning. They entered the open pasture, and Caleb pointed out ranch property lines and named the owners of the neighboring land.

When they approached a grove of trees, the trail narrowed. They would have to ride single file.

Caleb tipped his hat with a smile. "Ladies first."

Emerald hesitated, then nudged her horse forward. In the shade of the trees the temperature dropped. Emerald wanted to zip her jacket but knew she'd have to stop riding first.

Soon the trees parted so Caleb could ride beside her again. They heard a trickle of water and neared a small stream.

Though it wasn't the waterfall from the day before, it offered serenity. It reminded her of her mother's words: *opening my eyes to the many wonders of Your beauty*.

"You look deep in thought."

Looking up at Caleb she answered; "I was just thinking of something of my mother's that I read." Emerald hesitated. "She wrote of discovering the wonders of God's beauty."

Caleb leaned forward to avoid a low branch. "God is full of

wonders. Just look around." He pulled Roper to a halt, then dismounted. Holding his hand out, he helped her off her horse and then led her down to the stream.

Caleb hadn't secured the horses, but they grazed contently as he and Emerald walked away.

The trees thinned, and Caleb stopped and squeezed her hand. "Look."

She gazed at a beautiful meadow with a backdrop of mountains. Colorful wildflowers dotted the field.

"Come on." He pulled her hand and took off at a run through the meadow. He stopped to pick a large, bright flower for her and said, "Just one of God's many wonders." He picked another. "They're the same kind of flower, but each is unique. Out of millions, you won't find two alike." He handed both flowers to her. "Crazy isn't it?"

"It's hard to fathom." Emerald said, inspecting the flowers.

"Not just hard. Impossible."

He reached into his jacket pocket and pulled out a palm-sized Bible. "And do you know what the greatest wonder of all is?"

Emerald shook her head.

"God's love. No matter what season, what person, what you've done, what you believe, or how much time passes—God's love endures forever."

He took one of the flowers out of her hand and placed it in the Bible.

Emerald was silent. Then Caleb startled her out of her thoughts by passing the Bible to her. "You don't have your own, do you?"

"No. Well. . . ." She did have her mother's, but somehow that was private.

"I want you to have this one."

When she reached out to take it, his hand touched hers briefly. She felt warmth when he helped her mount her horse.

And when he led her through the meadow she felt something she'd never felt before.

Safe.

# Chapter Sixteen

PERSPIRATION DOTTED EMERALD'S FOREHEAD AS SHE focused on the hole for the wire. She bit her lip, barely able to hold the wire in her awkward, man-sized work gloves.

"Got it." Milt yanked the wire through the other end of the hole. The freckles on his face blended together, leaving his face blood red.

"Here, you work the knot on this one." He thrust the pliers into her hand.

Emerald nodded as she gripped them. Milt made this heavy-gauge wire, strong enough to hold back cattle, look as easy to tie as shoelaces. She turned and twisted the pliers, hoping her hands wouldn't blister as they slipped inside the gloves. Finally she had the stiff steel strands fastened.

"Good job, Emerald, you really picked up on this."

Emerald wiped the sweat from her face with her sleeve. With Milt's patient instruction, they'd soon have repaired all the damage the bulls had done to Jack's fences. She watched Milt removing his work gloves. Until today she'd only seen him briefly. He was out riding the pastures most of the time—especially now, as it was calving season.

Milt turned and spat tobacco. One thing she hadn't gotten used to. At least Jack didn't chew. Then Milt removed his hat to wipe the sweat from his forehead as they stepped back to look at their work. Only a few small sections of loose wire remained.

"Can you finish the rest on your own? I've got some feeding that I gotta get to."

Emerald hesitated before nodding.

"I'll come back and pick you up after I've finished." He handed her the pliers, then boarded the four-wheeler that had brought them there.

Emerald watched him roar away, then examined the next fence.

An hour later Emerald sank to the ground. Her stomach grumbled, deprived of lunch; it had to be three or four hours since they'd ridden out. She searched the cattle-strewn pastures for Milt. Why was he taking so long?

She closed her eyes and remembered the dream she'd had the night before—the first in a while. She had seen her mother again, but in a different way. Usually her mother appeared vaguely, a fuzzy version of the portrait in her father's study. But in this dream, she'd seen her mother's face for the first time.

Emerald leaned back against the fence post to wait for Milt and struggled to remember the woman's features, her expression. After a while she gave in to the sleepiness that overcame her.

∞

Jack slid off Denver, the young black gelding. The wind was picking up, and storm clouds loomed on the horizon. He led the horse out of the corral and back to the stables. When he stepped back outside the sky had darkened to an angry gray. He checked his watch. Almost four-thirty. Milt and Emerald should have finished by now.

He headed to the hay wagon, which was full of bales he'd picked up that morning. Then he fired up the tractor and hauled it into the barn to stay dry. That took fifteen minutes. By the time he had finished the wind had moved up to a howl, and he shivered. Lightning zipped to the ground in the middle distance.

Jack headed toward the house still wondering why Milt and Emerald were not back. What was wrong? Milt knew better than to be in the open pastures during a storm. From the kitchen he looked out the back window. No four-wheeler in sight.

His phone rang and with two long steps Jack reached the receiver, his heart jumping.

"Jack."

"Milt, where are you?"

"I'm at your dad's. I came over to feed, and—"

Jack interrupted. "Emerald's with you?"

"No, I left her to work on the fence."

Jack wanted to yell at Milt, but that would have to wait. "I'm going to get her."

He hung up and raced out. The truck would be useless for the high pastures, so he turned to the stable.

Jack forced himself to calm down. He shared the blame; he'd never given Milt instructions. Besides, Emerald had survived one storm stranded alone.

He saddled Houdini and rode out into the powerful wind.

∞

*She was searching. For what she couldn't be certain. She had to find the way. But there were so many different paths—and they were all dark. Anxiety rushed through her. She was looking for something, someone.*

*"Emerald, you have a mission." A man sitting in front of her. A blur. A vague memory from the past—or perhaps only a dream.*

*"Where?" she cried, frustrated. She couldn't remember. He always came and she never remembered.*

*She felt a familiar presence.*

*"Help me," she whispered, "Help me remember."*

*No answer. The one who called her name wouldn't help. Or maybe no one called her name. Maybe she was going crazy.*

*"Open your eyes, Emerald, and you will know you're not alone."*

*"Who are you?" she cried harder now.*

*"You know who I am, Emerald."*

*"No, I don't! I can't believe in someone I can't see!"*

*"Then open your eyes."*

∞

Darkness surrounded her. The wind roared, and cold cut into her. Great drops of rain poured from the sky like an angry wave. She tried to stand, but the gale was too strong. She had been told to open her eyes, but now this wrath was upon her. The voice said if she opened her eyes she would see she was not alone. A great feeling of evil filled her body, and she couldn't breathe.

"Emerald!"

It was Jack's voice.

"Emerald, wake up!"

Had she fallen asleep? She felt him shaking her body and opened her eyes to see his fearful face. He had come to save her. And hadn't he said he'd never come after her again?

She grabbed his jacket. "Jack, save me!"

A look of confusion crossed his face. His arms were strong and warm as they lifted her. She clung to his neck.

"Emerald, it's okay! I'm taking you back to the house!" The wind almost swallowed his words.

He threw her up on Houdini, then jumped up behind. Holding her securely in front of him, he kicked the horse to a full gallop. Emerald held on for dear life. Her heart raced and her breathing became slower, until she wondered if she breathed any longer.

∞

Jack urged Houdini on as he felt Emerald's body go limp. A fear built up inside him, more than just apprehension about being caught in the storm. What was wrong with her? Was this a psychotic episode? Was Emerald really sick?

*Pray for her.*

He prayed. But he didn't know what he was praying for.

∞

*"Open your eyes, Emerald."*

*"I already did."*

*She had opened her eyes to find herself in the middle of an angry storm.*

*"There are two ways of looking at something. We have our human eye, in which we see the physical and our spiritual eye, which is where faith comes in."*

*Caleb's words.*

*"Open your eyes, Emerald."*

*Emerald didn't know how. More frustration.*

*"Surrender, Emerald."*

*"All right. I surrender."*

*Warmth filled her. She was not alone.*

*"Follow Me."*

*Suddenly the man was in front of her. It was the same vision she'd seen during the dinner party in Philadelphia, the one that got her hospitalized and prompted her to run away. Only this time the haze slowly cleared until she could make out his full image. He was wearing jeans, cowboy boots, and . . . and a black-collared shirt with a small horse embroidered on it.*

*Now she argued with Bradford.*

*"He's a cowboy, Daddy!"*

*"Emerald, I do not want you near that man ever again, do you hear me?"*

*"I have to find him, Daddy!"*

*But Daddy didn't understand. It was useless. He wasn't going to help her.*

*Her memory went back to the man.*

*"You have a mission."*

*Now children's cries surrounded her. This time a child's face appeared, then another. She could smell something rotting. A woman was in front of her, helping the children, talking to people. Emerald could feel their need. But then their desperation turned to hope. The woman was helping them. The woman's voice rang out and could be heard above the cries of the people. "God has delivered me from the pit! He has brought me hope and a future."*

*Emerald choked.*

*The woman was Alexandra.*

*The woman was her mother.*

# Chapter Seventeen

JACK LAID EMERALD ON THE LARGE sheepskin rug in front of the fire to dry and warm. Her closed eyes twitched for a moment, then stopped. He studied her, afraid to move, to breathe. What's wrong with her? What do I do? He felt a sick feeling in his stomach. Maybe she was crazy. She hadn't shown any symptoms of psychosis until now.

He took Emerald's hand. It was cold. He squeezed and began to pray.

∞

Emerald opened her eyes. Surrounded by warmth, she looked into Jack's concerned face.

He smiled. "There you are."

Where had she gone?

She tried to sit, and Jack reached out to help her. His warm hand held hers securely. Her clothes were wet, but he'd wrapped her in a blanket. The fire lit the room, along with the floor lamp in the corner. Outside, hard rain lashed against the dark windows and made her shiver, despite the fire's heat.

What had happened? She'd had another vision—or dream. Had she spoken during it? Trying to remember, she stood on shaky legs and peered out the window into the storm, wrapping the blanket tighter around her trembling body.

Jack stood. "You need to get out of those wet clothes."

"Jack. . . ." Her voice was a soft tremor.

She crossed to him.

"Stay by the fire." He placed his hands on her shoulders and gently pushed her toward the fireplace where she sank back down on the rug.

He left the room, and a feeling of dread filled her. Maybe he thought she was insane. What if he told her she couldn't work on the ranch anymore? Told Kati and Caleb?

"I know this isn't ideal, but it's all I have." He held out a large, white cotton robe.

She took it but didn't move.

"Jack, what happened?"

"You were in the pasture when the storm came up." His voice was grim.

She studied his face, but it gave nothing away.

"Why don't you get out of those wet clothes while I make something for dinner?"

Emerald shuffled to the bathroom. She stared in the mirror at her wet, tangled hair and pale face. A nightmare back home, but not so bad here where makeup was pretentious. People around Canyon Ridge wouldn't mesh well in her world. She'd never have imagined fitting into theirs. Maybe she didn't. Maybe she wanted to so badly that she was only fooling herself.

Hot tears filled her eyes. Why was fitting in here so important? Maybe she was out of her mind. Daddy and Sidney certainly thought so. They'd prefer she be in a "special clinic" receiving treatment for her disorder.

Emerald closed her eyes and clutched her stomach. *Disorder.* Was a disorder behind the dreams and visions she'd had? Were they delusions and hallucinations?

∞

The aroma of steak and an unknown side dish filled the air. Emerald stepped into the hallway and checked the tight knot on her robe. The hot shower had refreshed her body, but inside she felt the same. With wet hair hanging down her shoulders, Emerald entered the kitchen.

Jack turned from the stove. "Almost finished. Why don't we eat by the fire?" He nodded toward the plates, silverware, and mugs he had set on the counter.

She brought them to the coffee table in the living room, and he followed with steaks and sweet potatoes. Then he brought napkins and hot coffee, filled the mugs, and said the blessing.

She looked at the sweet potato. Not something she'd ever liked. She took a small bite—warm, buttery, and sweet. "I've never had one like this. What's in it?"

He looked up from his steak. "Butter, brown sugar, and a secret."

She studied the distinct flavor. "Cinnamon?"

He laughed. "Yep."

"It's delicious. I'll have to tell my chef back home."

Realizing what she'd said she clamped her mouth shut. They finished the meal in silence.

*That was rich girl riding, probably English style.*

She'd just confirmed his spoiled-rich-girl image of her.

Rain slashed against the windows, and Emerald jumped. "It's raining hard, isn't it?" she asked in a shaky voice.

"Hail." Jack stood and took her plate. "I checked the weather while you were in the shower. It's supposed to do this all night."

"You checked the weather?" Emerald looked around the living room, knowing he had no television.

Jack gestured toward the computer then added, "Kati called from Caleb's and agrees that it's too dangerous with the hail to get you back to her house. So you can stay in the guest room. The bed's already made."

∞

Emerald lay in the dark. She heard no movement outside her room, so Jack must have already turned in. She couldn't sleep. When she closed her eyes the images were there. When she opened them, darkness met her. Either way she was doomed. She tried to control the pace of her heart.

Maybe she did need help. What if she'd fled because her disorder caused her to imagine things that weren't true? Another feeling fought off this fear. What if she really could open her spiritual eyes? She had, after all, seen the images in her vision more clearly today. And she'd seen her mother. Had her brain just associated children's cries with Alexandra? Or, had Emerald opened her eyes to something she couldn't see before?

She had to know. "I don't want to be insane. Open my eyes. I surrender."

A peace came over her. She wasn't out of her mind. How, she couldn't be sure. But she was sure that she wasn't alone.

"Emerald."

Eyes open, she sat up in bed. "Jack?"

No answer. She sat in the silence for a moment. A dream?

"Emerald."

She jolted up, pushing back her covers and creeping to the door. "Jack?" She cracked open the door and saw only the faint glow of dying embers in the fireplace.

She was hearing things.

∞

Jack opened his eyes and his heart thumped. A thin shadow stood over him. He froze until he heard Emerald's voice.

"Jack?"

He jolted up and saw her in the door frame. "What's wrong?"

"Nothing. You were calling me."

Calling her? Was she dreaming?

He had been restless, only finding sleep by resolving to quell all his concerns in the morning with a quick call to the psychiatrist. Even though he expected this Dr. Coffman would likely claim "Patient confidentiality."

"Jack?"

He realized he hadn't responded and cleared his throat. "I didn't call you, Emerald. It must have been a dream."

"Oh."

But she continued to stand there. She didn't believe him? Or was she questioning her sanity, as he was?

"If you want to wait outside, I'll be right there."

∞

"Sorry." Emerald's face burned. Jack must be sleeping in his boxers or. . . .

She rushed out of the room and closed the door. Huddled by the weak glow of the fireplace, it offered little heat. Emerald wrapped her robe tighter. What was she doing? She returned to her bedroom. He would think her mad for sure now.

# Chapter Eighteen

BRADFORD LOOKED AT THE PAINTING OF Alexandra. It was ironic that after all his nurturing, that nature had given Emerald a mental illness. Like mother like daughter. But that didn't change his love for either of them. Where once Alexandra was his world, now Emerald was. How could she do this to him, he agonized. Run off like this without a word? Didn't she understand that not knowing where she was was killing him? No, of course she didn't. As a psychiatrist, he knew someone as mentally disturbed as Emerald was not able to consider such things.

He had hired the best private investigators and not a trace of her could be found. There was no sign that she had been forced or kidnapped—which was a relief. He'd started worrying about that after a while, but the investigators assured him that her departure was seamless enough to suggest she had planned it for a long time. Chances were she wasn't even in L.A.—it had been some type of cover-up. Her brilliance and sneakiness was the one thing he didn't understand. Usually people with her type of illness suffered from confusion. Their lack of reality often left both their thoughts and actions jumbled and messy. Yet, Emerald's intelligence and foresight had made no mistakes, left nothing to uncover. When he'd shared this with Sidney, he'd seemed equally as disturbed.

Bradford massaged his temples, unable to put to rest the racing, unanswered questions in his head. Was she happy? Was she well? Was she safe? He glared at Alexandra's portrait, and left the room.

∞

"Caleb, how do you know when God speaks to you?"

Emerald rode beside him, studying his expression carefully. It was the first she'd spoken during this Saturday afternoon ride into the mountains.

Caleb had prayed that she'd open up to him. Now he watched her looking straight ahead. *What is it you're looking for, Emerald?* "Well, I believe God continually speaks to us, we just don't always listen."

"So God speaks to our hearts?"

"Yes. It's impossible for us to understand God through human logic. It is only when we open our hearts that He can be perceived."

"But how do I know God is speaking to me . . . and I'm not just imagining it?"

"You know when it's God, Emerald. You feel His presence."

"But how do I know it's His presence and not another?"

"God's voice is different from any other. His presence gives you courage and strength to do things you otherwise wouldn't be able to."

"Caleb, the first time I came to Cowboy Church your sermon was about God's calling on our lives." She hesitated. "Do you think He has a plan for mine?"

"Absolutely. Since the beginning of time God has known you and the plan for your life. And while you might not always know what that plan is, you have the promise that He will bring you a future. God gives you life, everlasting life."

Her face blanked. She needed peace that he couldn't give.

He stopped his horse. "If you wouldn't mind, I'd like to pray with you."

Her horse came to a halt. Doubt shadowed her face.

He smiled. "I just want to pray that the Lord will bring you peace and make it clear when He speaks to you."

He expected an objection, but she nodded silently. He nudged Roper closer to her horse, then took her hand. He felt it tremble slightly.

"Father, please let Emerald know she is not alone and that You have a plan for her life. Speak to her so that she may know it's You." His hand tightened. "Open the eyes of her heart."

∞

Jack clutched Dr. Coffman's business card. It had been two nights since the hailstorm. Was Emerald insane? Disturbed in some way? No. He didn't want to believe it. But was he in denial?

He looked down at the card. He wasn't sure why, but it felt like calling the doctor would be a terrible mistake. Maybe he should just talk to Emerald. Show her the card. Ask about the other night. But what if she didn't want to talk? And how would he ask her? *Emerald, are you a schizo?*

He sucked in his breath. No. He couldn't do that. And he couldn't give Emerald the benefit of the doubt any more either. If these episodes continued, she could get hurt—or worse. He pushed the thought aside. So far, all she had done was be frightened by a storm. Maybe the storm somehow triggered it.

He sat down on his sofa.

*Break down the wall.*

His heart thumped. The wall? Admitting it was hard, but yes, he had built a wall. From the beginning he had been afraid to get close to Emerald. He had walled his heart to her. She had run away three times, and she'd do it again. Eventually, women always left.

A long-forgotten pain began to surface.

*May.*

No, he wouldn't think about her. She could hurt him if he let her. But the memory was there, too vivid to dismiss. Long blond hair, bright blue eyes. Jack's high school sweetheart and former fiancé had been the prettiest girl in town. It was for her that he'd built the house. On the front porch, two days before the wedding, she hit him with the news.

*Sorry, Jack. I'm just not cut out to be a rancher's wife. I've lived in this small town my whole life—I want to get out.*

He never heard from her again.

At least May had left him before the marriage. Milt's Becky had left after seven years of marriage and two sons—one nearly a newborn.

Maybe, Jack thought, God put him in Emerald's life for a reason. Maybe she needed him to help her. It would be a big gamble. He could break down the wall only to have her leave again. Jack dropped his face into his hands. If that was God's plan, he didn't know if he could carry it through.

∞

Emerald watched Jack ride into the pastures where she was feeding. The past few days she hadn't seen him much, calving season monopolized his time. In fact, he'd hardly spoken to her–-except for working instructions. She had the feeling he was avoiding her and wondered if it was because of what happened during the storm.

She turned back to the goats who were waiting for their meal. She touched a gray one's head. At least she still had this fulfilling job and her beautiful home in Canyon Ridge. So what if Jack had become distant? She closed her eyes as a cool rush of wind ruffled through her shirt and swept her hair off her warm neck.

Last night she'd slept well. Since Caleb's prayer the week before she hadn't had any more dreams or visions. Yet that didn't give her any answers. She needed to know what her dreams were trying to tell her. There was still doubt in her heart, but one thing had become clear. She had to believe they were from God. She couldn't face the alternative—that she was insane.

Caleb had made believing sound so easy. Still, doubt tormented her. Could she be imagining everything? Even the presence that brought her peace? She looked into the clear blue sky. "God, I need to know You're here with me and You hear my prayers."

Emerald picked up the large buckets to carry back to the barn. A movement caught her eye and she whirled at the sound of horse hoofs. Her heart hammered at the sight of Jack charging toward her on Houdini.

He pulled the horse to a quick halt. "Emerald, I need you to come with me."

"What's wrong?"

"Milt fell off Dad's four-wheeler. His boys need someone to look after them while we take him to the hospital."

Jack reached out with one arm and yanked her over Houdini's back. "Hold on."

She struggled to get her right leg over the back of the saddle as he urged Houdini forward. They rode through a couple of pastures; and as they cleared an opening in a fence, a small cabin came into view. As they got closer, Emerald could see Tony's truck parked at the front of the house. Tony stood below the front porch attending to a crouched-over Milt.

She felt a knot in her stomach as Jack pulled the horse to a halt. Blood oozed from Milt as Tony helped him hold his head.

Jack pulled her down from the horse. "The boys are inside. They're pretty shaken."

He ran to Tony, whose face was pale. "He's having seizures."

Milt's legs shook. Emerald swallowed nausea as Tony and Jack fought to get Milt's writhing body to the truck. A trail of blood followed them. Her gaze went to the house. Thinking of the two small boys inside, she walked up the stairs with quivering legs as the truck took off. Her icy fingers wrapped around the door handle, then stopped. She took a deep breath, unable to turn the knob. What had the boys seen?

She entered and heard whimpering. The boys sat in the corner of the one large room on a bunk bed. The elder wrapped his arms around the crying younger.

"Hey, guys. Your daddy's going to be all right." The words caught in her throat. Could she reassure them of something she didn't know to be true? She looked down at their round fearful faces. She had to do something.

She sat beside them on the bunk. "My name is Emerald. What are your names?"

The elder sniffed. "I'm Hank. This is Patrick. He's only two."

Patrick looked up at her then hid his face in his brother's shirt.

"And how old are you?" Emerald asked Hank.

Hank straightened up. "I'm five. How old are you?"

"I'm twenty-two."

"That's old."

Emerald laughed.

Hank pulled away from Patrick, who was still clinging but showing his face. "We're hungry. Our daddy was supposed to make us lunch."

Good. Maybe they hadn't seen anything. She stood. "Okay, then. What do you guys want?"

Hank climbed off the bunk, then helped Patrick get down. Holding Patrick's hand, he took Emerald's with his free hand and led her into the small, tight kitchen that was connected to the room. "Daddy was going to make us grilled cheese. We'll show you where stuff is."

The boys pulled out the bread, cheese, butter and even a frying pan. Emerald followed, amazed at how Hank made the toddler feel important. Hank would give Patrick materials he couldn't reach so he could carry them to Emerald. Before long Emerald had grilled cheese sandwiches sizzling while the boys sat at the small square table munching on pretzels.

Finally, Emerald slipped each boy a sandwich on a plate with satisfaction. She was grateful that the first meal she had to cook in her life was a beloved dish she'd watched Molly make countless times during her childhood.

"We have to say the blessing." Hank pushed Patrick's plate away from his little hands.

Patrick cried out, but Hank hushed him. "Patrick, we have to pray for Daddy."

Patrick's eyes filled with tears.

Hank looked up at Emerald. "God will heal Daddy. He will make him better won't He?"

Emerald stared into Hank's hopeful eyes. Right. Milt taught these kids to believe. But what if Milt did not recover? Emerald pushed the thought aside. This small child asked one thing of her and she didn't know any other way to calm his fears. Struggling to play the part Hank wanted, she folded her hands as she'd seen Jack do and closed her eyes.

*Anything that you ask, believing in My name, shall be done.*

Her heart thumped, not knowing where the words had come from but she grasped for hope with all she had.

Hank leaned across the table to touch her hand, looking at her closely. "Did God just speak to you?"

She looked at him in shock. "What did you say?"

"Did God just say something to you?"

Emerald felt a strange tingle. This little boy believed. He believed God heard his prayers. He believed God would heal his daddy. And he believed that God had spoken to her.

Emerald squeezed the small hand. She had prayed earlier for a way to help her know God was really there. And He had just answered her prayer.

# Chapter Nineteen

JACK PARKED THE TRUCK AT MILT'S cabin. A dim light glowed from inside and he rushed up the steps, knowing Emerald was probably worried.

Emerald opened the door, weary.

"Are the boys asleep?"

She nodded. "They're in the next room."

Jack sank into Milt's worn-out armchair. Emerald sat across from him on the edge of the sofa. "So, how is Milt?"

"Well, he lost a lot of blood. The doctors didn't think he'd make it. But then something happened that nobody can explain: he stabilized and opened his eyes. He's still critical," he gave Emerald a tired smile, "but we think he'll be okay."

He noticed Emerald was crying.

"Hey, it's all right. You did great with the boys. Milt will be thankful to know you were with them."

"That's not why I'm crying, Jack. Hank suggested we pray for his daddy today. He believed Milt would be healed. And he helped me believe, too. We've been praying for him all day, and we just knew he would be all right."

Jack joined her on the sofa and wrapped an arm around her.

"God heard our prayers, Jack."

Jack nodded. Had this experience helped Emerald find faith? He pulled away from her, quite serious now. "Emerald, I need to talk to you about something."

She wiped her tears and looked at him.

"The other night you came to my room. You thought I called you and I told you, you were dreaming." He placed his hand on hers. His heart raced, but he had to do this. "I know you're battling something. I know the storm frightened you and . . . and at first, I didn't know what to think about it. But last night I had a dream that God was calling you."

Emerald sucked in her breath.

"I think He is trying to speak to you." He squeezed her hand. "And after my dream, something occurred to me."

Emerald watched him, silent, frozen.

"Have you ever heard the story in the Bible about Samuel?"

She shook her head.

"One night when Samuel is a young boy he is in bed, and he thinks he hears the temple priest, Eli, calling him. But Eli isn't calling him. After the third time Eli tells him to next time answer, 'I am here, Lord.' So Samuel does. It is God speaking to Samuel."

"You're saying—"

"I'm saying that maybe God is speaking to you."

Emerald stood and walked to the window. She saw only darkness.

*. . . and the many conversations we've had.*

Her mother talked to God.

"It's not that simple. My dreams are confusing. I never know what they mean. Sometimes I feel so. . . ."

"Christ is the mighty counselor."

Christ was a counselor? Like Sidney? She wasn't sure she wanted any part of that.

Jack strolled to the hook by the door where he'd left his hat. "You've had a long day. Why don't you get some sleep? Kati said she'd come in the morning to take over. Sally, the woman who usually watches the boys during the day, is out of town for the next two weeks visiting her mother. But we'll see that they're taken care of. My mother said she'd pitch in, too."

Emerald nodded, and Jack left. Later, after checking on the boys, she lay deep in thought in Milt's small bunk in the corner.

∞

After he finished praying for his full recovery, Caleb stood over Milt's bed and smiled.

"I hear the boys are staying with your mom and Emerald. Please tell them I really appreciate it," Milt said weakly.

"You know mom loves them and Emerald sure has taken to them."

"And they've taken to her, too."

Caleb looked at Jack, who was sitting across the room. He had remained silent during most of the visit. Caleb studied him now. His cousin had been acting strange lately.

"Emerald's learning to be quite a little cowgirl after all, isn't she?" Milt shifted in the bed.

Caleb glanced at Jack. "And quite a good rider, too."

"You two seem to have become close lately."

Caleb raised his eyebrows. What was that supposed to mean? "Yeah. We enjoy riding and talking. She's come a long way since she first came here."

Jack poured a glass of water from the pitcher beside Milt's bed. "Thanks to you, no doubt."

"Jack, don't make assumptions. Emerald is searching for direction."

"And you can help her find it. That's what all those sunset rides are for, aren't they?"

Jack could think what he wanted, but Caleb had only taken one sunset ride with Emerald and their rides had purpose.

"Just don't have her thinking she can talk me into letting her ride the pastures."

"Jack, I told you she was a good rider because she is."

"And I guess you would be a good judge."

Milt cleared his throat. "Boys?"

Caleb narrowed his eyes. "Maybe I'm not a rancher, and maybe Emerald isn't, either. But she's trying, Jack. And you won't give her a chance."

"Riding and herding cattle are two different things. It can be dangerous, and you're not the one who'd be liable if something happened."

"I'm not saying she's ready to herd cattle, but she enjoys riding. Have you even let her ride once?"

"I don't have time to baby-sit, Caleb. If she wants to be a cowgirl she has to be tough first. And with you around, she won't learn."

"Are you jealous, Jack?"

"You're a pastor, Caleb. I'm just warning you that you should remember that."

Jack stood, grabbed his hat, and left.

∞

"Emmy! Emmy!"

Jack looked up from his tractor to see Hank and Patrick rushing to Emerald, who was twenty feet away, her hands full of feed.

Caleb strode behind them with a smile. "Mom said they've been asking for you all day."

Emerald set the feed down as both boys leapt into her arms. "Did Kati go to that auction she wanted to go to with Pete?"

Caleb nodded, then looked down as the boys jumped excitedly.

"Ride, ride!" Patrick yelled.

"We're ready to ride!" Hank joined in.

Emerald looked at Caleb. "Are we going to take them riding?"

Caleb hesitated. "Well, actually I have a few things at the

church that I need to take care of this afternoon." He looked down at the boys. "Do you want to play on the church playground for a while?"

"We want to ride!"

"We want to stay with Emmy!"

Jack noticed Emerald glance his way. He lifted a bale of hay and carried it into the barn.

"Jack?"

He knew she would come after him. He turned to her; she was holding Patrick.

"You want to know if the boys can stay here."

She nodded.

Jack looked at Patrick's grin. "You almost done with your feeding?"

"They can help me finish."

He sighed. "It's all right with me as long as you look after them. I've still got work to finish."

"Okay." But she didn't move. "Is there something else?"

"The boys really want to go riding. Can we go?"

*We.* Caleb must have decided to go riding with them after all.

Patrick waved his hand excitedly. "Riding, riding!"

"Do what you like, Emerald. Just finish your work."

Jack walked past her and outside to the tractor waiting with hay. He brought the last bale in and stacked it. Leaving the barn, he found Emerald kneeling beside the boys at the corral with the goats.

He looked toward the house. Caleb's truck was gone and the realization struck him.

*"We" meant Emerald and me.*

He watched her and the boys. One of the goats bleated, and the boys giggled. Emerald laughed. With the kids, Emerald opened up. His remaining chores could wait. He saddled his two calmest horses and led them to the corral.

Emerald looked up as he approached and her eyes widened at the horses.

"Horses!" Patrick shouted.

"Are we going riding?" Hank jumped up and down.

"You three have a choice." Jack stopped just in front of them. He looked at Emerald's smile, and his heart jumped.

He turned his attention back to the eager boys. "You boys can ride by yourselves, while Emerald and I lead the horses around the corral, or," his eyes met Emerald's, "we can all ride together out there." He pointed to the pastures.

Patrick, clearly not understanding the question, shouted, "Ride, ride!"

"I want to ride out there!" Hank pointed past the fences and jumped even higher.

Jack looked down at Hank. "Hank, you've ridden with your daddy before, haven't you?"

Hank nodded, lifting his head high. "Sure have. Daddy said I'm a good rider!"

Jack turned to Emerald. "Why don't you ride with Hank, then." He looked down at the bouncing two-year-old. "That way I can handle this one if he starts getting antsy."

Emerald nodded, though she probably would've agreed to anything.

First Jack helped Emerald up into the saddle and put Hank in front of her. Next, he put himself and Patrick on his horse. The restless boys turned calm the moment they touched saddle leather. Emerald and Jack nudged their horses to a slow walk.

"What's your favorite thing about riding?" Jack asked after the boys' chatter died away.

Emerald smiled. "Easy. The wide open land."

The land? Even more important than the horses?

Half an hour later, they stopped to let the boys run off some energy. They chased each other; then Hank told Patrick that they were on a treasure hunt, and the two boys crawled around. Emerald's eyes lit up as she watched them, much as when she looked at the mountains, or on the first day she rode his four-wheeler.

"You're really good with them. Do you have younger brothers or sisters?"

"No." Emerald was quiet. "I'm an only child. I know I have cousins, but I've never met them. My father worked a lot." She hesitated. "I spent most of my childhood with nannies and tutors. I guess you can say I'm kind of a loner." She shrugged. "I've never been around children."

So he was right. Her eyes lit up because she was living life for the first time. He thought about her riding with Caleb so often. Had Caleb picked up on her need to live?

Emerald leaned against her horse, her hands stuffed in her jean pockets. Milt was right. She was becoming quite the little cowgirl. And all because he'd given her a chance to live and discover the woman inside. He smiled. Maybe he could help her after all.

One of the boys grabbed her, and she ran from Hank and Patrick, who were chasing her in circles.

Hank tapped Jack. "You're it!" He dashed away, and Patrick struggled to keep up.

Jack had just been tagged. He looked at Emerald's grin. He took off toward her, and she fled with a scream as the boys giggled.

# Chapter Twenty

CALEB WATCHED AS JACK PARKED THE truck, and Emerald climbed out. She was helping Jack feed now—formerly Milt's job.

He approached her. "So, how is 'real ranch work' treating you?"

She gave him a tired smile. "I'm kind of worn out. Do you think we could make it a short ride?"

He nodded, understanding. All their rides had been short–-if not cancelled—lately due to the extra responsibility Milt's injury had thrust on Emerald. He looked at Jack, who hadn't yet greeted him. Jack was working her too hard.

He turned back to Emerald and smiled. "Of course. We'll ride along the stream and you can let me know when you're ready to head back."

"Okay."

They mounted their horses and rode side-by-side in silence. He could tell she relished the quiet. Their eyes met. She smiled, then suddenly kicked her horse into a gallop, leaving him behind. Where had that burst of energy come from?

He nudged his horse forward, catching up but still keeping her in front. She tore off her cowgirl hat, and let her hair hang down her back. The wind wafted a lovely smell to his nostrils. Her shampoo? Caleb listened to her laughter and breathed in her scent. Emerald looked back, and her smile teased. When he reached her side and took her hand in his, she registered surprise, so he let go, then pulled his horse to a stop. He jumped off as she pulled to a stop a few feet ahead. He gently lifted her down from her horse. She felt so light; he'd have to tell his mother to feed her more.

Peering down at her, he wrapped his arms around her slender waist. His face loomed just inches from her soft, tender lips.

*No, Caleb. Tell her of My love. Tell her of My miracles.*

Caleb jerked awake, sweating. He sat up in bed and looked around his dark room. It was midnight; he was alone. No Emerald, no horses, no kiss. He inhaled deeply, but her scent was no longer there. He pushed back the covers and dressed in jeans, boots, and a white tee. Then he pulled a flannel shirt over the tee and buttoned only the middle buttons as he stepped outside into the cool night air.

Caleb headed for his small barn that was just large enough for his two horses. He saddled Roper and rode at a gallop through the moonlit prairie, the wind tearing through his shirt. He often rode at night when restless, or frustrated about a sermon. That ought to be his motivation tonight; he had yet to write a word for this coming Sunday—three days away. But Emerald dominated his mind. The dream. It left him feeling weak and vulnerable.

A cloud drifted from the moon, flushing Milt's house with light. He usually did not ride this far. He slowed his horse to turn when he noticed a shadow on the other side of the field.

The shadow moved again. An animal? A chill rattled him. Bears came out at night—and mountain lions. But Roper would let him know if either were around. On impulse, he leapt from his horse. Taking the reins, he spoke to Roper and led him toward the shadow.

He called out, "Is anyone there?"

No reply. Standing still, he was poised to jump back on Roper and trot away. Then Roper jerked, spooked. Something was there.

"Caleb?" a voice spoke softly.

Emerald crept from the shadow. She wore an oversized tee shirt with a work jacket and jeans.

"Emerald! What are you doing out here?"

"I couldn't sleep . . . had a dream and needed some fresh air. What are you doing here? You scared me to death!"

"I'm sorry. I guess I have the same answer. Trouble sleeping, I ride a lot at night."

Roper nuzzled Emerald when she stepped forward to stroke him. She nearly touched Caleb in the process. He held his breath. He breathed in her scent, just like in the dream. He wanted to pull her close, but he didn't dare move. How could he tell her he'd fallen for her?

"You shouldn't be out alone at night." Caleb stepped back, fearful that his lust would take over. "There are wild animals, you know." He took a scolding tone, trying to conceal his desire.

"I know. But I didn't come far from the house."

"Jump on Roper and I'll take you back."

She obeyed, and he could tell she expected him to get on with her. Instead, he led the horse to Milt's house then helped her slide down.

"Jack has you working hard enough; you should be able to sleep."

She didn't reply.

He re-mounted Roper and rode away, anguish washing over him. He hadn't told Emerald of God's love and miracles. He could try to justify it—this wasn't the time or place, or his personal feelings made it awkward—but he couldn't ignore the facts.

For the first time he could recall, he hadn't obeyed the voice of God.

∞

Emerald watched Caleb ride away, trying to make sense of what had happened. She tip-toed back to her room, careful not to wake the boys. Wondering if Caleb might return, she peered out her window and saw only faint shadows from the aspen trees near the house. She closed her eyes as she thought of her dream. Why had it led her outside? And was Caleb's presence there a coincidence?

Emerald pulled her mother's treasure chest out from under the bed. After opening the diary, she stared down at her mother's words, dated January fourth. Two months later than her last writing, where she had expressed her desire to sing praises. Alexandra's tone was different in this entry.

> *Oh, Father! Bring rest to my soul! The enemy attacks me, and I am tormented. I know where I should be but I cannot reach the mountain I am to climb. I fear that I won't make it. I know that this doubts You, which only brings more sorrow to my soul. I am torn between my husband, and where You are calling me. Please, don't make me choose. My heart longs to be with You, but I love Bradford, and it says in Your word not to seek a divorce but to honor the sacred commitment of marriage. If only You will deliver me from this torment and guide me.*

Emerald's hand trembled. Maybe God hadn't redeemed her mother's life from the pit after all. Alexandra had praised God only a page before for bringing her peace, and now she was crying out for deliverance from torment.

*I am torn between my husband and where You are calling me.*

Bradford didn't agree with Alexandra's beliefs. That Emerald knew already.

*Please don't make me choose.*

Did Alexandra mean she had to choose between God and her husband? Then why would she write of the commandment against divorce? Was religion coming between her mother and Daddy?

*. . . where You are calling me.*

Where was God calling her mother? Obviously someplace Bradford wouldn't let her go. Emerald remembered Caleb's sermon about the calling on people's lives, and the visions she had of the mysterious man.

*Emerald, you have a mission.*

Emerald closed her eyes. The man was a cowboy and her mother had a calling. She closed her mother's diary. She wanted to read more but was worried she wasn't ready. Her heart beat faster. She felt the answer was right in front of her, then something occurred to her. Maybe Alexandra felt torment because she knew her calling but couldn't get there. Maybe Emerald felt torment because she was close to her mission but didn't know what it was. For the first time she felt a real connection to her mother. Different women, different callings, different obstacles—but the same frustration.

Emerald was confused, but she did know two things: anything was better than being deemed insane, and if her mother found her answers, then Emerald knew she could find hers, too.

# Chapter Twenty-One

"Emmy, look!" Patrick screamed with pride as the baby goat sucked the bottle he fed it.

Emerald watched Hank and Patrick feeding the goats, their new favorite chore on the ranch. Kati was busy that morning, so Emerald had brought the boys with her to work.

Crossing her arms against the chill of the overcast day, Emerald turned to the sound of a truck. Caleb was arriving to take the boys to see Milt. Her heart thumped. He'd probably have a good excuse for his abrupt and bizarre behavior the night before.

She gathered the boys. "Caleb's here, time to go see Daddy!"

"Yeah!" They jumped in excitement and rushed to the truck.

Caleb stepped out and greeted her with his usual smile. "Sorry about last night, didn't mean to startle you."

His eyes were distant, his voice forced into an unnatural casualness.

Emerald was uncomfortable. "Don't apologize. We were both startled."

He adjusted his hat and glanced at Hank, who was trying to boost Patrick into the truck. "I better go. Have a good day."

She watched as he got the boys settled, then left.

"The boys excited about seeing their dad?"

She jumped at Jack's voice behind her. "Yes, we—" She turned around, cutting herself off as she realized how close he stood, almost touching her. Had he been there all along?

His dark eyes seemed to read her. His face said he'd sensed the awkwardness between Caleb and her. She hoped he wasn't waiting for an explanation.

"Ready to feed?"

"Yes." She released her breath in relief, thankful for the distraction of work, and climbed in Jack's truck.

He started the engine. "Remember your lesson yesterday about feeding in the pastures?"

She nodded. "Drive in circles, so the cattle don't just keep following and eating."

When they entered the pasture, the heifers plodded toward the truck for mealtime and the dogs jumped out the back of the truck bed to start herding the cattle where they needed to be.

"All right." Jack put the truck in park and got out.

She slid over to the steering wheel, hesitant.

He poked his head in. "You can drive a manual, right?"

She could. At least, she knew how. But with chauffeurs on call until a couple of months ago, when was the last time she drove anything, manual or automatic?

She wrapped her fingers around the steering wheel and nodded. She adjusted her rearview mirror to see Jack jump in the bed of the truck. Then he called out to move forward.

Tentatively, she pushed in the clutch and moved the stick to first gear. Then she released the clutch and hit the gas. The truck jerked forward, slamming her against the steering wheel. A loud thump and yell came from the back of the truck. Hitting the brakes, she shifted to park. Emerald looked out the back window, but Jack wasn't there. Her heart hammered. Where was he?

She flung open her door and dashed around the bed. In that sudden jerk forward she'd gone about thirty feet from where Jack now lay in a pile of spilled feed, surrounded by hungry heifers.

Hatless, he stood and limped toward her, brushing feed from his work clothes. "I thought you said you knew how to drive a manual."

"I did. But I've only driven one once. About six years ago."

"You've got to be kidding."

She didn't answer.

"You're not kidding." He staggered to the truck, climbed in the driver's seat and shut the door.

Emerald stood there, uncertain. He cranked the truck, then leaned his head out the window with an annoyed grumble. "Get in."

She timidly took the passenger seat. "What are we going to do now?"

"*We* aren't going to do anything. I'm taking you back to the house."

"But how will you feed?"

"I've fed before alone. It's not ideal, but I can do it."

"How are you going to drive the truck and throw out feed at the same time?"

"Put the truck in neutral."

"And let it roll while you're on the back?"

He glared at her. "It can't be as dangerous as you driving it."

"Why don't you let me throw the feed?"

"Oh, no." He shook his head. "I'm not going to take the chance of you falling off the back of the truck."

"So just because I can't drive, I'm incompetent?"

She watched his face in silence. Frustration rose. She didn't want him demoting her to cleaning stalls again.

Jack shook his head. "I guess if I don't give you a chance, the drive out here was a waste." He sighed. "Get out."

Emerald opened her door and leapt out. Despite his grumpy moments, she liked being with him. But she wasn't going to tell him that. No way.

∞

Jack glanced in the rearview mirror. She was doing well so far, though clearly showing signs of fatigue. She wouldn't make it to the pregnant heifers in the heavy pasture. Still, he had to admit that with calving season demanding extra attention and Milt out of commission, Emerald ended up being more help than he'd thought.

She shouted, and he poked his head out the window.

"Jack!" she yelled and pointed. "Look at the cow over there!"

"Where?" He looked and spotted a limping cow behind some shrubs.

"Isn't that kind of weird, Jack?" Emerald clung to the front end of the bed and leaned close to his window.

"Hold on." He swerved toward the animal.

As the truck reached the cow he noticed her belly dragging the ground. There was a sickness in his stomach as he shifted into park and jumped out.

"What is it, Jack? What's wrong with her?"

"Her stomach's ruptured. The calf could already be dead."

How had he missed the pregnant heifer? For any chance to save this calf, he had to work fast. He glanced at Emerald, who was staring in horror from the bed of the truck.

"Stay back."

Emerald watched as Jack examined the heifer, and in one swift move tipped the cow over. The heifer bellowed and kicked her legs and Jack stepped back to give her a second to calm.

Emerald felt her pulse quicken as Jack barked out instructions.

"Go to the glove compartment of the truck, I've got a knife in there."

She hopped out of the bed and brought the knife. "What are you going to do?"

She was beginning to think she didn't want to know.

But he answered without a thought. "C-section. Think you can stomach this?"

She hoped so.

"Good, cause I'm going to need your help."

He began feeling around the cow's lower stomach. "There is a triangle shaped area with no bones that is close to the uterus; I'm going to start there." He looked at her. "I'm going to need you to help hold up this layer of fat down here while I make an incision."

"Okay." She let him move her hand to where he wanted her to lift.

She watched as he sliced, expecting nausea to overcome her, but it didn't.

Jack was swift and masterful. He had clearly done this many times.

Within minutes he was lifting the calf out. "I need you to rub the calf while I milk the cow."

He laid the calf down in front of her and showed Emerald how to rub. She took over, and he got a plastic container with a tube from the truck.

He milked the heifer. "Now, hold him still."

While she did so, he inserted the tube into the calf's mouth and slowly slid it down his throat. "We have to be careful not to get it into his lungs."

When they finished feeding the newborn, Jack put the container with leftover milk back in the truck, then returned with his rifle. "Get in the truck with the calf."

Emerald struggled to stand under the calf's weight, and his hand gripped under her arm. He smiled. "Good job."

The two words gave her strength, despite what she knew was coming. After she pulled the truck door closed she heard the shot.

Emerald peered at the bloody calf trembling in her arms and saw her reflection shining in his big eyes.

*Sorry about your mom. But we saved you.*

∞

"We did it." Jack's eyes held more than gratitude; they showed admiration.

She sat on the couch as Jack started a fire.

"Hungry?"

She shook her head, too tired to feel hungry.

He brought his guitar into the firelight. Sitting in a chair across from her he played softly.

She watched him, the glow from the fireplace dancing on his tan face. He sang, and she felt her heart jump. She closed her eyes, letting the music speak to her heart.

*What is your desire, Emerald?*

An image of children flashed before her. Then her mother was there, reaching out to people in a third-world country.

"I think I have a mission."

Jack stopped abruptly. "What?"

She had said it out loud. She stood and moved to the fireplace, her heart thumping.

"Emerald." He stood beside her, and she could feel his hesitation before he touched her shoulder softly. "Talk to me."

She turned to face him, thinking his touch seemed natural, and she felt a longing to tell him everything. Instead, she closed her eyes and leaned into him, and his arms encircled her. She let her head fall against his chest, and her hand rested on his heart. She could feel its steady beat.

He caressed her hair and lifted her head. He touched her face, catching a tear. "Emerald, whatever you're battling, you're not alone."

His lips lowered to hers. They were warm, soft, and tender. She felt hers tremble beneath his. Her eyes closed, and she realized that here, her worries, questions, and fears disappeared. His touch took her pain away.

A pounding filled her ears. He pulled away abruptly looking

as startled as she. She was reluctant to let him go, but someone was at the door.

He hesitated, then went to answer it.

"Jack, I really need to talk to you." Caleb adjusted his hat and sized up his cousin. Confronting Jack daunted him, but he had to do it.

"Caleb, is everything okay?"

"May I come in?"

Jack glanced behind him. "Can it wait until tomorrow?"

"It's about Emerald."

"Caleb, now is not a good time."

"Jack, I've been thinking, and—" He pushed past him and stopped when he saw Emerald in the next room, facing the fireplace.

*So that's why she didn't show up for our ride.*

"I'm sorry; I didn't know you had company." His voice faded as he backed up and left, hoping she hadn't seen him. He'd come to tell Jack that Emerald was lost and searching for meaning. But now he stomped away, jealousy blazing inside him. Caleb jumped into his truck, cranked it, and did a U-turn out of the drive.

*Is your will My will?*

Caleb slowed the truck. Of course he wanted God's will, but surely His will couldn't be *this*? He was the one leading Emerald toward God. It was Jack who was messing that up. He gripped the steering wheel thinking he didn't understand any of this.

Caleb wanted God's will . . . he did. But he also wanted something else, more than he had ever wanted anything. As much as he told himself this was about Emerald finding the Lord, he realized that he had fallen in love with her.

# Chapter Twenty-Two

SIDNEY PONDERED GREG'S IDEA. HE COULDN'T say he was thrilled about it, but at this point he didn't have much of a choice.

"All right, send her in."

Ending the call on his cell phone he poured himself a drink from the bar in his living room. Greg had suggested that since Emerald threatened to talk to the media why not send Anna to an upcoming event the small town was throwing? Greg's logic made sense. Anna was a well-known reporter. So if Emerald was going to talk to the press, they could provide her the perfect opportunity. Anna had already been warned about Emerald's condition, and that she was most likely delusional. Shoot, she'd witnessed it first hand at the hotel.

Greg had told his fiancé that her interview at the event was really a hoax and she was to report directly back to him with any and all information.

Sidney downed his drink, then re-filled it. Greg was confident that he could convince Anna that Emerald was psychotic and that it was in Emerald's best interests that they find out the truth so they could help her. Best case scenario, Anna would get Sidney's disk back and that would be the end of it. However, if Emerald was planning on exposing them . . . well, they'd cross that bridge when they came to it.

No other evidence of his drug prescriptions existed. At least not past what had been called into the pharmacy. He'd erased all illegal prescriptions from the system at his practice and his computer was clean. He'd saved it all to one CD. The CD that Emerald now had.

∞

"I've got it." Jack wiped the sweat from his brow as he helped his dad herd the two heifers they'd bought at the auction down the ramp off their trailer and into the pasture.

Tony sighed as he closed the gate. "Well, Son, that was a good deal."

Jack nodded. "Surprised I got that price. I was sure old man Buck was going to outbid me."

Tony patted his son's shoulder. "He usually don't give up quite so easily does he?" he laughed.

Jack climbed in the passenger seat of his dad's truck. "Need to stop and check on the heavy pasture."

Tony nodded. He did a U-turn and headed toward the heavy pasture near the house. But Jack couldn't focus on the mother-to-be heifers. He thought back to last night. Caleb wasn't expecting Emerald to be there, and he hadn't planned on ruining a private moment between them. But he had. He had reminded Emerald of her missed ride, and Jack ended up taking Emerald home, knowing he'd never get the moment back.

"Got any springers in there yet?"

His head spun back to the present. "I think so. None seem as close as that heifer yesterday." He glanced at his dad. "First one to give birth and it had to happen in the main pasture—the only one we missed."

Tony pulled the truck to a stop. "Would be that way. Like I always say about calving, right when you're expecting the worst, everything goes easy. And, whenever you think you've got everything under control, well then, something you never expected happens."

Jack jumped out of the truck and Tony followed him into the pasture. "Plan to walk through here?"

"I usually ride, but earlier I told Emerald to ride through here and check on things."

"I see."

Jack recognized and accepted Tony's skepticism. No, Emerald probably wouldn't be able to tell anything. But she had helped save a calf's life; he needed to give her some of the responsibility she craved.

"Pete went with her." He watched his dad's face and realized it wasn't the heifers his dad was concerned about.

"You've really come to care about this girl, haven't you?"

Jack stuck his hand in the water pump to check the level. "She tries hard and she helps me out a lot."

"Caleb says she's come a long way since she first came here."

What was his dad insinuating? "She's come a long way, but I'm sure Caleb takes the credit."

Tony sighed. "She's heading in the right direction, but this is all new to her and we don't know anything about her. All I'm saying is for you to be careful."

Anger flared inside him. His dad was warning him not to have a relationship with Emerald.

Jack looked his father straight in the eye. "I don't care what Caleb says, and I don't care what you think. Neither of you know Emerald like I do and neither of you have a right to judge. I'm the one who spends all day with her." He turned and stomped back toward the gate. "My relationship with her is none of your business."

"Jack?" Tony called after him.

Jack barked over his shoulder. "You can take the truck home. I feel like walking."

∞

Jack climbed down the ladder with a rope in his hand. From his side view he caught a glimpse of Caleb entering the barn and scanning the shelves that were stocked with equipment and feed. Finally his gaze fixed on Jack.

Jack acknowledged him curtly, then turned back to work.

"Jack, you got a minute?"

"I'm busy."

"Jack?"

Jack threw the rope over his shoulder. "I've got work to do, Caleb."

"You know we can't avoid this discussion."

Jack sighed and dropped the rope. Crossing his arms over his chest, he faced his cousin.

Caleb adjusted his hat. "It's about Emerald. Jack, you've been working her a lot of long hours. Just look at her. She's exhausted."

"Since when is it your business how I work my employees?"

Caleb took a deep breath. "Since I believe the reason you're working Emerald long hours is to keep her from going riding with me."

"It's calving season. Everyone knows that. There's a lot harder work to come." *And why do you care so much if she rides with you?*

Caleb's eyes held his. "I'm not questioning your ranching decisions. I'm just asking you to consider Emerald's needs."

"I guess you would be the one to know?" Anger rose inside him as he watched his cousin. *Why is Caleb bugging me about Emerald now?*

"She's confused, Jack. She needs to find peace." Caleb was speaking like a pastor now.

*Emerald* needed peace. But Caleb wasn't the only one who could help her find it. Jack straightened. This time Caleb didn't know everything. He was using his profession to analyze a woman he wanted to know.

"So I guess, Caleb, the only place she can find peace is in the sunset?"

The knot in Jack's stomach loosened as he saw his cousin's face change to a deep shade of red. It wasn't jealousy that had generated his comment. He simply knew more than Caleb this time around.

But Caleb didn't think so. His eyes narrowed. "Do you care about Emerald, Jack?"

"Yes, I do."

"That's what I thought. So now the more important question would be, which do you care about more? The physical Emerald, or her soul?"

Jack stepped closer to Caleb; he wanted to knock that smirk right off his cousin's face. "You may think you know everything about Emerald, and what she needs. But you don't. And how I care about Emerald—" He smiled. The victory was his. "—is none of your business."

The tension was interrupted by a noise outside the door. Jack took a step past his cousin and saw Emerald in the doorway, hands by her sides. He didn't have to wonder how long she'd been listening. Her face said long enough. Caleb's expression said he was just as surprised as Jack to see Emerald standing there.

"I can't believe you, either one of you," she said as she turned and left the barn.

"Wait," Jack called as he followed her into the dimming daylight. But Emerald was gone, leaving him with a bad feeling about what had just happened.

∞

Jack watched Emerald as she fed the horses in the corral. On this chilly day, one of Kati's work jackets hung loosely on her, and her hair hung over one shoulder in a braid. Emerald barely acknowledged him, then continued her work. She hadn't spoken about the night before—or anything, really—since Kati had dropped her off.

Emerald dumped the last bucket of feed into the trough. Opening the gate she approached him, chin held high.

"What do you want me to do next?" The question was cool and businesslike, asked purely out of duty.

"Come with me."

He led her to the stables and she followed, not struggling to keep up as she once had. Emerald had come a long way since that first day on the job—soon to be two months ago.

When they reached the entrance he said, "I know how it must have looked last night. But you have to understand that Caleb and I had our disagreements long before you ever came into the picture."

She stared awkwardly, then turned away. It was clear she didn't want to address the subject. "What do you want me to work on?"

He led her to a stall with one of the newer fillies. "Getting to know your new horse better."

She flushed, but her gaze fell. "Thanks, Jack."

He sighed, knowing it wasn't what she wanted. "Of course, you are awfully stubborn. Maybe that horse doesn't fit you after all."

Squelching her effort to reply, he walked down two stalls to the black gelding she loved. "Perhaps Denver would suit you better."

Her eyes widened. "Jack, you don't really mean—?"

He grinned. He'd made the right decision. "You've proven yourself to be quite a capable ranch woman. A true cowgirl has to have her own horse, doesn't she?"

Pure joy covered Emerald's face, and relief flooded over him. No matter what Caleb thought, he knew exactly what Emerald needed.

∞

Emerald sat alone at Kati's kitchen table with a cup of hot mint tea and her mother's diary. Milt was home from the hospital now, but the boys were staying with them until he finished his rehab. Kati had taken him dinner that night, and the boys went along for the visit.

She ran her hand over the smooth surface of the book that she hadn't fully read yet. Her mind had stalled on the previous night when she'd walked in on Jack and Caleb's argument.

*Do you care about Emerald, Jack?*

*Yes, I do.*

*So now the more important question would be which do you care about more? The physical Emerald, or her soul?*

She shivered. What kind of a question was that? If someone cared about her they would care for her entirety. Body, heart, soul or whatever someone's explanation of the human makeup might be. And how dare either Caleb or Jack try to determine who she was or what she needed. A familiar anxiety crept over her, constricting her breathing.

*Daddy.*

He always claimed to know what she needed. And relying on him had almost landed her in a "special clinic." She shook. The last person who supposedly looked after her needs had let her down. He isolated her and assumed she was crazy.

Emerald opened the diary with trembling hands and turned to her mother's next writing, dated February 20th. She clearly remembered the previous entry. Would God bring Alexandra the answers she sought?

> *Dear Father, I rejoice in Your Name for my spirit prays to Your Spirit and Your Spirit intercedes with mine just as Paul's! When I search diligently for the answers and do not know what to pray, Your Spirit 'intercedes with groans that*

*words cannot express' (Romans 8:26).*

*I call out to You and do not hear an answer. I search for You through man's explanation, but I cannot find You. I participate in religious practices and attend services that promise Your presence but I do not feel You. It is in the still quietness that I surrender to You, that I admit my logic will never come close to grasping Your entirety. It is in the moment when my desire to be with You becomes more important than understanding You. It is then that I feel the fullness of Your presence.*

Emerald reread Alexandra's words. Not at all what she had expected. She wasn't sure what she'd hoped for and she sat quietly, trying to understand. Outside the sliding glass doors, the sky was turning dark blue to herald the onset of night. She stepped onto the front porch and settled on the swing. The sun moved to the horizon, leaving its unmatchable stream of colors behind. Hearing a truck's engine, she expected to see Kati returning home, but it was Caleb who parked in the driveway.

He climbed out and tipped his hat to her. As he approached the porch, she slowed the swing to a stop.

"Mind if I join ya?"

She couldn't resist such honest sincerity. Despite her resentment about the night before, she patted the seat beside her.

"I can only imagine how you must feel about last night." He faced her, his eyes truly sorry.

Removing his cowboy hat, he held it between his legs. "The truth is, both Jack and I have come to care a great deal for you and we both want what's best for you. It just seems, like everything else, it's one more thing we don't agree on."

Caleb and Jack cared for her. The problem was she didn't know what to do with that.

She thought of Jack's kiss. It felt wonderful, but it had created awkwardness. He was a typical man following his desires.

She needed it to be that. She couldn't let someone care for her; that would lead to control.

And then she realized that Jack and Caleb weren't Bradford and Sidney. They weren't trying to lock her away. They were trying to help her find her way. *They really care about me.*

She waited for the anxiety to come, but for some reason it didn't.

She looked at Caleb, who was waiting for her reply. Yes, maybe he was directing her along an uncertain path toward a mysterious God. But he cared for her in a much different way than Daddy or Sidney. It wasn't at all logical, but it brought her closer to finding what she sought than anything ever had.

She smiled.

He stood up from the swing. "Want to go for a ride?"

She looked at him in confusion. Kati only had an old mare. "On what?"

"I meant in the truck."

∞

The truck pulled onto the main road, then headed up the steep, winding road that led higher into the mountains. When they reached a wide spot, Caleb pulled off the road and parked. Flashlight in hand, he helped her out of the truck and led her up a craggy cliff. Sitting on a boulder that overlooked the town of Tussle Springs, they watched lights flicker in the grayness below. A sleepy orange moon now hung over the horizon.

"Wait until it gets completely dark." Caleb's voice was soft beside her. They sat for a long time in silence until the brightest stars speckled the black sky.

"The Little Dipper." She pointed as Caleb removed his work jacket and hung it over her shoulders. She looked at the shadows from the moonlight as they fell on his handsome face. "It's just beautiful."

He smiled. "And you probably thought once the sun set and it grew dark it was over." He turned back to face Tussle Springs. "It's never over, Emerald."

There was something about Caleb's comments that reminded her of her mother's. "Caleb, when do you feel the presence of God the most?"

"Times like these."

His hand covered hers and she accepted the comfort it offered. The desire to share with him was there, and without thinking she found herself opening up to him about her mother's journal and prayers. Enrapt, Caleb listened with an occasional nod.

She finished with the writing she had just puzzled over that evening. "So, what do you think?"

"That your mother was searching for answers." His eyes met hers. "Just like you."

# Chapter Twenty-Three

EMERALD SAT ON DENVER. THE STEADY rhythm of the horse's slow trot down the main road brought an unusual stir of emotions. Denver belonged to her. She glanced at Jack, riding alongside on a horse called Silver Bullet. He'd surprised her that morning by suggesting they go for a ride—into town.

When they reached the main drag, Jack headed left, toward the shops. "I have a few supplies I need to pick up."

They hitched their horses in front of a feed and supply store. When they entered, her nostrils filled with an odor ten times stronger than what was in Jack or Kati's barn. Jack gave the clerk his list of needed supplies. The clerk smiled and asked about the ranch. Yes, everyone in the town seemed to know everyone else. Emerald leaned against the counter while the man led Jack to the back of the store to fill his order.

"Well hi, honey, how ya doing?" A plump woman with short, curly red hair waved to Emerald from the aisle.

Emerald greeted her.

The woman put a stack of papers on the counter and shook her head. "I printed fifty bulletins and then realized I spelled the scripture reference wrong!"

Emerald looked at the mistake. She'd spelled Romans "Romens." The bulletin was for the Cowboy Church service this coming Sunday, and Emerald realized she recognized the woman from church.

"Ah, ain't nobody gonna notice that." The woman's husband appeared, glancing over her shoulder.

While the couple argued politely, Emerald read the top bulletin. The cover said WELCOME TO COWBOY CHURCH as usual, but under it in bold letters now appeared: WHERE WE BELIEVE IN THE MIRACLE-WORKING OF GOD! Emerald's breath caught as images of children crying out for help appeared.

*They need healing, Emerald.*

She began to tremble as more images emerged. More cries. People hungry, searching desperately for something.

*Show them the way, Emerald.*

*I can't.*

Her chest felt heavy; she couldn't breathe.

*Do not be overcome by fear. Do not let the enemy confuse you.*

But who, Emerald wondered, is the enemy?

∞

Jack glanced down the aisle to the front of the store where Emerald spoke to Mary and Doug from church. He froze. Emerald didn't look right. She was pale. Too pale. He rushed to the front of the store where he gently took her arm.

"Come on."

She leaned against him and he wrapped his arm around her waist. Her hand grabbed his free one and clutched it.

"Is she all right?" Mary and Doug stopped their conversation and turned to them.

"She'll be fine, just needs some air."

He led Emerald out and sat her on a bench, where she continued to shake and cling to his hand.

"Just take deep breaths; you're going to be all right."

She leaned back against the bench and her breathing seemed to steady, but the look in her eyes disturbed him. Why was she so terrified?

Emerald's breathing eventually slowed and she loosened her grip on Jack's hand. Jack still watched her. She had done this before—but during the storm. What could possibly explain this attack?

He stood. "I'm going to get you some water. Will you be all right for a minute?"

She nodded, and he returned a few minutes later with a bottle of water and a granola bar. "Here, it'll get your sugar back up."

She opened the bar and took a bite. After chewing and swallowing, she looked a lot better.

"Low blood sugar," she whispered hoarsely.

He nodded but didn't reply. They had missed lunch. But he had a feeling that wasn't the reason at all.

∞

Jack rode through the heavy pasture to examine his heifers, but his mind was not on the cattle. It was on Emerald. Why couldn't he get her to open up to him?

Was Caleb having better luck with her? He remembered his cousin's question. *Do you care more about the physical Emerald, or her soul?*

How could Caleb have the nerve to ask him such a thing? Jack slowed his horse to a trot and then to a stop as realization struck him. Caleb prayed for Emerald, and she responded to him. Jack turned his horse back toward the house. No, he wouldn't go to Emerald just to beat Caleb.

*Tell her you love her.*

Love her? Did he? No, not possible. He only cared about her and wanted to help. He frowned, knowing that was a lie. Okay, so he cared about her a lot. And yes, he did care about her soul.

∞

Caleb rode next to Emerald, with Denver and Roper keeping a steady trot. Today they rode through the pastures to the little stream. He watched Emerald's wavy, sandy hair hanging loose over her light sweater. She seemed relaxed today, with a new glow.

Anguish washed over him and the deep pain came back. He tried to shrug it off, but it only grew until his entire being ached with yearning.

"Caleb, what is it? Are you still embarrassed about the other day? I told you, it's okay."

Emerald's soft voice brought him back to reality and he forced a smile. "Then everything's fine."

But he wasn't fine.

Emerald pulled her horse to a stop and slid off. "Let's walk to the meadow from here."

Caleb got off his horse, and she took his hand in hers, tightly and securely. Leading him to her favorite meadow of wildflowers, she seemed stronger today. He closed his eyes and took a deep breath, trying to let the beauty around him take over him as it usually did.

"Tell me how you do that."

"What?" He opened his eyes to see Emerald studying him closely.

"Every time we come here, or climb the peak, you always breathe like that—it's like you're breathing in the very meaning of life."

"If I could breathe in the very meaning of life in one breath––believe me, I would."

She faced partly him and partly the mountains, her fingers loosely interlocked with his. Her face held a soft radiance, like a beautiful, yet fragile, flower. He craved to touch her, to kiss her, to love her, to bring her peace, to put the broken pieces back together. But there was a pain that stopped him. Why? Was it fear of losing her—or of never having her?

Emerald's fingers tightened around his. She stepped closer and with her other hand she touched his face so gently, only the heat proved her fingers were there.

He closed his eyes in fear that if he moved she might be gone. Her hand rested on his cheek as her face drifted into his. He felt the warmth of her closeness. He opened his eyes and something drew her to him. She needed him, and when her lips lightly met his he knew; he may not be able to breathe in the very meaning of life but when her lips touched his, he'd found it. She was so soft, sweet and tender. Unable to resist, he took her in his arms and kissed her.

But somewhere, in the midst of this glory, his pain resurfaced, stabbing into his heart, stealing the moment he had dreamed of, and ripping out his soul. He pushed away the one he had longed for more than anything else.

She looked at him, hurt.

"I can't," he whispered hoarsely.

His legs felt ready to crumple. He turned away from her, drained. It had taken everything within him to say those two words.

∞

Caleb stood two feet away from her now, his back to her. Emerald was stunned—talk about awkward.

"Caleb . . . I'm sorry."

The truth was she had believed his love could fill her emptiness. His touch offered her great comfort, but his kiss had felt nothing like Jack's.

"I love you, Emerald." Caleb closed the space between them. His hand went to her hair and he breathed the next words close to her ear. "That's why I had to pull away. I can't offer you healing or wholeness."

He pulled back enough to touch her face. "Forgive me."

Her lower lip trembled, and he caught it with his thumb.

"I've been selfish, only thinking how much I love you."

"I don't understand."

"I wanted to help you find healing, Emerald. But I became so caught up in my feelings for you that I didn't realize until you kissed me, " his voice became raspy, "that the reason it hurt so badly was because I can never bring you wholeness."

"I love you, Caleb," she whispered. She really did. Maybe not in the romantic sense she'd tried to make it, but she loved him. He listened to her; he made sense of her insanity.

Sagging back he replied; "No, you don't, Emerald. I realized I had to choose between my desires and something I want even more than to kiss you and hold you in my arms."

A tear ran down her cheek and touched his thumb. "What's that?"

"For you to find your answers, whatever they may be." He smiled. "I can't get in the way of that."

She drank in his words and smiled, sadly, as he continued.

"As much as I want to help you, I've done all I can. I have to let God do the rest."

She closed her eyes and nodded, more tears flowing.

He led her back to their horses and helped her mount, then they rode back to the ranch in silence. But they were not alone. Emerald felt Him, and she knew Caleb did too.

# Chapter Twenty-Four

THE SUN LOOMED HIGH ABOVE THE mountains at Emerald's favorite spot in Kati's pastures. To escape the heat, she moved to the shade of a juniper tree. She removed one of the small white berries, rolled it in her hand, then inhaled the fragrance. Then she looked up at the sound of a four-wheeler. Jack tooled through an adjoining pasture and headed toward the house.

She waved, and he turned the vehicle her way. "Plan to sit in the pasture all day?"

He laughed before she could answer. "I have tickets to a rodeo tonight. My dad and I were going but it seems Mom made other plans for him." He smiled. "Want to go?"

"I've never been to one before."

Jack adjusted his hat. "Well, its one of the things cowboys do for fun. Of course, you can say no if you want to."

"I'd like to go."

He climbed back on the four-wheeler. "All right. We'll feed early and I'll pick you up at five. We'll grab a bite of dinner at Martha's before we go."

She watched him ride off. A date? Jack was full of surprises.

∞

Jack watched Emerald from across the table. At first she'd seemed uncertain about their date, but now she was relaxed.

They ate Martha's famous barbeque brisket sandwiches. Emerald put hers down, then grabbed a napkin to catch the sauce dribbling down her chin.

"They are messy, but oh, so good." Jack took a sip of his Pepsi.

Emerald looked around at the small, packed restaurant. "All rodeo fans?"

"Most. As you've probably noticed we get a lot of people from the next town over when we have a rodeo."

Emerald sipped her lemonade. "Do you go to rodeos in Tussle Springs?"

"Sometimes. But ours are better." Jack grinned.

After dinner they headed to the arena. Emerald recognized only a few in the crowd from around town. Stands with hot dogs, cotton candy, and ice cream flanked the entrance, almost like a fair. An announcer's voice blared over speakers throughout the area, and children dressed in cowboy boots and hats passed by.

"Hey, Jack!" a little girl that Emerald recognized from Cowboy Church rode a pony with the number twenty-seven written on a piece of paper attached to the saddle pad.

"Hey, Jenna! When do you go up?"

"Not 'til tonight. Will ya watch me?"

"Wouldn't miss it for the world." Jack's smile and voice, particularly around children, warmed Emerald's heart.

He slung an arm around her. "Ready to go watch some steer wrestling?"

She nodded.

They went to a separate arena where a man rode after a steer. He swung the rope but missed the steer. He nudged his horse forward. Closing in he swung again and the rope caught around the steer's neck. He jumped from his horse, ran to the steer, knocked him on his side, then tied his feet together.

When he finished, boos filled the crowd and Emerald looked at Jack in surprise.

"He didn't make as good a time as the guy ahead of him," Jack explained, as the man threw his hat on the ground with a curse word, then grabbed it and left the arena, his horse trailing after him.

"Ever watched roping before?" Jack leaned against the fence.

"No."

"Well then, I'm just going to have to show you how it's done." he said it matter-of-factly, as if he had no other option. Then he swung his legs over the fence.

A few cheers formed in the crowd. "Yeah, Jack's up! Go, Jack!"

The announcer's voice came over the speakers. "Jack, you're not in this competition."

Jack laughed, "I am now."

The announcer laughed. "Jack, you weren't registered—"

"Ah, let him!" someone yelled.

"Yeah, we want Jack!"

The crowd roared. Not only did everyone know Jack, they loved him.

Jack pointed to Emerald. "This beautiful young lady's never seen roping before and I promised to show her how it was done."

The announcer chuckled. "Okay, okay. Bobby, let him ride your horse."

Jack winked at Emerald then went to the sidelines where he embraced a man she guessed was Bobby. The man laughed as he pointed to Emerald and said something. Emerald felt the stares of the crowd and heard their whispers.

*Now the whole town will call us an item.*

Jack mounted the horse. The gate opened to release the steer and he was off. He closed in and swung his rope, looping it around his neck the first time. With incredible speed and ease he swung off his horse, turned the steer on his side, then bound his hooves. He stood, and pride covered his face as the crowd roared. Then he jumped back over the fence.

Emerald gasped. "You made the best time. No one will be able to beat that."

He laughed. "No, probably not. That's why mine never counts any more."

The older man who had loaned Jack the horse stepped closer. "It's an unwritten rule that Jack can never compete in roping. He was our champion for the past nine years. Nobody can beat him."

"That's not true," Jack protested. "The fifth year Millie Brown's boy won."

"Only 'cause you felt sorry for him."

Another man offered Jack a beer, and Jack declined. But still he talked and laughed with the other men, all of whom were drinking. Jack didn't seem to need alcohol to have a good time.

Feeling the two lemonades she'd had at Martha's, Emerald ducked away to find a bathroom. She spotted a row of porta-potties and sighed. Yes, this was cowboy country.

She exited the porta-potty and headed back toward Jack.

"Emerald? Emerald McGintay?"

She turned to the woman calling her name and her smile faded. No. It couldn't be. Not here. Not now.

*Anna Lockingdale.*

Was she delusional? The shoulder-length blond hair, long thin legs and beautiful face was hers all right. Only thing missing was the business suit. She wore cowgirl garb, or rather, a touristy attempt at it. Emerald turned abruptly and smacked into Jack.

"Whoa, what's the hurry? The bull-riding hasn't even started yet." His effort at humor didn't help.

Anna persisted. "Emerald. It's you!"

No escape. Jack would confirm her identity. She'd been found. After a moment she faced Anna.

Anna laughed in disbelief. "I can't believe it's you! It's really you!

∞

Jack stopped short at the beautiful blonde who seemed to know Emerald. She held a cell phone in one hand and a notebook full of papers in another. But it was the glimpse of the small black mike clipped to the collar of her shirt that stopped him in his tracks. She was a reporter. His mind whirled to a snooty reporter who'd come out last year to the event.

The woman fluttered her long lashes his way. "Who is this, Emerald?"

Emerald didn't reply.

"Well, the gossip columnists have been buzzing about you for weeks back in Philly. Nobody's seen a trace of you and your father certainly isn't talking." She reached out and touched Emerald's arm. "My station manager sent me here to cover the event––and I can't believe you're here."

Jack turned to Emerald, whose face had become pale. In fact, she looked ready to faint. And if Emerald's experience with Anna had been anything like his last year with Rachel, he knew why. He had to protect her.

Without consideration, he threw his arm around Emerald's waist. "My wife's privacy is her right."

The reporter's mouth hung open and her blue eyes widened. Jack grabbed Emerald's arm before anything else could be said.

∞

Emerald's legs were weak but somehow she managed to walk as Jack took her to the truck in the gravel parking lot. She climbed in, trying to control her trembling. How could he have said she was his wife?

Jack cranked the truck and headed toward the ranch. His face was grim and hard.

*What were you thinking, Jack?*

"Emerald, you have to tell me what's going on."

She looked at him, outraged. "Me? What did you just do?"

"I just saved your tail."

"You just saved me?"

He didn't reply.

She looked out the window at the tunnel of pines they drove through. Not only would her father know where she was, he'd find out through the headlines: EMERALD MCGINTAY FLEES HOME AND MARRIES COWBOY.

Her heart stopped, and her breathing stilled. Why didn't it sound so bad? If Daddy thought she was married, it would limit what he might do to get her back, wouldn't it? Her stomach knotted. Not if he challenged the marriage on grounds of mental instability.

Jack parked the truck in front of his house. "Emerald, I want to help you, but I can't if I don't know how."

She tried to swallow the lump in her throat. "The damage has already been done." But she knew it could get worse.

"What damage? And I'm not talking about my part in it. I saw your face; you looked like a deer caught in headlights when that woman recognized you."

Her boots shifted his rug around on the floorboard. "She's a reporter from back home." She lifted her head and fixed her eyes on a small aspen tree near the house. It looked so thin and alone; most of the time aspens grew together. "She's done lots of stories on my father, Philadelphia's number one psychiatrist. He owns the largest psychiatric clinic in the nation."

He leaned forward. "Okay. So you don't want your father or anyone to know where you are. Why?"

She lifted her chin. "Because I'm a grown woman and have a right to live anywhere I please, and even keep it from my father if I choose."

He held her gaze for so long, she felt she'd break. "What are you running away from?"

Her heart pounded in her ears "What makes you think I'm running away from anything?" But she'd already made it clear she was.

He sighed. "Emerald, if you're in some kind of trouble—"

Her head spun. "Don't assume something you know nothing about." She immediately regretted her fierce tone.

"Fine." He dropped his gaze, shaking his head as he climbed out.

Emerald followed him inside the house where she commandeered a living room chair. Why couldn't she just tell him? What did it matter, now that she'd been found? But it would matter if Jack thought she had an illness.

Jack ran his hand through his hair, then dropped onto his knees in front of her. "Emerald, I've come to care about you." His eyes deepened, and her heart fluttered. "A great deal. If you have a problem . . . of any kind . . . I want to help you. I *will* help you."

It would be so easy to tell him everything. But she couldn't. She just couldn't. Her eyes dropped, and he stood. When she lifted her gaze to meet his, a mixture of hurt and frustration crossed his face.

"Well then, I guess I'll take you home."

He didn't understand. And she couldn't change that without risk. But it could be too late. She may have already lost everything.

# Chapter Twenty-Five

JACK PUT MORE WOOD ON THE fire. Maybe he made a mistake telling the reporter that Emerald was his wife. He had told Emerald that it was to protect her, but could he have also been protecting himself?

He lay on the sofa and gazed into the fire as his memory went back to his first encounter with Rachel. She was pretty, yes, and had a vibrant energy and spontaneity about her. It had been attractive. Then.

Jack reached for the coffee mug on the table in front of him and stared into the cold brew. The bubbly city girl had traveled west last year to write her "first big story." Something about the ranchers' dying way of life. She seemed anxious to learn about his ranch, and it felt good having a pretty girl take such interest in him.

He took her to dinner, then brought her back to his place. They wound up by the fire with beers, and she asked why he wasn't married. In a drunken tirade he'd spilled May's story.

The phone rang, interrupting the memory. Jack was slow to get up, and he dumped his coffee in the kitchen sink before answering.

It was his father. "Jack, I heard Rachel is in town again."

*Gee. Less than an hour. What took the rumor mill so long?*

"It isn't Rachel, Dad. It's another girl. From what I know she isn't tied to Rachel."

Tony sighed. "I'm sure she'll be heading out first thing tomorrow the way I hear folks have been treating her. You know that hot shot reporters are not welcomed in this town."

No reporters were after what had happened.

"Dad, don't worry, I'm fine. Reporters are attracted to stories; once this reporter finds there isn't anything of interest here, she'll leave."

*Or had she found one?*

Jack's gut tightened as he hung up the phone. If Emerald did come from a big name in Philly, would this reporter write about their so-called marriage?

He went to the barn, where he saddled Houdini. He needed to check the heavy pasture. What was done was done. If this reporter was anything like Rachel, she'd only care about a good story, regardless of who got hurt in the process. He'd have to deal with the fallout. Again.

∞

"Heard your first rodeo was pretty exciting." Kati said from across the kitchen table as Milt's boys shoved down macaroni and cheese.

"Yeah." Emerald forced a smile. The last thing she wanted was to re-live it. "I watched Jack rope a cow."

Kati shook her head as she poured Patrick more juice. "You know that's not what I meant."

When Emerald didn't reply, Kati sighed. "Jack didn't tell you the story about him and Rachel, did he? He's always been kind of embarrassed about it."

"Rachel?" He'd not told her any story.

"She's the reporter who came out to cover the rodeo last year." Kati said answering her question. "Then she did another story on all of us 'hick' ranchers."

So Jack's concern wasn't entirely about Emerald running

from her past. Unfortunately, with the potential story bubbling, it brought her little relief.

Emerald sat up in her chair anyway. "Tell me."

Kati lifted a sleepy Patrick to her knee. Her lips formed a tight line as if she were debating what to share. "A year ago this reporter, Rachel, wrote a story on Jack. He thought it was going to be about his life as a rancher."

Kati laid her cheek across the top of Patrick's head. "But it was much more than that. Jack got drunk and trashed May Durham, his ex-fiancé. Nasty woman ran away two days before the wedding," Kati said shaking her head. "Rachel quoted every word. Made all cowboys look like backward idiots."

"Ouch." Reporters showed their subjects no mercy. The thought made her stiffen.

"And if that weren't enough, Rachel did extra research and reported that May is living the high life married to some rich stockbroker in New York. Doesn't claim to remember Jack."

Kati stood and hoisted Patrick to her hip. "At least some good came of it. Jack hasn't had a drink since."

Reaching out to Hank with her free arm, she turned away from Emerald. "Come on boys, time for bed."

Emerald watched Kati take the boys, pitying poor Jack. Such humiliation, and he probably never saw it coming. Was that why he'd told that lie today? To make Anna think this good-for-nothing rancher had bounced back from May and snagged himself a McGintay?

For a moment panic filled her; then her beating heart slowed. Jack didn't know who she was. Did he? He had her name and an Internet connection. He could have learned almost everything about her; how many other Emerald McGintays could there be? Emerald propped her elbows on the table and let her face fall into her hands. How could she have been so naîve?

"You know he cares deeply for you, honey."

Emerald looked at Kati, standing in the doorway. "What?"

"Jack. He may not say it out loud for fear of being hurt or humiliated again." She went to the stove and turned down the burner the teapot was on. "You know the worst part about cowboys is their pride. Especially for someone like Jack, who's been hurt."

Kati smiled as she headed to the door. "Don't let him fool you. I know my nephew and if he's ever harsh or foolish, it's because he's trying to protect this." She touched her heart, then turned and left the kitchen.

∞

Emerald awoke with a start. Her heart pounded, and her head spun. Daddy had found her. He and Sidney had admitted her to a "special clinic." They'd told Jack and Caleb she was crazy.

She pushed her damp hair back from her face and tried to control her breathing. It was just a dream. But it could happen. She stood from the creaky bed, steadying herself on the post. No, she wouldn't let it happen. Daddy might find her, but he wouldn't take her away. He could not force a legal adult to go with him.

Unless he had her declared incompetent. Could he do that?

She thought of Jack and Caleb. Her father couldn't fool them, could he? They were different from any men she'd ever met. They looked at her as a person instead of a possession, or a broken flower needing attention and care just to survive. She swallowed hard as images began to surface.

She looked at the shadows of the aspens fluttering outside her window. Maybe she should tell Caleb. He was wise; he'd probably know what to do. He'd tell her the voice she always heard was God—proving she wasn't insane.

*If you have a problem . . . of any kind . . . I want to help you. I will help you.*

Remembering Jack's caring voice brought her warmth.

Caleb was the logical choice. He'd helped her come so far. But telling Caleb didn't seem nearly as comforting as telling Jack.

Caleb had chosen God over her. He followed a Higher Being and would always look to Him for direction. What if God told him not to help her? Or revealed to him through her father and Sidney that she was indeed insane? Could she fully trust a man who would always look to another instead of making his own decisions?

While Jack also believed in this God, he was different. *I will help you.*

Jack would help her, no matter what.

Emerald dressed in jeans and a sweatshirt, then quietly left the house. Feeling a chill, she thought about going back for Kati's work jacket. Instead, she crossed her arms against the wind as she went to Kati's stables. She saddled the old brown mare. Kati had let her ride Sadie Girl around the property before. Leading the horse outside of the stables she coaxed her with soothing tones.

With only a half moon to guide her, Emerald mounted the mare bareback and nudged her forward through the adjoining pastures to Jack's ranch. Surely the horse would be able to avoid fences, trees, and ditches. Jack would think her foolish for riding at night. But Caleb did it all the time. Besides, if she didn't go now, she feared she never would.

∞

Emerald clutched the reins. She'd come a long way, but just over the next bluff she'd see Jack's house. Passing through the heavy pasture, she heard a sudden, sharp cry. A slight movement caught her eye. Moos filled the air, and the cattle stirred. An animal passed through the heifers, and fear pricked her skin. Too large to be a coyote, it was a wolf.

Sadie Girl shied. Unbalanced, Emerald clung to the mare's

neck as Sadie broke into a gallop. Emerald's grip on the reins nearly drew blood. She didn't dare glance behind her; she knew wolves were fast. Why did the animal activists bring them back into Colorado?

If she could just make it to Jack's house . . . but the mare turned in the wrong direction. Emerald tried to turn Sadie Girl back, but she needed all of her strength just to hold on. The mare tore through a patch of trees, and branches cut her face. She could feel no pain, only fear. If the wolf didn't get them, the horse would surely throw her to her death.

Then another movement caught her peripheral vision—a larger shadow. She wanted to scream, but no sound left her throat. The animal came closer, but the mare slowed. It was a man on a horse. He came nearer, then grabbed her reins and rode beside her until the mare slowed to a stop.

Her breathing was ragged, her body fatigued.

"Are you all right?" Jack's voice.

"I think so." Relief flooded her.

He brought the horses back to the barn and suggested she go into the house. Emerald was grateful for the comfort of the sofa, and quivered more from the adrenaline rush than the cold.

Jack entered a few minutes later with a rifle, presumably just used on the wolf. He set the rifle against the wall and got a large quilt. He wrapped it around her, then started a fire. His face was grim.

After the flames rose, he was back by her side. "Are you hurt?"

She shook her head, unable to speak.

He touched her face, and she winced. "You're bleeding."

He dressed her wounds with the kit Caleb had used to bandage her hands.

"What were you doing, Emerald? You could have been hurt a lot worse."

*Or killed.*

"How did you know about the wolves?" she asked.

"I heard them. That's why I keep the heavy pasture close to the house."

She remembered the cattle running and crying out in fear. "Were any of the cattle injured?"

His jaw tightened. "We lost our calf."

The tendons in her throat grew taut. The calf they had worked so hard to save. She had bottle-fed him special formula every day until Jack encouraged another calving heifer to nurse it.

"When?" But she already knew the answer. "You could have saved him if I hadn't—"

Jack stood. "It doesn't matter now. It's over. The important thing is that you're okay. Now why don't you go lie down for a while, we've got a couple more hours before the sun rises."

She nodded as she pulled herself up on weak legs. She headed to the guest room while she heard Jack go outside. He was checking on his cattle—to take care of damage he could have prevented, if not for her.

Hot tears flowed. The calf was dead, and it was her fault.

∞

The morning sunlight streamed into her room, but Emerald was already awake. She went to the bathroom to wash her face and run her fingers through her tangled hair. When she finished, she opened the front door to a warmer breeze than the night before. She spotted Jack walking towards the barn with a shovel. Had he been burying the remains of their calf?

She closed the door and went to the kitchen. Jack came in a few minutes later and she heard him showering. Though she couldn't cook and scarcely knew how to work the simplest appliances in her kitchen back home, she felt she should make coffee. Rummaging through the cabinets, she found a can of Folgers.

She studied the coffee maker; it was different from hers. Less complicated, she realized, fumbling with it for a while. Finally the sound of coffee grinding and steaming met her.

Emerald sat on a kitchen chair and waited for Jack, who appeared with fresh clothes and wet hair. "You're making coffee." He wasn't smiling, but his tone sounded normal—not what she expected after last night.

"Yes, I would have made breakfast, but I don't know how."

He pulled bacon, then a carton of eggs from the fridge. "You learn when you're a bachelor."

*Without a chef.*

Had he remembered her remark? If he did, his face held no sarcasm.

Jack whipped the eggs together with milk and grated cheese. He placed the bacon in the fryer, and soon it's aroma filled the kitchen. Good thing he wasn't making one of his Colorado steak omelets. She wouldn't have been able to stomach it.

Emerald watched his face for signs of resentment, but his expression remained bland as he scooped the bacon from the skillet and poured the eggs into it.

"I'm sorry, Jack."

"Me too." His voice was sorry, but not angry.

Still, the hurt tore at her heart. How could he forgive her?

He set her plate down in front of her, then bowed his head. "Heavenly Father, we thank you for this meal and for protecting Emerald last night. Please continue to watch over her. Amen."

He still cared about her. Even now.

Jack took a sip of his coffee, then gagged and spit it back in his cup. "How much did you put in there?"

"I filled it up to the top."

"And the water?"

"I only put in enough for one cup, since I wasn't drinking any."

Jack stared at her as if she were from another planet. He set the mug aside and poked a fork into his bacon. "Need to cut down on my coffee anyway."

*Okay, so maybe it was a good thing I didn't make breakfast.*

She looked down at her plate. Finally she scooped up a bite of eggs and forced them down.

When Jack finished, he didn't clear the dishes. Instead, he watched her.

*Here it comes.*

"What is it, Emerald?" he finally asked. "Why were you riding through the pastures in the wee morning hours?"

She took a sip of her orange juice to buy more time. If she told him the truth now, she'd have a reason behind such an impulsive and stupid act. She grabbed her napkin and dotted her mouth. He was waiting. A knot formed in her stomach as reality hit her. If she told him about the dreams and visions, it would look as if she acted upon them in dangerous ways.

"Emerald just talk to me. It will be okay, whatever it is."

She bit her bottom lip. How did she want Jack to see her? Did she want to remain the spoiled little rich girl with a chef who didn't know how to use a coffee pot?

Or become Emerald with an illness?

"I'm sorry, Jack. But there's really nothing to tell." The lie stuck in her throat.

Jack's gaze cut through her. Finally, he stood, picking up his plate. "Church will start in a couple of hours. I already called Kati and told her what happened; she's on her way to pick you up so you can change clothes."

∞

When church ended Emerald was the first to leave. As soon as she stepped out into the warm sunlight she spotted her. Anna.

Anna was standing in front of a Lexus SUV. Obviously a rental.

What was she still doing here? She glanced around at the few people starting to exit the building. There was nowhere to run to. And most likely, Anna had already revealed her whereabouts.

"You don't want to talk to me do you?" Anna said as she approached Emerald.

"No."

"You don't have to."

"But you're going to hang around here until I do."

Anna laughed nervously. "I'm still here because of my job."

"Find any interesting stories here?"

She was quiet for a moment. "Will you get in the car with me for a few? We won't drive anywhere and I'm parked where you can see people coming out the church door."

Emerald glanced back at the steady flow of people who were now exiting the church. Neither Jack nor Caleb were anywhere in sight. Kati had told her earlier she was going to stay for a while after church to try to sell some pies with her sister-in-law, Jack's mom, Libby.

"Why not?" She could think of a million reasons but the truth was none of them mattered once Daddy knew everything anyway.

She opened the car door and slipped in the passenger seat. Despite the new leather interior, the car smelled of cigarette smoke.

Anna slid in and said, "I asked around town. You're not really married to Jack."

"No."

"What a relief."

Emerald darted a look at her. "That doesn't mean I haven't found a home here."

"You're living with Jack's aunt?"

"Yes." She sighed heavily. "Look Anna I know you're just trying to get information together for a story here and it's probably not even worth the effort in asking, but could you please just leave me alone? Leave this town alone? They dealt with a nasty story last year and don't want any media around."

"I sort of figured that one out on my own." Anna said. "Emerald, if there's something else going on, you can trust me."

Emerald's head spun. "What do you mean by that?"

"I mean, it looks like you don't have anyone to talk to."

"I have plenty of people to talk to here."

"But what are you doing here?"

"I told you already. Making a home."

"And you're happy, here? You plan to stay long term?"

"As long as this town will have me. I love it here. Why do you ask?"

Anna studied her for a long moment, then asked, "What will you do if your father comes for you?"

"Tell him to go home." Emerald's eyes narrowed. "I'm not going back to Philly."

Anna swallowed hard. "Good. I don't think you should."

"What?"

"Your father—and others—will find out you're here, Emerald. But remember that he can't make you come back."

Was there a secret message Anna's eyes were trying to convey?

"One last thing, Emerald."

"Yes?"

"If you ever have a story to tell the media, don't tell it to me." Her face was grim." I like you. In another time and place, we could be friends." She smiled, softly. " I hope you listen to what I have said."

Emerald opened the car door and watched as Anna drove away, struggling with what had just happened. And feeling, strangely, free.

# Chapter Twenty-Six

On Monday, Emerald went to the corral where Denver was with the other horses. It was a misty, foggy day, and she'd worn her jacket since that morning. Denver neighed when he saw her, bobbing his head.

Jack had hardly spoken to her since she'd left his house yesterday morning, except to give work instructions. Cold and businesslike. And she didn't know how to change that without making things worse.

She smiled as Denver came to meet her and she touched him, speaking sweetly. She'd finished her chores early so she could spend time with him before Kati took her home.

"He's always taken to you. That's why I chose him."

Jack walked up to her, slapping the dust from his pants. The sides of his mouth parted in a slow smile.

"You should do that more often," she said.

"What?"

"Smile like that. It's nice."

He laughed and looked at the horse. She enjoyed making him uncomfortable.

Jack seemed to be in a better mood, so she decided to take a chance. "Jack, I was thinking. I could ride Denver home so Kati wouldn't have to pick me up."

Jack was quiet for a moment. He had every reason to protest, given what happened the last time she'd ridden by herself.

He nodded. "Okay, we'll saddle them up."

*We.* He would ride with her. He had every reason not to trust her riding alone.

The sound of hooves approaching them caused both to turn. Pete rode up in a huff. "Jack, one of the cows is in labor—been watching her and she's been down almost two hours now!"

"All right, I'm coming," Jack glanced back at Emerald. "Sorry, I can't ride with you today."

She nodded and watched as he hurried to the stable and thundered off to the heavy pasture to assist with another birth. He sure did care about his cattle.

Emerald turned back to Denver and sighed. Would he be upset if she rode alone? It was during the day. She knew the way back to Kati's—in fact, it was quicker than the main road. Time to prove her independence and capability as a cowgirl.

"Come on, sweet baby—we're going for a ride."

∞

She saddled Denver in just a few minutes. She felt exhilarated as he began to move beneath her in a rhythm that became her own. Then she squeezed him lightly until he shot forward with incredible speed. The wind tore through her, and the mist seeped into her skin and dampened her hair. Energy seemed to soar through both woman and horse and they became one, understanding each other. They were free.

Emerald asked Denver to slow, realizing she had plenty of time. Her attention drifted to the mountains, mostly hidden by low lingering clouds. But some of the fog had parted, unveiling the mountain face with a soft shimmer of pink.

Hadn't she wanted to go up there ever since she saw it from the bus? What was stopping her? She made an instant decision and patted her horse. "Denver, we're going to the Divine."

What a strange thing to say.

Soon they were climbing the many winding crags. When she came to a shallow slope beneath a high ridge, she hesitated. A foggy façade peeled back from the mountainside, and a few pines crowded the narrow trail. Enough room for one horse—if she was careful.

Emerald gently encouraged Denver as they wove up the trail closer to the Divine. She could feel the presence of the mountain pulling them up the slope, and knew that Denver sensed it, too.

When they broke through the mist she knew she had entered into Divinity. Here was the soul of the mountain. Here was the place she had longed to be since the first day she arrived at Canyon Ridge. Out of everything else here—her rides and hikes with Caleb, the wildflowers, the sunsets, the night skies—this trumped them all. The ridge blazed with light while clouds bathed the woods below. She closed her eyes and breathed in the beauty—the energy, the power. Then she cried.

But her entire body still desired something. She had thought that once she found this beauty, this Divinity, she would be satisfied. But now she discovered that she wanted to carry this presence with her all the time.

There was no denying it; she'd found what she had been searching for her entire life. Emerald couldn't explain it in words, or by human logic. It wasn't logical, but she knew it was God.

Emerald remembered her mother's words in the journal. Alexandra had written of uniting with the Spirit of God. Now Emerald understood.

And it was happening to her.

∞

Jack rode to the house. The birth had taken a lot out of him. Thank God the heifer had nursed right away. Jack passed the corral on his way to the stables and noticed Denver wasn't there.

He frowned. Emerald wouldn't have taken him on her own, would she? Maybe Caleb took her for a ride. Jack forced away any stab of resentment and instead whispered a prayer for Emerald. An hour passed as he worked with a filly. He looked up at the sound of a truck's engine. Kati.

"Emerald's not here," he said. "I figured maybe she'd gone riding with Caleb."

Kati shook her head. "No, I don't think so. Caleb said he had some counseling at the church today."

Then Emerald had taken the horse on her own. "Well, she's probably already home, then. She's riding Denver."

"You worried about her riding alone, after the other night?" Kati offered a small smile. "You know you don't have to worry about wolves during the day."

Jack knocked the dust from his pant legs. "She rides well, most of the time. But if the horse tripped or shied, I'm afraid she wouldn't have the seat to stay on."

She certainly hadn't known how to handle Kati's old mare the other night.

∞

The light faded, and Emerald realized Kati would be wondering where she was. But she'd found what she'd been searching for!

*Wait until I tell Kati! Wait until I tell Caleb and Jack!*

A cry came from the rocks, and Emerald jumped as a badger darted past them. She shrieked, and Denver lurched forward as she grabbed the reins. "Whoa boy, whoa!"

But the horse launched forward up the craggy peak, going almost straight up at a 90 degree angle. Emerald screamed as he slid on the rocks and lost his footing.

She fell backward and cried out in pain as her head cracked against a boulder. The animal's body landed on her with full force, pushing all the air out of her lungs. He thrashed, then staggered up. She fought to breathe, but the pain was too great. Time froze. Then blackness was all she knew.

∞

After finishing his work, Jack went straight to the kitchen sink to wash. Why did he feel something was wrong? He'd checked the heavy pasture again, and both heifer and new baby were doing great. Everything else on the ranch was fine.

The phone rang, and he jumped. Grabbing a dish towel, he dried his hands then answered.

"Jack—"

Kati. She sounded strange.

What is it?"

"Emerald never came home."

"You sure?"

"Yes, I'm sure. She's not here"

"Where are you calling from?"

"Caleb's cell."

"I'm going to look for her." His breath had quickened, and urgency surged through him.

"Okay. Caleb's looking for her, too."

Caleb had likely come to the house to see Emerald. But none of that mattered now. Jack hung up the phone and ran to the stables.

∞

Something penetrated her. She was air, floating. She could feel nothing. Just air, and space and . . . and someone was with her.

*Emerald, you're not alone.*

No, she guessed not. Funny how she had always considered

herself alone, yet no matter where she went, a familiar presence followed.

Caleb said he wanted her in the arms of God. Maybe now that was where she was.

*I'm dying. I found the Divine and wanted to be a part of it.*

Had her prayer been answered? Had her search ended with death? A peace overcame her, and she stopped fighting for air. Air didn't matter. She'd found what she'd been searching for.

# Chapter Twenty-Seven

JACK PULLED SILVER BULLET TO A halt as he approached his cousin.

Caleb shook his head. "No sign of her."

The words unsettled Jack. It would be dark soon. Not much time to find her.

Caleb sighed. "She probably just wandered off. We both know if you don't know the land it's easy to get lost."

Jack could see Caleb was worried. Jack had been praying the last fifteen minutes that they would find Emerald.

He looked up into the mountains and he knew.

"She's up there."

Caleb followed his gaze up the peak. "How do you—"

"I just do." Jack faced his cousin, his face grave.

Caleb opened his mouth to say something, but Jack had already turned his horse. "I'm going up."

∞

Caleb watched his cousin in amazement. Why in heaven's name would Emerald try to climb the peak alone? Just didn't make sense. Much more logical to look by the stream or the meadow—places he knew she'd gone riding with him.

*Follow your cousin.*

Caleb hesitated. He didn't want to follow Jack. Surely he'd have a better chance at finding Emerald, looking in places he knew she'd choose. Besides, the logical thing for them to do was split up.

The voice inside him insisted. *Follow your cousin.*

Caleb sighed and turned his horse.

∞

Jack climbed the craggy peak, struggling between the power that was pulling him forward and his brain telling him he was being stupid. He tugged Silver Bullet's reins, doubt seizing him. If Emerald were in trouble elsewhere, he'd lose precious time.

He looked back down the trail and caught a glimpse of Caleb, who never followed anyone but the Lord.

*Follow Me.*

Jack urged his horse forward. Even when he reached the narrow ridge leading up, the presence pushed him onward. He coaxed Bullet on up the path. The horse's ears pricked forward at a whinny from beyond the trees and Jack's heart stopped.

Denver.

The horse limped around the junipers toward him, and Jack caught a glimpse of a yellow shirt. Emerald, sprawled on the rocks.

He dismounted and rushed to her. Emerald's eyes were closed; her ragged, shallow breathing came as a gurgling sound, and her chin was bent toward her neck. He knelt beside her.

"Don't!"

Anger surged through him at Caleb's interruption.

"Don't touch her, Jack. Don't move her. Her neck could be broken."

Jack looked at Emerald's still body. He forced himself to focus. Her shirt was torn, and he could see a fragment of it on an adjacent rock. There was blood smeared across several rocks, as if she'd dragged herself from one to the other. If she'd been able to move, she probably hadn't broken her back. He felt for a pulse and was alarmed to find it so faint and fluttery.

Behind him, Caleb fell to his knees and cried out in anguish.

Jack forced a sob down his throat.

"Praise the Lord that she's alive!" Caleb cried out behind him. But it didn't bring Jack the relief he'd expected. Emerald wasn't awake. And she wasn't breathing normally.

"We have to get her to a hospital." Jack tore off his shirt. "Here, help me."

Caleb helped him tie the shirt around Emerald's head wound.

"Call nine-one-one, then ride down to lead them here. We don't need to waste time with them getting lost." For once Jack gave orders, and Caleb followed without arguing.

Caleb mounted his horse. "I'll get the truck and bring it to meet you. Nine-one-one will come from Tussle Springs. You can follow them to the hospital."

Good thinking, Caleb. Jack held Emerald's cold body against him.

*Please Lord, don't let her die.*

∞

*Follow Me.*

The hand stretched out in front of her. This was the same hand that had led her to flee from her home; the hand that had brought her to Canyon Ridge Mountain, to Jack and Kati and Caleb and Cowboy Church. To a life so far from what she had ever known.

She took the hand. Would she go to heaven now? But the place she entered was not what she'd expected. She was in her home again, in Philadelphia. She was a little girl.

Someone came to the door. Her nanny came to the room she was playing in and knelt down beside her. "Darling, you have a visitor. It's a very nice man who was a friend of your mother's. He'd like to speak with you."

The man was nice. He was slightly overweight and wore jeans and a black collared shirt with a cowboy on it. He was warm and friendly, and Emerald liked him. He introduced himself as her mother's pastor.

"What's a pastor?"

The man laughed and held out a book she'd never seen before. "This is the Bible."

He said her mother had loved her very much—and God loved her.

"Who is God?"

"He is calling you. I know it may be hard for you to understand now, but you have a mission from God."

*You have been searching for Me, Emerald. Your mission is from Me.*

# Chapter Twenty-Eight

When Jack pulled up to the emergency entrance behind the ambulance, he threw the truck door open. The next few moments seemed like an eternity as Jack waited for the staff to scurry to Emerald's aid. He fought his fear when he sawEmerald on a back board with an IV.

A doctor came. A nurse shoved the chart with Emerald's vitals to the doctor, who asked, "What happened here?"

"She fell from her horse."

The doctor shouted orders to his staff as they rushed Emerald to the ER. Jack tried to follow, but a nurse pushed him back. He watched in desperation as they took her away.

A few moments later Caleb burst through the emergency entrance. "Do they have her? Is she okay?"

"They took her back."

Caleb's face dimmed as he handed Jack a work shirt. "Had an extra shirt in the car."

Jack took it. He'd forgotten he was no longer wearing one.

"All we can do now is pray." Caleb's voice was shaken.

Jack turned to face his cousin. "Then pray like you've never prayed before."

∞

Time passed slowly. Jack brought a cup of coffee from the machine to Caleb. Caleb accepted it, feeling nausea wash over him. It seemed like an eternity before the doctor finally came out. Both Caleb and Jack got up to meet him.

"How is she?" Caleb's heart raced.

The doctor's face was grave, and Caleb felt the sickness in his stomach grow.

"We don't know how long her oxygen supply was cut off. We put in an endotracheal tube to assist in ventilation and took x-rays of her spine and neck to rule out fractures of her vertebrae.

"So that's good, right?" Caleb asked.

"The CT scan did show some possible brain swelling that we're closely monitoring."

Jack took a step back, as if to prepare himself for the worst. "Will she be all right?"

The doctor's face didn't change. "At this time we cannot tell what her mental activities are without knowing how much oxygen deprivation she had."

Caleb turned to Jack, who was struggling with as much emotion as he himself was.

Emerald had to be all right. She had to live. She just had to.

∞

Emerald's mission was from God. She'd been searching for her mission, but what was it?

*Follow Me.*

Emerald still held the hand, but now familiar cries filled her ears. She was in a third-world country. People surrounded her, reaching and crying out to her, begging for help. They were hungry, diseased, dying in a poverty stricken land. Was this her mission? To feed and care for these poor, suffering people?

The cries faded, and the people around her were different. She was no longer in the third-world country; she was in . . . New

York City? Once again, large crowds of people surrounded her; only here no one cried out to her. No one even noticed her. They rushed along busy sidewalks, fought for taxis, and immersed themselves in cell phones, iPods, and PDAs. It was the normal organized chaos of New York City. But no one needed her, so why was she here?

*This land is just as diseased as the first.*

Emerald looked around in bewilderment. No, that didn't make sense. Suddenly, new images flashed before her. Teenagers on the street, shooting up. Others offering their bodies in exchange for deadly daily cravings. Greed, violence, sickness, despair. So many felt alone.

Then she was in a shabby apartment full of children. A man beat a woman in front of her children, who cried out to their daddy to stop.

Another apartment, a young boy alone, a gun in his hand. He had never felt loved or accepted. His father had deserted him; his mother went from boyfriend to boyfriend. He'd been sexually abused. He was failing school. He was stupid. Worthless. Alone. No one would ever love or accept him. He put the gun to his head and pulled the trigger.

Now she was in a bar. A man had just lost his job. He had a wife and three children to support. Bills were piling up; they were going to lose their house. He drank. He felt completely overwhelmed, so he drank more, to numb the pain, the anxiety, the overpowering feeling of helplessness.

Realization struck her. These people were starving, but not for food. Starving for worth, acceptance, love, purpose. Struggling to exist in a world filled with drugs, sex, violence, and selfish acts. Struggling to find fulfillment.

*Your mission is to show them the way.*

∞

Jack and Caleb followed the doctor to the ICU cubicle where Emerald lay hooked to wires and tubes. Machines monitored every aspect of Emerald's life.

Tears burned behind Jack's eyes. He clutched her icy hand in both of his as he looked at her still body and the white bandage around her head. He could hardly bear to look at her crushed throat, at the tubes breathing for her.

Caleb went to Emerald's other side. For a moment the two cousins, once as close as brothers, stood in silence, watching the woman they each had come to love. Suddenly Caleb knelt down, burying his face in the bedding, and began to weep. Jack turned and left the room.

Caleb was acting as if she were going to die. His jaw clenched.

*God, I won't accept her dying. I won't.*

∞

Sometime later, a hand touched Jack's shoulder and he turned to see Libby's compassionate face.

"Mom." He hugged her; thankful Caleb had called her on the way to the hospital.

Tears filled Libby's eyes. "Oh, honey, I'm so sorry. I am so very, very sorry."

"All we can do now is pray for her." Kati appeared behind Libby with two other women from church.

Libby nodded in agreement. She squeezed her son's hand, then the women left to go to Emerald. The women stood outside her cubicle watching through the window. Usually no one but family got into the ICU, but Emerald's doctor was an old friend of Caleb's.

Caleb was still on his knees, praying. The women placed their hands against the glass and joined in his prayers. Jack could see their lips moving, and the caring compassion in their eyes, on their faces. He was so blessed to be part of this community, this family of people. But while he knoew they cared, he also knew they could not share the depth of his pain.

Jack turned away, unable to join them. He had to stay strong; he preferred to pray alone.

# Chapter Twenty-Nine

CALEB SAT AT EMERALD'S BEDSIDE. SOME time had passed since his mother and the ladies had left. They were going to stir up Canyon Ridge and get everyone praying for Emerald. He watched Emerald, alive but motionless.

*Tell her of My love and miracles.*

Caleb's breath suspended. "I was supposed to tell her," a knife sliced through his chest, "but I never did."

"Tell her now."

Caleb looked up to see Jack standing over him.

For a moment Caleb didn't know what to say. With shaky legs he stood, leaning over her still body. *Will it do any good now?* His mind told him it was too late. She couldn't hear him. He had disobeyed the voice of the Lord and now it was too late.

"It's your choice, not hers. It was you who chose not to talk to her," said Jack. "Surely God cannot be so unjust as to punish her, not let her hear what she needed to hear because one man didn't speak up. God is bigger than that, Caleb."

Caleb's mouth twisted. "You don't know how much that means to me."

He looked at Emerald, hoping Jack was right.

*I do give second chances.*

Could God really give him a second chance? He thought about Jonah, who had disobeyed the Lord and was swallowed by a large fish. But then the fish spit Jonah out. God heard Jonah's cries, saw his heart had changed, and gave him a second chance to make things right.

He looked at Emerald. If he obeyed God now, could he make things right?

"Emerald, God loves you." He hesitated. "God has called you and He has a special plan only you can do, people only you can reach."

A fire burned within him, and he felt a sudden power in his words. The voice of the Lord was speaking through him.

∞

Caleb stopped talking and tears ran down his face. Emerald's cold hand still remained in his, but there was no movement or sign that she heard what he was saying.

Caleb repeated his plea. "He can heal you, Emerald."

"He *will* heal you, Emerald."

Jack reached Emerald's bedside and clasped her other hand, and when he looked at Caleb, his face held a new light.

"Emerald, God is going to bring healing to your body. James 5:16 says, 'pray one for another, that ye may be healed.' He also says in Matthew 7:7, 'Ask and you shall receive.'"

Caleb marveled at the power blazing through his cousin.

Jack's voice grew stronger. "Isaiah 53:5 says 'by his stripes we are healed' and—"

Jack wasn't just asking for healing; he believed it was happening. Jack was talking as if Emerald was already healed. Could their faith be enough?

∞

A man's voice said her name. It was a voice she knew. Caleb. At first Emerald couldn't understand him. All his words ran together and when she looked around, no one was there.

She had thought she was dead. But then why would she have seen the third-world country and New York City with all the people who needed her help? She was still air with no existence, no life. And again she heard Caleb's voice.

Emerald struggled to digest what Caleb was saying. He was talking to her.

"You are healed, Emerald."

The voice that spoke to Emerald now was Jack's. She wasn't dead? She was no longer on the mountaintop? Wherever she was, she knew God was with her.

Breath and life entered her body. She was going to live. She was going to carry out her mission.

∞

Jack awoke groggy and stiff from sleeping in the hospital chair. He massaged the crick in his neck with two fingers before going to Emerald's still body. She was going to be all right. He knew it.

Caleb walked in, offering a cup of coffee. Jack took the cup and smiled at his cousin. "Thanks." None of the animosity between them mattered any more.

The doctor entered the room. "Good morning."

Jack managed a nod of greeting. No, it wouldn't be a good morning until Emerald was back with them.

"I'm afraid Emerald's brain activity is minimal," the doctor said. "She went too long without oxygen."

Caleb cut in. "But she's breathing some on her own."

"Yes, but as to when she'll wake—or what condition she'll wake in. . . ." The doctor's face looked grim. "I think you should contact any relatives if you haven't done so already."

Caleb and Jack exchanged glances as the doctor left.

"She mentioned she had a father," Caleb said.

Jack sank down to Emerald's side without a response.

Caleb rested his hand on Jack's shoulder. "I just talked to your mom. She said all the folks Canyon Ridge want to have a prayer meeting at the church for Emerald. I think it's a wonderful idea. Everyone is going to meet at Cowboy Church at ten this morning."

Jack nodded.

Caleb placed a kiss on Emerald's forehead, then turned to Jack. "You coming?"

Jack shook his head. "No. I don't want her to be here alone."

Caleb nodded, then left.

Jack tried to settle into the chair he had pulled next to Emerald's bedside. He wasn't going to leave her. He bent down and kissed her hand. She would come back to him. She would.

∞

As Caleb drove to the church, a big part of him wanted to turn around and go straight back to the hospital. *He* should be with Emerald, not Jack. But Caleb knew that now was not the time for jealousy or hostility. Jack cared for Emerald, as did he. And right now the only thing that mattered was Emerald's recovery.

"Lord, please heal her." Then he remembered Jack's sincere prayer. "I believe Emerald is healed."

When he arrived at Cowboy Church, the building was packed. Caleb hadn't seen that many bodies at one service since Easter. He looked around at all the neighbors who had stopped their lives to pray for the Lord to heal a woman most of them didn't even know. A new appreciation and love for his community overflowed in him at the sight.

Caleb went to the front of the church and lifted his Bible. "The Bible says when two or more are gathered in the Lord's name, there He will be also."

And they were just that. A community of people who had

come together to pray for one of their own, and he felt love for every person there.

∞

Warmth touched Jack. His eyes widened, and he lifted his head from Emerald's bedside. His hand touched Emerald's. It was warm—no, hot—to the touch! Her face looked different, too, no longer pale. He touched it. It, too, was warm.

Suddenly, incomprehensible words met his ears. He opened his eyes to see Emerald's mouth moving. His fingers tightened around hers as tears of joy came. Her eyes twitched, then slit open. She was alive. She was healed.

∞

"She's healed, Caleb! She's healed!"

Caleb clutched the receiver of the church office phone, his heart jumping in a moment of disbelief. But why disbelieve this miracle? He hung up and raced back into the church, still full of people.

# Chapter Thirty

JACK STOOD IN THE HALL OF the hospital. A flood of people had been in and out of Emerald's room since he'd raced down the hallway announcing Emerald's awakening.

"Jack!" Caleb embraced him with tears of joy.

Jack grinned broadly. "They removed the inter-tracheal tube and Emerald is breathing completely on her own. Her brain activity is normal, and she can speak and comprehend everything. No medical test can explain it." Jack laughed as he remembered the look on her doctor's face. "Caleb, even the doc said it's a miracle!"

Caleb smiled. "Just wait until her father hears."

"What?"

"I heard from the ladies at church that her dad, Bradford McGintay, arrived in Canyon Ridge last night looking for her. He should be on his way here soon."

Jack's jaw dropped. "We've got to warn Emerald."

Caleb looked at him in astonishment. "Warn? Jack, it's her father."

Caleb didn't know the details of what had happened with Anna Lockingdale, so of course he wouldn't understand. Then again, Jack didn't understand it himself. But one thing was clear––Emerald didn't want her father to know where she was.

Caleb's hand touched his shoulder. "Jack, I know you think Emerald is running from something, but she just survived a serious accident and also accepted the Lord. Isn't it possible that changes things?"

Fury filled Jack. His cousin always assumed that salvation ensured a smooth ride all the way to heaven. But Jack could testify that sometimes the road was even rockier than before. "You give her the news, then."

"All right." He turned and headed toward her room.

∞

Emerald smiled when Caleb entered the room. She was tired of all the doctors and nurses who had poked and prodded since she had awakened. Caleb gently lifted her from the bed in a hug, then placed a kiss on her cheek.

"Everyone's been praying for you! The entire congregation is on fire now from this miracle!"

Emerald squeezed Caleb's hand. "I found what I've been searching for."

She told him about her visions, how she had questioned her sanity.

Caleb's face brightened. "So all along you were searching for who your mission was from—and it was from God?"

"Yes." Then Emerald felt her heart pull. "What is it, Caleb?"

"This morning a few people in church informed me that someone is in town looking for you." He studied her closely.

Her chest became heavy, and she found it hard to breathe.

"Emerald, it's your father."

She closed her eyes as if hiding behind the lids.

Caleb took her hand and held it firmly. "Whatever it is, Emerald, God is with you."

She opened her eyes but could not respond.

The nurse entered the room. "Poor girl's had so many people in and out of here for the past few hours, she's probably exhausted." She checked Emerald's vitals.

Emerald wondered if the monitors were registering that she was about to have a heart attack, but the nurse just shooed Caleb into the hall.

Emerald closed her eyes again, and Caleb's words rolled through her head.

∞

Caleb entered the waiting area where Jack sat. "She wouldn't say anything, but I have a feeling there is more healing that needs to occur for Emerald."

Jack stood without responding and went to peek into Emerald's room. He knew he was interfering between her and her father.

She stirred. "Jack."

"You're awake." He stepped into the room.

She looked up at him with a tired smile. "I couldn't sleep."

He pulled up a chair and sat down beside her. "Could've fooled me. The nurse and Caleb said you were exhausted."

And she still looked exhausted. Dark circles had formed under her eyes.

"My dad's coming." The words seemed to contain volumes more information than they stated.

He placed his hand on hers. He frowned. It was cold again.

"Jack, can I ask you something?"

He smiled warmly, squeezing her hand. "Anything."

"Promise me you won't let him take me away."

His heart lurched. She seemed so weak, so vulnerable. The healed and renewed Emerald was nowhere in sight.

He leaned forward, placing his other arm around her body. "No one is going to take you anywhere except for home, where you belong. The ranch is your home, Emerald, and it needs its cowgirl back."

Her face lit up, and her smile was all he needed.

*There's the new Emerald.*

He wasn't letting anyone take her anywhere.

∞

Two hours later, Jack left the hospital cafeteria, having barely stomached their interpretation of a Reuben sandwich. He took the stairs to Emerald's floor, where Kati was visiting.

As Jack left the stairwell, two men in suits and ties exited the elevator at the opposite end of the corridor and turned toward him. The older man had gray-streaked brown hair and was balding. He looked confident and confrontational. The younger man had an olive complexion and dark hair slicked back. He looked familiar. Jack's heart stopped. Dr. Sidney Coffman?

Sure enough, the men stopped outside Emerald's room.

Jack swallowed. "Dr. McGintay?"

Bradford's eyebrows raised. "Yes?"

"I'm Jack Evens. Emerald works on my ranch."

Bradford's dark eyes met his, challenging. "Yes, I know."

Sidney and Bradford turned and entered Emerald's room. Real polite. Like he was too beneath them to matter. Jack stood outside the open door and watched Kati look up, and meet the men with a smile.

Bradford gave her a simple nod of greeting, then turned to his daughter. "Emerald! You're all right!"

"Hello, Daddy."

Kati stood. "I'm Kati Graham." She stretched out her hand.

Both men shook her hand and introduced themselves.

"This is the woman I've been living with, Daddy," Emerald said.

"I see." Bradford turned to Kati with a forced regard. "Thank you for taking care of my daughter."

Kati nodded. "Emerald has been such a blessing in all of our lives." She squeezed Emerald's hand.

"If you don't mind, Mrs. Graham, I would like some time alone with my daughter."

"Of course." Kati squeezed again. "I'll see you later, honey."

Jack watched Emerald's face as Kati left the room. He needed to know if she wanted him to get them out or if she wanted them to stay.

As if sensing his question, Emerald shook her head slightly.

Sidney turned to Jack in the doorway and promptly closed the door. Dr. McGintay's time alone with his daughter apparently involved this Dr. Sidney Coffman. It made Jack's spine crawl.

Kati touched his shoulder lightly. "She's going to be fine."

The words did not reassure him.

∞

Emerald watched her father's faux smile turn to frustration.

"Emerald! Do you have any idea how worried we've been about you? You disappear and I don't hear anything from you for over two months! As far as we could trace, you were on a plane to L.A.! Then I woke up Monday morning to the headlines saying you'd been discovered at some rodeo in cowboy country."

Sidney hadn't told him she'd called him. Twice.

She looked at Sidney who raised his eyebrows as if to ask, *would you rather I told him you threatened his livelihood?*

He was gloating as if he had done her a favor and knew there was no way she could tell on him. Emerald was tempted to wipe that smug look off his face. Her eyes came back to her father, who was struggling with emotion. How could she make her actions look any better by telling him she had called? He would be even more betrayed if he knew his own daughter had threatened him if he dared to find her.

"This morning a man in town said you had been in a terrible accident and weren't expected to live. Do you have any idea what we've gone through to find you, then hear that news?"

"I'm sorry," she whispered hoarsely. She had never seen her father cry before. Her heart twisted. She'd never meant to hurt him.

"The best news I've heard since you left was at the front desk when we found there had been some kind of mistake in your diagnosis." He gave a tired smile. "I felt myself actually be able to breathe because it was the first time in two months that I knew you were all right."

She wondered if he still would have come if he'd been aware of her threats. She glanced at Sidney. He obviously hadn't thought she'd act seriously on them, or he would have never put his own career at risk.

She met her Daddy's eyes and sucked in her breath. "My diagnosis wasn't a mistake, Daddy. I almost died. But then—"

"You beat all odds." Bradford cut her off, leaning forward and grabbing her hand with a smile. "I guess you're my daughter after all."

Sidney cut in. "Emerald, the important thing is you're all right, and we've found you. From now on your father and I are going to make sure you receive the care you need."

Bradford nodded.

Emerald reminded herself of Jack's promise. *No one's taking you anywhere except for home where you belong. The ranch is your home, Emerald.*

Her daddy's phone rang and he answered it, giving the driver instructions where to park.

Sidney leaned forward and whispered, "You can thank me later for keeping your secret. I assume you're keeping mine."

The statement was numbing. She had no idea what it meant and sucked in her breath. She didn't know how Jack would keep his promise. She prayed he'd find a way.

# Chapter Thirty-One

BRADFORD AND SIDNEY HAD BEEN IN the room for three hours. When Sidney left to take a phone call and Bradford walked out shortly after, Jack saw his chance.

He peeked into Emerald's room. "How ya doing?"

Emerald's face looked strained.

"I brought you something." He handed her a page he'd scribbled on from a front desk notepad.

*My Father, who has given them to me, is greater than all; no one can snatch them out of my Father's hand. I and the Father are one. John 10:29*

She read the verse silently and then looked up at him. Her eyes said he'd chosen the right verse.

Then Bradford walked in. "Emerald, I won't take no for an answer on you getting rest. You need to sleep whether you want to or not and that's final." He frowned. "I spoke with your nurse and she agrees it's vital if you want to get your health back. None of this was ever an issue when you were at home in Molly's care."

Emerald didn't answer.

Bradford turned to him. "So you are the man responsible for subjecting us to such distasteful gossip?"

Jack glanced at Emerald's tightening face. "I explained everything."

Bradford's gaze penetrated him. "So, Emerald's been . . . working for you?"

He nodded.

Emerald's eyes dropped and he could feel his anger rising. Her father made it sound so immoral.

"She's come a long way since she's been here. She's learned to ride, feed, and even birth a calf."

Color drained from Bradford's face, and he cleared his throat. "Well, Emerald. Seems you've managed to become a hired hand. I'm just going to step out and find a place to wash up."

Emerald closed her eyes. "Germs."

"What?"

"Daddy's terrified of germs. It's been a paranoia of his as long as I can remember. He also discontinued my riding lessons when I was young for fear I'd break my neck."

Jack's gaze drifted to Bradford, who was striding down the hallway. He'd never make it on a ranch.

Emerald yawned. "I'm tired."

She looked it. Much more worn down than earlier. "Why don't you get some sleep, then? It is getting late."

Her eyes closed, and she didn't respond.

Jack stepped back outside and waited until Bradford returned from the bathroom. "She's asleep." Maybe now they'd leave her alone.

"Good."

Caleb approached behind Bradford with an outstretched hand. "You must be Dr. McGintay."

Bradford shook his hand. "Yes?"

"I'm Caleb Graham, pastor of Cowboy Church." His eyes gleamed with pride at the words he spoke next. "Emerald's pastor, Sir."

Bradford gaped and his face paled. He looked from Jack to Caleb, then his eyes narrowed. "I suppose you boys have discovered my daughter's love of adventure. I just hope her little experiment hasn't fooled you. Emerald doesn't believe in God. I raised her to think, not be deluded."

Caleb's face registered surprise. "That may be so, Sir, but Emerald has chosen—"

Bradford smiled coldly as he interrupted. "I appreciate everything you men have done for my daughter, but Dr. Coffman and I have it covered from here." He returned to Emerald's room.

"Did you hear that?" Jack asked his cousin in disbelief.

Caleb shook his head. "I had a feeling that Emerald and her father's relationship needed healing but I don't think I was ready for that." Caleb sighed as he added, "Why don't you go home, take a shower, get a decent meal and a good night's rest?"

"I don't want to leave her."

"Jack, it's late. Her father is with her, you'll just end up spending the night in the waiting room." He smiled wearily. "We'll come back in the morning when we're fresh. At least we know she's all right now."

Caleb was right. Bradford would probably spend the night in her room, and Emerald would be sleeping anyway. He was tired. He glanced one more time at her slumbering form before following Caleb.

∞

Emerald awoke, startled.

Her father stood over her. "Come on sweetheart."

She looked around the hospital room, groggy and confused. A nurse solemnly removed her IV, and another stood by the door.

"Here we are," smiling wide, Sidney rolled in a wheelchair.

"What's going on?" Emerald asked, bewildered. But her words didn't sound right. A sudden anxiety developed inside her.

Daddy pulled back her covers, then the nurses stepped forward and lifted her body from the bed to the wheelchair.

She tried to resist but couldn't. It was like a nightmare, only she knew it was real.

"No. . . ." Nothing more would come out. "Where are you . . . taking me?" But her words slurred. Anxiety turned to horror.

"We got you discharged, darling. You'll have your own nurse to care for you now."

"What? No. . . ." She couldn't manage more than two words. Why couldn't she move? Her body felt like lead, immobile.

Sidney hung a jacket around her shoulders, then spread a blanket over the bare legs below the hem of her hospital gown. They rolled her outside, and the staff and patients they passed became a blur.

She tried to call out to them, but the words didn't form.

Outside, a black limousine waited. Sidney lifted her from the wheelchair and set her in the back seat while the driver held the door for her father on the other side of the car.

She watched helplessly as they pulled away from the hospital. She should be fighting, but she couldn't. Her head fell sideways, and she went back to a sleep—a very strange sleep.

∞

Jack and Caleb reached the hospital at seven-thirty the next morning. Jack rushed straight to Emerald's room with Caleb close behind. He peered in, saw the stripped bed and took a step back to check the number.

Caleb flinched. "Jack—?"

Jack felt as if someone had punched him in the chest. He opened his mouth but couldn't speak.

Caleb looked in the room and said, "They must have moved her."

His cousin waved down the hallway at a nurse. "Ma'am, can you help us?"

"I'll try."

"Where have you moved Emerald McGintay?"

"Miss McGintay has been discharged, sir."

"Discharged?" said Caleb. "There must be a mistake."

The nurse shook her head. "No, Dr. McGintay checked her out in the middle of the night."

"But how could he do that?" asked Caleb. "Wasn't she supposed to be under observation?"

"I'm sorry. That's all I can say. Our patient records are confidential."

Jack spoke for the first time, the tendons in his throat tightening. "They took her against her will."

Caleb looked at him in surprise. "Now, Jack, we don't know that."

"Give me your keys."

"What?"

"Go see what you can find out from the front desk. In the meantime, I need your keys."

Caleb opened his mouth to protest again, but Jack cut him off with a fierce look. Jack snatched the keys from his cousin and left the hospital. Caleb wouldn't find anything out that they didn't already know. Jack just wanted his cousin occupied.

He cranked the truck and floored it to Tussle Springs—the nearest town with hotels. He knew most of the owners personally, and within an hour he'd obtained Bradford McGintay's cell phone number from the guest registry at the Mountain View Inn.

∞

Kati arrived at the hospital with the purse Emerald had left at her place, and Caleb dialed directory assistance for Philadelphia, gave the address on the license, and got Dr. McGintay's number. It connected him with an answering service.

"I need to get a message to Dr. McGintay immediately. Tell him Caleb Graham is trying to get in touch with him. He can call me back at this number." Caleb gave his cell number, then hung up.

He looked at his mom who said, "Let's go get some breakfast while we wait."

But before they had reached the truck, the cell rang. Caleb exchanged a quick glance with his mom before answering.

"This is Dr. McGintay, Caleb."

"I just got to the hospital to find that Emerald's checked—"

"You called earlier than I thought." Amusement filled his voice.

"What?"

"Never mind. As it turns out, Emerald has decided to come home. I have a nurse who will care for her from here. She didn't want to have to spend another minute in that dreadful place."

*No way. Not the Emerald I know.* "Can I talk to her?"

"She's sleeping now."

Something was wrong; he could feel it. Maybe Jack was right.

Bradford spoke again. "Caleb, there's a situation that you know nothing about. My daughter. . . ," he hesitated, "Emerald has a condition. She has schizophrenia."

Caleb processed the words. No, impossible.

Bradford sighed. "I know that you and this other man have come to care about my daughter. But if you want to help her, you'll just let this go. Emerald comes from a completely different world. I know my daughter. For her to have given up Julliard, her music, her social groups and class, everything she's worked so hard for—to work on a filthy ranch. . . . Well, it's quite obvious to everyone who knows her that she has a problem. But from now on I am going to see that nothing like this ever happens again and she receives the treatment needed."

Treatment? No. Emerald wasn't schizophrenic. She couldn't be. He would have noticed it before now.

"Dr. McGintay—"

But the line was silent. Caleb hung up the phone with a sick feeling. He thought of all of the time he'd spent with Emerald over the past two months. There was the night he'd found her outside his mother's house in the dark. That was a little strange. Was that schizophrenia? Perhaps he'd been so blinded by his feelings for her that he missed it.

Kati touched his shoulder. "What is it, Son?"

He met her concerned eyes. "According to Dr. McGintay, Emerald has a medical condition we weren't aware of."

Kati's lips formed a tight line. "We'll just have to pray, Caleb. God healed her once."

Caleb forced a smile for his mother, struggling to decide whether Emerald could have been in need of additional healing or not.

*Leave her in My hands.*

*But she needs help.*

*I healed her once*

*Yes, but this is different. Now, Dr. McGintay had control.*

*Do you trust Me?*

*. . . Yes.*

∞

Jack returned to his house, frustrated. He'd tried Bradford's number multiple times only to have his call go straight to voicemail. An engine sounded in the driveway and he stepped out on the front porch.

Caleb got out of Kati's truck with Emerald's purse. "I called Dr. McGintay, Jack."

Jack sighed. "Me, too. I didn't get an answer."

"I spoke with him."

"What did he say?" He heard Emerald's voice whisper in his memory. *Jack, promise me you won't let them take me.*

Caleb hesitated and Jack was jarred by his cousin's expression. "What did he say?"

"He said there's a lot that we don't know about Emerald."

"What are you talking about?"

"Her father said she has schizophrenia."

"You don't believe him?" But even as he asked, thoughts and memories swarmed through his mind. The night he'd found her in the storm and brought her back to the house. Her early runaway attempts. The inexplicable desire of a wealthy city girl to choose a laborer's life in Canyon Ridge in the first place.

Jack refused to believe Emerald was mentally disturbed. But he remembered Dr. Sidney Coffman's appointment card. She'd been in treatment at one time. Emerald was fine now, wasn't she? Fine until her father and Sidney had come. Then she had changed into a different person.

*Promise you won't let them take me, Jack.*

Something tightened inside him. They'd taken her. *And I wasn't there to stop them.*

# Chapter Thirty-Two

EMERALD OPENED HER EYES TO FAMILIAR pink flowery wallpaper. Her bedroom in Philly. She tried to sit up, but her head ached. Sunshine peeked in through the dark burgundy drapes and panic filled her. How had she gotten there? The bits of her memory were faint. Flashes of her father's private jet and a limo.

Anger accompanied the panic. Why hadn't she done anything to stop them? She must have slept the entire time! She pushed back the covers and stood, but everything began to spin. She fell back to the bed; something was wrong with her.

Before long her door opened and Molly walked in with a tray. "Well hello, dear. Welcome home."

*Home.* She felt sick. This was not her home. Her home was in Canyon Ridge with Kati and Jack and Caleb and the community that she had come to know as family.

"Here, dear. Try to eat a little." Molly placed the tray of soup on her lap but Emerald pushed it away. "Where is Daddy?"

Molly hesitated. "I'll be back." She set the tray to the side and left the room.

Soon after, Sidney entered. Emerald, how are you feeling?"

"Where's my father? You brought me home without consent!"

"Your father had to go to the office. He was in the middle of a rather important crisis when all of this started." Sidney set a leather bag on her nightstand.

She frowned. "Sidney, I don't live here any longer!" She once again tried to sit up, to ignore the spinning. "I'm going home, Sidney. I'm leaving right now!"

"I know you're frustrated, but we can talk this through. You're not thinking clearly." Sidney opened his bag and put something together. A syringe filled with fluid.

"What are you doing?"

She fought him as he held her arm down. "It's all right, Emerald, everything is going to be all right."

She screamed, but no one came to help.

*No one's taking you anywhere except home, to the ranch where you belong.*

What had happened to Jack's promise? She grew sleepier until her thoughts fell into a bunch of jumbled puzzle pieces that didn't fit together.

∞

Bradford gripped the receiver. "How is she?"

"She was a little paranoid when she woke up."

He closed his eyes. Sedated again? "Sidney, wasn't there some way around it?"

"I would have never sedated her if I hadn't felt it was absolutely necessary."

He sighed. No, of course Sidney wouldn't. He was on edge. The suicide case and now Emerald found physically injured from a ridiculous accident and mentally in danger from lack of treatment.

Sidney cut into his thoughts. "Have you made your decision yet?"

A fresh unease stirred within him. Sidney still wanted Emerald sent away for psychotherapy, even though she'd disappeared from home last time he suggested it. Now Emerald didn't trust him anymore. She'd completely pulled away.

"I can't make this decision now." How could Sidney understand what it was like to love someone and then lose her? Emerald was all he had. Maybe now she was home things would change.

∞

Sidney ended the call. Impatience surged through him. He had to convince Bradford that Emerald needed to be sent away. At this point, having her locked up was the safest thing. Truth was, from what he'd witnessed thus far, her mental psychosis was probably severe enough that she may not be capable of exposing him, if she'd even looked at the disk at all.

But why go through his jacket and take it without reason?

He'd searched all her belongings and there was no trace. It was very likely it could be back at Canyon Ridge. From what he'd witnessed, the people there were too backward to know what they had. But he couldn't take the risk. There were ways to get the truth out of her. He just had to find a time when Molly and Bradford weren't hovering over his shoulders.

∞

Emerald lifted her heavy eyelids to the darkness in her room.

"Help me."

*Follow Me.*

But her body ached and denied her the strength to get out of bed, much less escape. She was completely helpless. She fought the despair but her eyelids drifted closed. Paralyzed by a dark fear; she could almost hear the room whispering to her.

*That's right, Emerald. Everyone's deserted you and your God has forsaken you.*

A sick feeling formed in her body. She heard the anguished cries of her visions.

*You can't help these people. You can't even help yourself.*

"No, no, no," she whispered, then she once again slipped beyond consciousness.

∞

Emerald awoke to more pounding in her head as sunlight crept through the edges of her drapes. She sat up, this time with less difficulty. She noticed a pitcher of water on her nightstand where her cordless phone had once lain.

She drank until her parched throat and tongue could function again. Cautiously, she set her feet on the floor, then trudged slowly to her bathroom to splash cold water on her face. Next she looked for a pair of jeans in her closet. No Wranglers there. She settled on a pair of designer denims never meant to come into contact with saddle leather.

Emerald peeled off her light blue Christian Dior nightgown. Molly must have dressed her—but as with much of the past few days, she couldn't remember. Clad in the jeans and a black tank top, she crept to the Victorian style phone on a small table in the hallway.

Whom should she call? Kati didn't have a telephone. And, as she had never used a phone while she was on the ranch, she didn't know Jack or Caleb's number.

She lifted the receiver and called information.

"Jack Evens, Canyon Ridge Mountain, Colorado."

The telephone rang seven times. Was he outside working?

She was about to hang up when the line clicked.

"Hello?" He sounded out of breath.

"Jack." Tears of joy stung behind her eyelids.

"Emerald?"

"Jack, I'm in Philly. I think they drugged me." She choked on a sob.

No answer. The phone was dead. She whirled around to discover that Sidney was pressing the receiver hook down.

"Let's not do anything hasty without thinking of the repercussions."

She wanted to lash out at him, but forced the anger down. He would drug her again. She had to try a different approach.

Faking a dumbfounded look she asked, "What have I done? I'm sorry, Sidney. I guess I really am schizophrenic." She paused. "Is Daddy home now?" He was her best chance.

Sidney didn't even crack a smile at her schizophrenic remark. "He'll be home for dinner. Why don't we have some lunch? Molly should have it prepared." He spoke warmly, convincingly. "It's been a while since you've eaten."

She plastered on a smile in response. She had to cooperate, for now.

Sidney led her to her father's study. Sitting on the couch, she waited. He returned quickly with Molly, who carried a tray of cucumber sandwiches.

She forced a bite down as Sidney stretched out in front of her in one of her father's chairs.

"Who was it you called, Emerald?"

Accepting that he'd probably heard her, she decided not to lie. "Jack."

"Your cowboy husband?" He flashed a strange smile.

She swallowed a sip of her mineral water. "Yes."

"So what led you to cowboy country, Emerald?"

She studied his relaxed face. Her answer, she knew, would only confirm in his mind that she was crazy. "God did."

She finished her sandwich, and he nodded toward her plate and two pills lying on it.

"No, Sidney, I won't be drugged again."

Sidney leaned forward. "Relax. This will help you feel calm. It's similar to what you were taking before you left."

She pushed the plate away. "I'm not taking them, Sidney. I don't need them." She left the room, her back stiff.

∞

Jack hung up the phone. Emerald had been cut off.

He dialed *69 and grabbed a pen, but the recorded voice said it was a private caller.

*Shoot.* Jack's online efforts to find this unlisted number had been futile, too. He stared at the solemn face on Emerald's driver's license. They had been disconnected. Obviously something was wrong.

Jack returned to the barn to care for the stock. But the hard work gave him no relief. Emerald asked him not to let them take her. He had no idea whether that constituted a kidnapping, but it sounded like she said something about being drugged. Had they drugged her? Surely he'd heard wrong.

Finished feeding the animals, he headed back inside for his truck keys. He floored the truck out of the drive and headed toward the church.

Caleb was watching an instructor who worked at the therapeutic riding center. A child perched on a docile mare was learning colors and direction by first pulling left on a lemon yellow rein, then right by pulling on a red rein. Lemon for left, red for right.

Caleb walked over to the truck. "Jack, good to see you. What's up?"

"Emerald. They took her, Caleb. Against her will."

Caleb's jaw tightened. "What do you suggest we do?"

"Go get her."

Caleb was silent. The horse and rider turned another circle around the corral before his cousin nodded. "All right. Let's go."

# Chapter Thirty-Three

"DADDY, PLEASE. I WANT TO GO back. I made it my home, Daddy, I love it there."

Bradford's face softened. She was working him down. *Just a little more time with him away from Sidney, please.*

"Sweetheart, I know how you feel. All that I'm asking is that you take a little time here to know what you really want."

"I know what I want, Daddy, I want to go back home, to Canyon Ridge."

Pain flickered across his face. Calling Canyon Ridge home upset him. "Sidney tells me you won't take any of your medication. I'll tell you what. If you agree to take the medicine now, then I promise I will be more open to this idea of Canyon Ridge as home."

Why should she agree to this? She was twenty-two, free to make her own choices. But did that mean leaving Bradford behind? If she could just get his blessing.

"All right." What would it hurt to take a couple of pills, anyway?

"That's my girl." Bradford placed a kiss on his daughter's forehead.

∞

Emerald returned to her room. She'd try the phone again after everyone was asleep. She lay on her bed and realized her mother's Bible and journal were still at Kati's. She knelt by the bed, desiring to once again be with her new friends, living her chosen life.

"Father, please help me. Show me the way."

It was a simple prayer. Right now, she could think of nothing else.

A light tap sounded on her door. "Emerald, Dr. Coffman's here to see you."

Sidney waited at the bottom of the stairs with one of his most charming smiles. He reached out to her as she descended the last three steps. He led her to her father's study, the most private sitting area in the house. She dropped into the sofa against the wall as he turned a chair toward her.

"Your father told me you took your medicine."

*Sure, gloat. Why'd I have to give him the victory?* That medicine was for her father, not Sidney.

Sidney's face turned more serious. His eyes narrowed. She knew what that meant. He was about to probe inside her mind and search for the madness he was sure he'd find. She should just leave. Two months in Colorado had proven she didn't need Sidney.

"Tell me more about your adventure in cowboy land."

Adventure? He thought it was an act of rebellion. Just another stage of her disorder. Emerald remembered her father's earlier coaxing. She couldn't bear the thought that he must feel the same.

"Canyon Ridge Mountain is the nicest town I've known. An old western town where the people are like family. Kati gave me a home. Jack gave me a job. Caleb gave me faith."

"So, it was like a fairy tale? Three wishes granted?" His condescending smile didn't change.

She laughed in an attempt to break free of his disparagement. "Sidney, I hate to break it to you, but Canyon Ridge is not a fairy tale. I have the calluses on my hands and the freckles on my nose to prove it."

"So you think you really became an old West cowgirl out there, don't you?"

"I learned that pride comes from hard work."

"What else did you find in this little speck of a town?"

"I found what I've been searching for my entire life." Even though she was trying to sound rational, she couldn't keep her awe of the experience out of her voice.

"Did it match your fantasy?"

"No, not at all." She never expected to find answers there.

"And how has this experience developed?"

She closed her eyes. "He showed me my calling."

"I see. You have a calling now." His lips turned downward. "And what's that?"

"To reach out to people, the hungry, the diseased." She had to stop telling him all this. She knew what he'd say, how he'd use it against her.

Sidney leaned forward. "So in all the world God has called *you* to end world hunger and poverty? Emerald, you couldn't even make it at Julliard by yourself. How do you think you're going to be able to do this calling in places far more difficult than plush, protected Julliard?"

And there it was. Sidney aimed to make her reasoning sound ridiculous. Part of her wanted to lash out at him. Yet, the other half of her mind listened. She had to admit that her claim didn't seem very possible. She swallowed the lump in her throat.

Sidney leaned back and crossed his legs. "Helping people is a good thing, Emerald. You can certainly do that. But then again, don't you think that anyone who puts his mind to making a difference to better humanity can and will do so? Look at your father and the clinic. He didn't do that because God called him. He did it because he's a good man who decided to do a good thing.

You don't need religion to do that."

Her mouth went dry. What Sidney suggested was that God hadn't called her with any specific plan. This desire to help was entirely a decision of her mind, not a calling. She fought off a sense of unease.

*No. Sidney was wrong.*

"Emerald, do you think that possibly your need and desire to be important created a voice that told you that you were? That maybe you made the decision a long time ago that you wanted to be something different, special, so you created a way to become that person? Then you created this image of something larger than you to tell you that you belonged and had special meaning."

No, not possible. She'd felt the presence so strongly. It had been outside of her, not just in her mind. It had been real.

Sidney crouched forward. "Emerald, this is not a bad thing. It's good. It is putting reason behind a motive that couldn't be explained before."

He stood and moved beside her. "You don't need a higher being calling your name to give you meaning or purpose. You can make a difference and find your own calling without putting some childish notion of a booming-voiced God behind it. It's you, Emerald. You are who you are. And now you can stand up to the woman you are without fearing or waiting for someone to acknowledge you or give you permission to be that woman."

"Others believe this too, Sidney. Are they all schizophrenic?"

He laughed. "No, of course not. Just uneducated ranchers who don't know any better."

"What about the millions of people in the world who believe there is a God? Some of them are very educated: scholars, doctors, professors!"

"You're right, Emerald. For many it's childhood programming. Others find a false comfort in believing. But Emerald, millions of people believe in God without dreams and visions."

She jumped up and stood just inside the doorway now, knowing what he was insinuating.

"It's a trick of your mind."

She left the study, shaking. She reached her room and sank to the floor. Sidney's words haunted her mind.

*Your need and desire to be important created a voice that told you that you were.*

No, she'd heard God's voice. It had been real. If she could just hear it now, for assurance.

*Follow Me.*

"Where?"

There was no answer.

∞

Bradford looked up as Sidney entered his office. "I think we've just taken a huge step."

Setting his paperwork aside, Bradford lowered his glasses. "Is she—?"

"We just opened the door to the possibility of her creating this 'higher being' as a way to find meaning and purpose. As a way to permit herself to be the woman she desires to be."

"Permit herself?" Emerald didn't need permission to be the woman she wanted to be. He'd already let her do the things she needed to do to be that woman.

Sidney settled into the chair across from him. "Bradford, did you not tell me that your acknowledgment and approval was important to her as a child?"

"Well, yes. Of course it was. I was her father."

"Yes, but you gave restrictions. Set parameters. Perhaps, you were a bit overprotective."

Bradford's mouth went dry. Sidney was suggesting Emerald's illness was his fault? That he had warped her mind and made her have hallucinations to get approval? That was nonsense. Any psychiatrist knows that children who lost a parent at a tender age were vulnerable because of the parent who died, not the one who lived.

"Alexandra died so young."

Sidney's face showed surprise at the mention of Alexandra. Understandable. Bradford rarely mentioned his deceased wife.

"She had ridiculous notions; she believed God was calling her." The buried pain resurfaced. "I loved her, so I let her go. She went as a missionary to a third-world country. Was only supposed to be there for two weeks. She was five months pregnant with Emerald. She didn't return home after the two weeks. God was still calling her to be there. Week after week passed and she didn't have God's permission to come back yet."

Bradford laughed, to cover a sob. "Turned into three months. Emerald was born there prematurely. Alexandra was eight months into the pregnancy. She gave birth in a little hut in the middle of Guatemala with no doctors or medical help. To this day I still don't know how that little girl survived. But she did. Unfortunately, Alexandra wasn't so lucky." He gathered his stack of papers together. "I never knew the actual medical cause of my wife's death.

"So yes, maybe I was a bit protective. Anyone would be. From fifth grade on, I schooled her at home with tutors. All her hobbies were indoors with private instructors. I worked hard her entire life to protect her from the fate Alexandra met. So you can only imagine what it was like when I found out she thought she had a calling from God."

Sidney stood. "I had no idea."

Bradford nodded. "All that matters is that my daughter is all right." His eyes met Sidney's. "I will do whatever it takes. Anything."

# Chapter Thirty-Four

JACK LOOKED UP AT EMERALD'S HOUSE. The three-story brick estate was magnificent with its perfectly manicured landscape. Leyland cypresses lined the drive, and a black iron fence encircled the yard.

He and Caleb left the rental car parked off the side of the road and approached the gate. It had a speaker box with a round, red button. Jack leaned forward and buzzed the home.

In a moment a man's voice sounded from the speaker. "Yes?"

"Jack Evens and Caleb Graham are here to see Emerald McGintay."

"Miss McGintay is not expecting anyone."

"No, but she'll want to see us." Jack made his voice sound confident.

A few moments passed while they waited for a response. Finally, the man's voice returned. "I'm sorry, but Miss McGintay is not receiving guests at this time."

Anger flashed across Caleb's face. "Then have her tell us that herself."

"I'm sorry. Miss McGintay will not be changing her mind."

"Then we'll just wait here until she does." Jack's voice held a mixture of anger and stubbornness.

Caleb leaned forward. "All we request is to hear her voice and know she's all right. If she doesn't want to see us we want to hear it from her."

Minutes of silence. He and Caleb exchanged stares. Would the next sound they heard be police sirens?

∞

Bradford looked at Riley, his driver, who waited for his answer. He should turn them away, call the police, and get a restraining order. Still he hesitated.

Emerald would be upset when she discovered her cowboy friends had been there and he'd refused to let her see them. She'd only retreat further, go back to seeking this nonexistent God who supposedly gave her the permission he denied—to be herself. It was almost humorous. But if he wanted any hope of getting his daughter back, he had to let her think she had some control over her own destiny—even if it was a lie.

He took a deep breath. This would be tricky.

∞

The man's voice returned. "Dr. McGintay will receive you."

The gate opened, and Jack and Caleb walked down the long drive and up the brick stairs to the mahogany double doors.

A man in a formal black suit admitted them. He led them to a spacious living room with rich green and gold drapes and a grand piano beneath a large crystal chandelier. Jack's steps sounded unnaturally loud on the marble floors. He realized for the first time how alien Emerald must have felt in his world. He saw Caleb tracing the carved woodwork.

Soon, Jack would have her out of here.

Bradford entered the room, smiling. "It's spectacular, isn't it? The house was built in 1866." He crossed the room to the bar. "Can I get you men something to drink?"

Caleb adjusted his hat. "No sir. We're just here to see Emerald."

Bradford put a couple of ice cubes in a glass, then filled it with Grand Marnier. "You two have certainly gone to great lengths to contact my daughter."

He sat in a brown leather chair across from Jack and Caleb. "She's recovering well physically from the injuries she received at your place. But she's been struggling quite a bit emotionally these last few days."

Jack fought to contain his impatience. He couldn't tell if Bradford was going to let them see her or not. If not, he would search the house—with or without Bradford McGintay's permission.

Caleb stepped in to answer. "We understand Emerald is struggling with something right now. That was clear from her phone call. We'd just like to talk to her and help her in any way we can."

Bradford looked puzzled at the mention of a phone call, but nodded. "I'll let you see my daughter on one condition. You cannot, under any circumstance, mention anything about God."

Jack saw his own surprise mirrored on his cousin's face.

Bradford stood. "My daughter never believed in God before her condition. Now I know you're a pastor, and your intentions are probably good. Even so, I'm her father and one of the best psychiatrists in this nation. I will not allow her treatment to be disrupted by your beliefs and influence. Your carelessness could be extremely dangerous to my daughter right now."

Caleb stepped toward Bradford. "No offense, Dr. McGintay, but your daughter's relationship with God has completely turned her life around. It has given her meaning and—"

Bradford put his hand on the doorknob. "Those are my terms. Abide by them or leave."

Caleb shook his head. "I cannot agree to such terms."

Jack was annoyed. Caleb was losing track of their purpose, was going to get them thrown out and barred from the property so they couldn't do anything at all.

Bradford took a sip of his drink. "Well, then, I think it's for the best."

Jack looked at his cousin in disbelief. "I agree to the terms, even if my cousin does not."

Caleb looked at him, surprised.

Jack turned to Bradford. "Where is she?" He had made a promise to Emerald, and he would fulfill it. He wouldn't need to mention God.

As if considering whether he could go back on his word, Bradford turned to the doorman and gestured toward Caleb. "Riley, please show this young man out."

Bradford turned back to Jack, and scanned his western attire. "I'll get my daughter."

Jack sat on the sofa as Bradford and Caleb left the room, but his inner joy was immeasurable. He would see Emerald. He was going to bring her home.

∞

Bradford climbed the winding staircase to his daughter's room. Overprotective. Responsible for Emerald feeling she needed permission from a higher being. His throat tightened as his hand closed around her doorknob, then stopped. What was he doing? He couldn't just walk into her room anymore; he'd lost those privileges even before her condition began. He tapped on the wood panel, then clenched his fist in annoyance as he waited.

The whole situation was a mess. Letting those men in his home so he could get his daughter back. Giving her control so he could regain his. Making it look as if he was giving her a choice–
–in likely the false hope that she'd trust him again.

Emerald's soft voice came through the door. "Come in."

His heart melted at the sight of his daughter sitting in the pink armchair in the corner, reading a book. She'd barely eaten the past few days, and her sweat pants—wherever the dreadful things had come from—looked baggy. Her normally wavy hair hung in lank strings.

Pain for her tore at his heart. He was overwhelmed by the desire to hold a little girl with pigtails and ribbons on his knee again, to hear her laugh, to play the piano with the joy and satisfaction she had when she was a child. But that little girl was gone. He could no longer pick her up as he had when she skinned her knee. He could no longer stop her tears with a Barbie Band-Aid, or make her laugh with a new doll when she was sad.

He forced the emotion down. "Emerald, you have a visitor."

She set her book down and looked at him, something flaring in her eyes. Hope? The possibility almost caused him to retreat from his plan.

"Jack Evens is waiting for you downstairs."

Joy crossed her face; then her expression closed to him. "I'll be down in a minute."

Bradford wanted to suggest she not see him. Maybe she wasn't ready for this. What if bringing this part of her fiasco back corrupted everything he and Sidney had accomplished toward her recovery in the last few days? But it was too late now. If he changed his mind, he would be controlling her again. He forced himself to leave the room.

∞

Emerald's heart jumped as the door clicked closed behind her father. Jack had come for her after all! She knew he would help her. He would tell her the truth.

Emerald had spent the past two days trying to find answers. She'd wanted to forget Sidney's suggestions, telling herself it was just a scheme for him to get what he wanted. Doubt, however, still plagued her. She was halfway to believing that it was her imagination that created the voice that she heard.

It was with great hope and anticipation that she ran down

the stairs to see Jack, but when she entered the living room, where Jack waited on the plush sofa, she was hit with the sudden realization that he did not belong in this mansion anymore than she did his ranch. He looked as out of place here as she must have there. The realization choked her.

Jack stood, and his mouth deepened into a smile. She'd missed that. A part of her wanted to tell him to carry her away, but she couldn't bring herself to say the words.

What if he knew her doubts? He and Caleb were so proud of her and her miraculous healing; she had seen the tears of joy in their eyes. What if he knew she'd spent the last two days locked in her room questioning whether it had been real?

"Emerald." He wrapped his arms around her, but his warmth didn't dispel the dark shadow that clung to her. She stiffened.

His eyes deepened. "Come home, Emerald."

Her heart jumped at the simple words. She so badly wanted to say yes.

"I made my father a promise." She clutched at the excuse, knowing there was much more than that. Could he see through her? Feel the doubt that attacked her?

She turned away. "I'm sorry I left the way I did."

*I was drugged, Jack. They took me in my sleep.*

But the truth wouldn't come out, and Jack looked as if she'd shoved him across the room. Emerald wanted the doubt and darkness to go away. She wanted Jack. But instead, she stood there, chilled by her inability to reach past the prison of her fears. She sat in an armchair and Jack followed suit, sitting on the couch across from her.

She should just tell him. Tell him she was having trouble believing, and tell how Sidney was eroding her faith. Jack would understand.

"What's wrong, Emerald?"

Tears stung her eyes. "What if I'm crazy, Jack?" She dropped her head to her hands, unable to believe she'd just come out and said it like that.

"You're not crazy, Emerald." Jack was quiet, his eyes penetrating. "What is it you're afraid of?"

The tears pushed forward. "I'm afraid that what I thought was God's voice is really just my own, my clinging for existence and a way to find purpose."

"Emerald, you know the truth."

But did she? Emerald expected Jack to say something more, but he didn't.

She studied his handsome face. Sidney suggested the community she'd found only supported her because of their lack of education. Shame filled her for even considering the possibility sitting here in front of Jack. Swallowing hard she tried to grasp the faith she'd had, but it was gone. Evidence of reality was too strong. She stood, unable to take this anymore. It hurt too badly.

"Thank you for coming, but I need some time." She forced her legs to move out of the room and back up the winding staircase.

∞

Jack's heart sank as Emerald left the room. He wanted to run after her, take her in his arms and carry her away. But he couldn't. And he knew it. The visit hadn't gone at all the way he'd intended. He had prepared for her to be different—but not this unreachable, cold woman.

A deep pain cut through him as he let himself out of the house. Caleb met him outside the gate with hopeful eyes.

Jack could only shake his head. "She's not the same woman." The words did something strange to him. He felt as if saying them out loud had turned his heart to ash.

# Chapter Thirty-Five

SPRAWLED ACROSS HER BED, EMERALD FOUGHT sobs. He'd left without her, and she'd let him. She should have gone with him—she'd wanted it with her whole heart. But she feared living what might be a lie.

She closed her eyes as voices clashed in her head. It was a constant battle between promises of peace and the torture of her doubts. If this was what He'd done for her, God had to be an invention of her mind.

Emerald went to her nightstand, dumped out a dose of pills, and swallowed them. Sidney said the medication would help the voices calm down and make things clearer. But it hadn't worked so far.

A knock sounded at her door and Molly peeked in. "Your visitor left something for you." She set Emerald's tote on the floor against the wall and shut the door.

Emerald stared at the bag. Jack had brought her things to her. She should be grateful, but all she felt was regret. As long as something of hers was left in Colorado, she'd had hope of returning. Not any more. As she crossed the room to the bag, memories flooded her. The night she stuffed it with clothes and felt something pushing her forward. The day she arrived in Canyon Ridge. Her first ride on a horse. The beauty of the mountains.

Opening her bag, she found her clothes—all of them, even her work clothes. Her mother's treasure box was missing, but it had been under the bed. Jack wouldn't have thought to look there. But her mother's journal was there.

Emerald lifted it out and closed her eyes. Was it her imagination or did the book bring a certain presence?

Sitting on her bed, she opened the book and paged through.

Her hand stilled on the first of the pages she had not yet read.

*Dear Heavenly Father,*

*This morning as I awake to look out at the morning sun, I know that I have many reasons to praise You! This child that I have growing inside of me is Your child, and I know that You have called her. My husband does not yet understand why I must go, and sometimes, I find myself questioning the timing. The timing of this child, the timing of my calling. But You have created this daughter, and have called her to Your purpose. And You have also told me that now is the time to go. So I will walk by faith and not by sight. I only pray that You will touch my husband's heart.*

*I trust You with all the obstacles that stand in my way. And I continue to follow You even when the path is not clear.*

*Resting in Your love and grace,*

*Alexandra*

Emerald touched her mother's handwriting. The letter struck her as odd. Where was her mother going? Why was she leaving? She said she had to follow God. Had she left Daddy? No, that didn't seem right.

One other thing. How had Alexandra known her baby was going to be a girl? Emerald shifted her eyes to the top of the next page, but it was blank—as was the rest of the book.

*That's it? That's all Mother wrote?*

No, wait. Between the pages, she saw ragged shreds of paper. Someone had torn out the final entry. Disappointment washed over her. Now she would never know where Alexandra went or what had happened. Or what her calling had been.

∞

Jack watched as the vast mountains beneath the aircraft came into view. He never liked leaving home. Returning had always been a relief. But this time was different. He felt no pleasure in the Rockies beckoning him home to the ranch.

He'd returned without Emerald, left her in Philly. And nothing had ever felt so wrong. Yet when he'd asked the Lord to show him another way, the answer had been, *Wait.*

He and Caleb exited the plane with the same silence between them they'd maintained the entire flight. Caleb placed his hand on Jack's shoulder. "Why don't you go ahead and get the truck? I'll take care of the luggage."

Nice of Caleb to remember how much Jack hated airports. Traveling wasn't something he'd done often and all the people and craziness made him anxious. He offered a tired smile of thanks as he left for the parking garage. As he pulled up to the curb outside the baggage claim, he looked for his cousin. Caleb wasn't out yet, but no airport police were urging the traffic forward. Must be a slow travel day.

Jack jumped out and went to the passenger side, where he pulled the seat forward to put the luggage in the back. A piece of paper fluttered to the floor.

He picked it up. The paper was thin, and light pink flowers outlined the edges.

> *Dear Father,*
>
> *As I prayed with Pastor Keith today, You confirmed that I was doing the right thing. Even Bradford has accepted the trip. I leave next week. As I anticipate this journey I feel a strange stir within. It is a great joy and sadness at the same*

*time. But I know I am in Your arms, and Eternal Blessings Church will continue to pray for me while I am gone.*

*Please help me not to fear, but to trust in You.*

*Alexandra*

The page must have fallen out of Emerald's flowery pink journal, Kati's late addition to his luggage as he departed for Denver. But it wasn't Emerald's writing, and the signature was "Alexandra."

Caleb approached with their bags. "Here ya go."

Jack stepped back for Caleb to put the luggage in the truck, then climbed in behind the wheel. After he'd pulled out, he glanced at Caleb thoughtfully.

"What?" Caleb asked.

"Here." Jack handed him the note. "Does this belong to Emerald?"

Caleb paused to read it. "It must be from her mother's journal. She told me a little bit about her mother's writings. They made a great impact on her faith."

Thoughtful, Jack took the paper back from Caleb. The cousins were silent the rest of the way home, and after he dropped Caleb off Jack headed back to the ranch, still in deep thought.

Entering the house, he dropped his bags. He went to the sofa and re-read the letter. "Eternal Blessings Church," he whispered. For some reason it felt significant.

He lit the fireplace, then went into kitchen to make dinner. Hope flickered in his heart.

He looked back down at the letter. *What should I do?*

∞

" Greg, I need to know the exact words the maintenance woman said."

"What? Sidney what's going on?" Greg asked in surprise from the other end of the line.

Sidney sat down behind his desk. "I don't think Emerald took the disk."

"How can you be sure?"

"I questioned her under the influence of sodium pentathol."

"The famous truth telling drug. Brilliant, Sidney."

"She doesn't know anything about the disk. Did the women actually describe Emerald?"

Greg was quiet.

"Greg?"

"No. I don't think so. She was Hispanic and it was hard for my guy to understand her."

"Then how do we know it was Emerald?"

"We just assumed it was since she was the only woman up there spying."

Sidney was tired and frustrated and it didn't look like things were going to get any better in the near future. Greg's voice was grim "I just can't imagine what other woman it could have been."

"I can't think about it this moment. I've got to go."

"Hey, don't lose it, Doc."

"I won't."

"Take a Xanax."

"I already did."

∞

Emerald awoke groggy and disoriented. Last thing she remembered was Sidney interrogating her in Daddy's office. He must have drugged her again. She thought of his announcement earlier.

*Your father has decided it is best to send you to psychotherapy. Emerald had cowered on the sofa in her father's study as Sidney pronounced judgment. He probably had anticipated another escape attempt.*

*There's no reason to be afraid. Sara will accompany you and see that you have all the care you need.*

Sara, the new nurse who shadowed Emerald's every movement. Each day seemed to bring a new restriction on her freedom.

But Emerald had just nodded, too dispirited to argue. There was no use in it. Maybe she did need help. Maybe she'd find her way. She had to know if she had been living a lie. Her mother's journal hadn't contained any answers, only good reason for her doubts. Alexandra had clearly gone down a path with no way back.

Emerald slid from her bed and sank to her knees. She had no more tears, no emotion. She'd lost all hope. As each day passed, Canyon Ridge seemed more and more like the fairy tale Sidney suggested it to be.

She buried her face in the soft bedding, unable to even whisper a prayer.

∞

Jack stood in front of Eternal Blessings Church. The stirring inside him said this was Emerald's hope, but now that he was here, he couldn't understand how. He stepped inside the large sanctuary with high vaulted ceilings and stained glass windows that depicted Jesus and His disciples.

"May I help you?" The woman had long dark hair that hung down her shoulders and an armful of papers with a small leather bag on top.

At her warm smile, Jack relaxed. "I think I'm looking for Pastor Keith—is he here?"

The woman's eyebrows rose. "He retired years ago."

Jack's heart fell. "Is there any way I can contact him?"

The woman studied him. "We don't usually hand out his number without asking him first." She didn't turn away. Perhaps she noticed his desperation. "I was just on my way to the bank." Her face softened. "But that can wait. Why don't I see if I can reach him for you?"

"Thank you." He followed her to an office, and within minutes a search in the files had yielded Pastor Keith's phone number.

The lady dialed the phone. "Good morning, Pastor." A pause. "I'm doing very well. There is a young man here who would like to speak with you, if you can give him some of your time." She nodded, then handed Jack the telephone.

"Pastor Keith? My name is Jack Evens."

"God bless you, Son." His voice was warm with the patina of age. "What can I do for you?"

"I'm not sure quite how to ask this other than straight out. Did you know a woman by the name of Alexandra McGintay?"

Silence. "May I ask why?" The voice had turned hesitant, guarded.

"Yes, Sir. If her daughter, Emerald McGintay, doesn't find the truth of her mother's life and death, her father may have her committed to a mental institution."

"Are you at the church now?"

"Yes sir."

"I'll be there in twenty minutes."

Jack hung up and met the puzzled look of the woman. "Thank you, Ma'am."

He left the office and returned to the main sanctuary where he looked at a stained glass window that depicted the Pieta, Michelangelo's famous sculpture of Mary holding Jesus's broken body.

Had Emerald's mother worshipped here? More critically, would the truth about Alexandra set Emerald free?

∞

Emerald sat at the breakfast table across from her father. She bit into the English muffin and poked at her uneaten poached egg. She'd had a rough night, had even awakened from crying out in her sleep. Sara had given her something to help her relax. Supposedly. It had put her back to sleep but hadn't stopped the turbulent dreams and voices.

She set her fork down.

*Emerald, I am the Way the Truth and the Life.*

*You are imagining this Emerald, creating this voice in your head.*

The telephone rang and after a moment Molly came to Bradford's side and whispered.

Bradford glanced Emerald's way, then shook his head.

Molly left the dining room, and Emerald studied her father while making another pretense of eating her breakfast.

The phone rang again, and Molly again returned to the dining room. This time her whisper was louder. "He won't take no for an answer."

Her father's answer was low but sharp. "Block his number."

"Jack?" Emerald whispered.

Molly nodded, then left the room again.

The phone rang a third time, and her heart jumped. Her father looked at her but said nothing. She studied the food on her plate.

Agitated, Bradford raised his voice several notches. "Molly, just take care of it."

"Yes, Sir."

Emerald pushed back her chair. "He'll just find another way, Daddy. Let me handle it." Ignoring her father's look of surprise, she darted out to the hallway phone.

Receiver in hand, Molly took a stern tone. "I'm sorry, but you must not call back, or—"

"I'll take it, Molly." Emerald grabbed the phone from Molly and waved her away.

Molly stood flummoxed, then left the hallway.

Emerald sighed and spoke into the mouthpiece. "Jack, I'm going to a psychotherapy hospital. I leave tomorrow and will be gone for three months."

"Emerald, listen."

"I have to go. Please don't call back." She placed the phone on the hook with trembling hands.

She shouldn't have forced herself to hear Jack's voice again. She tried to calm her breathing as she turned back toward the dining room. The insistent ringing of the phone stopped her. That stubborn cowboy wasn't going to give up.

She grabbed the phone. "Jack—"

"I'm here with your mother's pastor."

"What?" she whispered.

"I found a page that fell out of Alexandra's journal. You have to know the truth, Emerald. I'm coming to get you."

No words could come out of her mouth. Her heart lurched as she hung up the phone.

Her father stepped into the hallway. "Emerald, don't answer the phone again! I'm taking care of this personally." He stopped, stunned at the look on her face. "Are you all right? What did he say?"

Without answering, she left the foyer and went up to her bedroom, unable to think. Truth. A page from Alexandra's journal. Was it Alexandra's last entry?

Emerald stood staring out the window until a gray Buick pulled up to the gate. An old man climbed out of the driver's side door, and Jack came around from the passenger side. He had come for her. And he was bringing her mother's pastor.

∞

Jack buzzed the gate, determined. Her heart sank. Her father would never admit them. She was going to be sent away and drugged. Even here she was locked away, away from Jack, away from home, away from the blazing fire of the Divine on the mountaintop. She closed her eyes as her legs crumpled, and she sagged into the chair in the corner of her room.

She couldn't breathe. Part of her wanted to move, to run, to fight this prison—to run to the arms of a higher being. But what if there was no higher being? What if she was only surrendering to delusions her mind had created? Maybe it was the medicine. Maybe it took her strength away, stole her freedom and her choice.

Sirens wailed in the distance. Daddy had called the police. He would have Jack and the pastor arrested. He would get a restraining order against them. Shouting from outside. She opened her eyes. It was her father, yelling, cursing.

Emerald struggled to her feet and peered out the window. Jack was standing on the hood of the Buick to boost himself over the gate. Her breath stopped. Jack was breaking through the security her father had designed to keep her locked away—and to keep people like him out.

Police cars pulled up to the property just as Jack swung from the top of the gate to the ground. He was coming to save her. To bring her the truth that would set her free.

*Go to him.*

She listened to the voice and all of a sudden she knew. She knew she didn't need any drugs, and she knew her Daddy and Sidney were wrong. She was not sick. Definitely not. Resolve gathered within her and she bolted down the stairs.

Bradford stood in the doorway, shouting angrily. Molly and Sara stood behind him and peeked out the windows.

"Oh, honey. Go back upstairs." Sara rushed to her.

Emerald pulled away from her and tried to peer over her father's shoulder. "Jack!" she screamed through the open door.

Bradford turned to her, shock covering his face as he grabbed the knob and tried to shove the door closed. "Emerald, get back!"

"No! You can't keep me here against my will!" She pulled the door away from him just as Jack reached the front porch.

Pushing past her father, she reached Jack's arms. "Take me away, Jack." Tears of joy fell.

He grinned. "Did I ever tell you I won't take no for an answer?"

Her legs were weak, but his strong arms around her waist held her up as he carried her down the driveway.

The gates opened and police officers rushed up the drive. The elderly man was in handcuffs.

A large officer switched on a bullhorn. "Put your hands up and let the girl go!"

Jack glanced at Emerald with warm and reassuring eyes. "It's going to be all right." He released her and raised his arms.

She wanted to cling to him. She ran down the driveway to the officers. The one with the bullhorn shouted at her. "Ma'am, step back."

"No. My father's holding me against my will. These men came to rescue me!"

Time stood still.

"The woman says she is being held against her will." The officer finally motioned the team to lower their weapons.

"I want to get out of here, right now." Emerald looked back at her father, who was still standing in the doorway, but she was too far down the drive to see his face. Would he deny her freedom? Tell the officers about her condition? No, he just stood there, silent. She felt pierced by regret for him.

She got the bullhorn from the officer and spoke through it. "Daddy, if you love me, you'll let me go, and with your blessing. Please."

Emerald's voice trembled with tears. She glanced at Jack. His expression showed he knew how hard it had been for her to do that.

Bradford turned to Molly. After a few minutes the maid

walked down the long drive and spoke to the officers. "Let the men go. Dr. McGintay doesn't want to press charges."

Jack came to her side and grasped her hand in his. Together they walked through the open gate. She was free.

# Chapter Thirty-Six

EMERALD SAT WITH JACK INSIDE THE old church that her mother had attended. With his arm around her, she felt safe. He wasn't going to let go; his grip promised that.

Pastor Keith sat on her other side. He was a heavy man, probably close to seventy. He'd been in handcuffs earlier today, risking arrest and jail for a girl he didn't even know. As an adult, at least, she'd just learned that Pastor Keith had known her as an infant.

"You look very much like her." His voice was soft, and his smile reminded her of the warmth she had held onto in her visions.

"I never forgot you. I just couldn't remember who you were or why you'd visited," she said. "I remembered you saying I had a mission. But it wasn't until recently that I realized what I had been searching for."

Jack squeezed her hand. She glanced at him, and his gaze engulfed her, telling her she could do this.

"I need to know the truth. I need to know what happened to my mother." Her voice cracked. "What was her calling and why did she leave my father?"

A veil of sadness dropped over Pastor Keith's smile. "Your Mother grew up in a Christian family, but when she met your father she strayed from her faith for a while. She never stopped believing, though." The old pastor's eyes twinkled. "It's amazing how when God gives His children a purpose, they have it for the rest of their lives." He was quiet for a moment. "But it is their choice whether they're going to live up to it—or not."

"Did she?" Her question was a whisper.

Their eyes locked, and Emerald's tension released in the sudden warmth.

"Your mother joined our church not long after your father came to practice here in Philadelphia. It was hard for her, to come without your father, to believe in something with her entire heart and not have a guarantee that her husband would share it with her." He shook his head. "But she just kept on praying, believing, and trusting that one day her husband's heart would change."

"It never did," said Emerald.

"No, but your father's life is not over yet."

She thought about that for a moment. How could Pastor Keith still hold out hope for her father? Bradford still thought faith was insanity, even after all of her mother's prayers. He'd never understand.

"Your mother had a calling to the mission field."

"My mother was a missionary?"

The pastor nodded. "In every sense of the word. She shared her faith with everyone she came in contact with. Reached out to people all over the city."

She tried to imagine her mother walking around with a Bible and telling Daddy's partners and their society friends about God. Tough to envision.

"So why did she leave my father?" Perhaps she'd misunderstood her mother's journal. Maybe Daddy had wanted her to leave. She sure couldn't visualize him living with a modern-day disciple.

"It wasn't that she left him. And she didn't want to travel without him, Emerald. Every year our church has a group that takes a mission trip to a third-world country. She prayed about it the first year she was with us but hadn't felt called to go. The second year she felt strongly that she needed to go. So she did."

"When she was pregnant with me?" Confusion twisted her heart. "My mother wrote in her journal that her calling and her pregnancy happened at the same time. God ordained a pregnant woman to go off to a place as unsafe as Guatemala?"

Keith's eyes glistened and she wished she could take back the judgment she'd made in her desperation to know the truth.

"Emerald." His voice was so soft she questioned if he'd really spoken. "Your mother was only supposed to be gone for two weeks. Your father had agreed to that much. But after the two weeks passed, your mother didn't feel released to return home yet."

Emerald struggled to make sense of it, but she couldn't. Maybe her mother's mission had been more important than her unborn child.

"I know what you're thinking," Keith said with a glance. He'd read her mind. "If you'll allow me to finish telling you, I pray that you will feel at peace with the closure you find."

Emerald glanced at Jack and he nodded, as if urging her to listen. She then turned back to Keith.

"Alexandra remained in Guatemala until she gave birth to you prematurely at eight months." He wiped moisture from his eyes. "It was a true miracle that you lived."

"But my mother died." Her throat tightened as he handed her a worn piece of paper.

"But she wrote this before she did."

The words were almost illegible, but after looking closer she made out the letters.

*I have lived out my calling. I have brought a daughter called by God into the world.*

"Elizabeth, my wife, had remained there with your mother, but she had gone to the next village to help and minister there when your mother's labor began. Your mother stayed with a midwife named Rosita. When Elizabeth returned to bring you home, Rosita gave her this letter," he was quiet for a minute, "and she said that a prophet had journeyed a long distance to see you."

"What do you mean?"

"Rosita said there was no way for this man to know who you were or that you'd been born that night. He said God told him you would touch millions of people." Tears escaped his eyes and he didn't bother to wipe at them. "The prophet blessed you, and that blessing will remain with you as long as you live."

Emotion came through the old pastor's voice. "You asked how she could get her pregnancy and her calling at the same time . . . Emerald, *you* were her calling."

"I don't understand."

"Your mother didn't choose a mission trip over you." His warm hand reached forward and cupped her cheek. "God called her to go *for* you, so the prophet could bless you."

The warmth from his hand felt hotter and hotter, until she realized the heat was inside of her pouring out. Tears flowed down onto his hand. She had wondered if Alexandra cared for her at all. Now, for the first time in her life, she felt the impact of her mother's sacrificial love.

# Chapter Thirty-Seven

EMERALD PULLED DENVER TO A STOP beside Silver Bullet and looked up at the high ridge she had climbed the day of her accident.

Jack lifted his reins. "Ready?"

She took a deep breath. "Yes." She nudged her horse up the narrow, grassy path with Jack behind her. When they broke through the tunnel of pines, she gasped. She didn't see the blazing light above her as she did the day of her accident. But it was still beautiful.

Jack swung down from his horse, then helped her to dismount. They stepped carefully to an overhang that offered a breathtaking view of the valley below. Sitting on a large boulder, Emerald stared at the craggy curves of the mountains that swept around the valley, leaving it the bottom of a bowl. A canyon. Her home. Canyon Ridge. She closed her eyes and breathed in the scent of the junipers.

He touched her shoulder. "You all right?"

She smiled. "I've never been better."

She'd been back home for two weeks now. Calving season had kept her and Jack busy with births—but thankfully, no more coyotes.

She looked at him. His face was so gentle, so caring. He never once questioned her sanity.

"Jack, what do you think my calling is?" She'd never voiced the question until now.

His gaze met hers, and his mouth deepened into the smile she'd fell in love with.

"To bring the world to God, one person at a time."

Simple, yet perfect. Jack didn't have the answer; he didn't know any more than what they both had learned from Pastor Keith. Yet, he knew she had come this far.

His eyes engulfed her, igniting a fire inside her stomach. He slid his thumb across her lips. "I know what my calling is."

"What?"

"To spend the rest of my life loving you."

He pulled her to him and kissed her. Gently, he pulled away just enough to look into her eyes. "Emerald, will you be my wife?"

This time, her tears were from joy. "Yes." It had taken both Jack and Caleb to bring her to this point in her life, but only Jack owned her heart.

He cradled the back of her head and kissed her again. She breathed in the scent of his skin and surrendered to the warmth of his body. He felt perfect. Her entire being craved him. She had never felt so complete.

∞

Emerald opened the box from Philadelphia. It was her tote bag, full of clothes and her mother's journal. She took a deep breath as she opened it and leafed through the pages. With the bag containing the journal in her hand, she went outside to the corral where Jack was training a new gelding. She watched him for a moment, thinking about her father. Would Daddy feel differently if he knew the truth about Alexandra?

Jack noticed her and dismounted. He climbed over the fence, grabbed her, and kissed her. "How is my beautiful bride?"

She couldn't stop the giggle. "Missing her husband."

"Your husband might need a rubdown when he comes in."

"Is that so?"

"Yep." He pulled her close and kissed her again.

Finally, she pulled away. "At this rate, you'll never finish!"

She held out her mother's journal for him to see.

He lifted his eyebrows. "So your father sent it to you."

"I guess." She bit her bottom lip.

"What is it, baby?"

She clutched the book to her chest. "I don't know. I just worry about him."

He reached out to her. His hand brought warmth and safety. "Do you think you need to see him? I know it hurt that he missed our wedding."

"I know; it's ridiculous."

"No, it's not."

She dropped the book to her side. "I'm going to go start dinner."

"Don't burn the house down."

"Ha, ha."

∞

Hours later Emerald and Jack finished the meal she'd prepared. She'd followed his recipe for a Denver omelet—or as Tony would say, "Texas omelet."

Jack set down his fork. "As good as any I've made."

"Wait until tomorrow night," she laughed. So far it was all she could cook.

"I guess it's time to teach you how to make something new." He regarded her tenderly. "Not that I wouldn't eat an old shoe if you cooked it, baby."

They laughed and teased as they cleared the table and washed dishes. Afterward, in the living room, he started a fire. She waited for him to play the guitar, but instead he pulled out the Bible.

"I'd like to read something to you. It's from John 14:16-17. *And I will ask the Father, and he will give you another Counselor to be with you forever—the Spirit of truth. The world cannot accept him, because it neither sees him nor knows him. But you know him, for he lives with you and will be in you.*

"The Spirit of Truth is the voice you hear, Emerald. Without the Spirit of Truth, when you came here you would have never listened to what any of us had to say, and we would have been doubtful that God was really at work."

"You're saying I need patience."

"I'm saying you can expect some to reject you because they do not understand. But you can also expect the Holy Spirit to speak to them." He smoothed her hair back from her face and kissed her cheek lightly.

Though fear threatened her, she knew she needed to see her father, so she went to the kitchen and picked up the phone.

∞

Outside the large mansion that had once been her prison, Emerald shivered. Jack's smile comforted her, so she forced one back. She pushed the red buzzer, the gate opened, and they walked through. Emerald felt as if they were light entering into a prison of darkness.

She walked beside her husband, feeling a power surge through her. Her mind told her she was foolish for returning, but she knew she needed to be here.

Molly opened the door and smiled. "Emerald, welcome . . . back." She'd started to say *home*. But this wasn't Emerald's home anymore.

"Thank you." Emerald stepped inside the house that had once haunted her. But the trembling didn't come; the anxiety wasn't there. She felt peace.

Molly led Jack and Emerald to Bradford's study. As they sat

down, Jack leaned in close to her ear and whispered. "God's timing."

He was warning her the visit may not turn out as she hoped—and that it was all right if it didn't. She met his eyes, and smiled.

Bradford entered. "Emerald."

For the first time in her life, she saw her father as a nervous and hesitant man. She kissed his cheek. "Hi, Daddy."

He sat on the chair across from them. "I'm sorry I didn't come to the wedding. I had a patient. . . ."

"It's all right. That's not why I'm here."

"Then, why?"

She smiled. A familiar presence was with her, and she could feel its warmth filling the cold, empty house. Jack quietly slipped from the room, leaving father and daughter alone.

Emerald told Bradford about the voice and the dreams and the presence. How she had found God in a small Western town called Canyon Ridge Mountain. "This was the same God Mother knew. And the love she witnessed, too."

"Some God of love, to take her away and kill her," said Bradford. "You expect me to believe that is perfect love?" His skepticism was obvious, but at least he'd listened.

Emerald reached into her bag and pulled out the flowery journal, then leaned next to him against the arm of his large leather chair.

Surprise rippled across Bradford's face.

"You can't look past my mother's death, Daddy. What about what she left behind?"

"A daughter without a mother? A husband blaming himself for her death because he should have stopped her from going?"

He jumped out of his chair. This was more emotion than he'd ever shown before. Then she remembered that Caleb had told her that anger was hurt misplaced. She looked at him now and realized how deep his pain must be. Bradford felt Alexandra had deserted him; that she had chosen God over him. Emerald had to make him see the truth. So she told him about Alexandra, how hard it had been for her to stay after the rest of the mission had returned to Philadelphia.

"So why did she? Emerald, you can't go by what these people say. I know you want to understand your mother, but you can't justify her leaving us behind."

She opened the journal.

His face registered shock as she flipped through the pages. "Her diary?"

"It's all here, Daddy. Her love for you. Her love for me. She knew I was going to be a girl. She didn't want to leave you . . . but she knew that going on that trip was something she was supposed to do."

She got up from the armchair and took a few steps closer to him. After reading a few pages from the journal, she told him Pastor Keith's story—and about the prophet blessing her.

Tears flowed. "You see, Daddy, Mother loved us both. She loved us so much, that she wanted to share God's mission with us. It was the best gift she had to give you. It hurt her that you didn't want it."

"A gift? More like a thorn in my flesh. She would have been better off putting a knife straight through my heart and twisting it." His eyes blazed. "Is this what you want, Emerald? To justify your mother's past? Is this the same gift you want to give me? This is how you repay me for dedicating my life to you? I can't believe you'd be that cruel."

The words cut deep, and she prayed for strength.

*This is twenty-two years of buried hurt. Be patient.*

Her father was muttering under his breath. "And I didn't reject her work. I let her go." He sounded defensive.

*He's been carrying around guilt for her death all this time.*

"But you didn't support her. You didn't understand, so you withdrew. And that hurt you. You believed she was choosing

God, this trip, over you." Emerald stepped closer and placed her hand on his shoulder.

Moisture in his eyes again, he pulled away. "You make this all sound like a fairytale . . . but it's not. I have lived a lonely life. I know I've had you, but—how can you think you were better off without a mother?" He choked back the tears. "If you had known her you could never think that for a second."

Her mother had been willing to die if it took that for her husband to know God and her daughter to receive her calling.

"My mother wrote in her diary that she felt you were punishing her for feeling like she had to honor her calling. That you told her she was supposed to be with you, not God."

His fist hit the wall. "That's all I need, Alexandra judging me from beyond the grave! She was supposed to be with me. Even religious people say that. 'What God has joined together, let no man put asunder.' That's in the wedding vows."

"But Daddy, that's the point. It wasn't man. It was God who called her. The only man who put you asunder was you, in your choice to not go with her or support her."

Tearing away from her, he crossed the room to lean on the windowsill. Looking into the darkness outside, he remained silent. Just like when she was a child, he used silence and frigidity to keep her in line.

"Are you going to do the same to me, Daddy? Cut me out of your life because I don't follow the path you think I should?"

He flinched, and a sob caught in her throat.

"You don't have to reject something just because you don't understand it. You could try being more open."

"So my mind can became as warped and disillusioned as yours and your mother's?"

*He's afraid.*

"It doesn't have to be this way, Daddy. I know you're afraid you're going to lose me like you did Mother." She placed her hand over his on the windowsill. It was trembling.

"I'm not going to reject you just because you don't understand." She smiled as her tears came harder. "I love you, Daddy. I'm never going to stop caring. I want you to have the peace that I do—the peace Mom did."

Bradford remained silent, absorbed in the blackness the window reflected.

Emerald slipped from the room, and left him contemplating the darkness.

∞

Emerald left her father's estate with her heart aching. But the next morning with Jack at the hotel, she felt peace. Maybe her father hadn't responded to anything she shared. But she had reached out and at least he knew now the truth about Alexandra. Deep down she knew she'd done the right thing.

As she and Jack left the baggage claim at the Denver airport, a woman's voice shouted their names. It was Anna.

*Oh, great.*

Dressed in jeans and a t-shirt Anna reached them in a hurry, struggling with her luggage.

She finally set the bags at her feet and met Emerald's eyes with a smile. "I changed my mind."

"What?"

Emerald felt Jack's hand on her shoulder. He was ready to bolt from the nosy reporter.

"If you want to talk to the media . . . I'd like you to talk to me."

Emerald glanced at Jack. She patted his hand, letting him know she could take the conversation from there. He nodded and left with the luggage.

"Anna, what makes you think I want to talk to the media?"

"Because I think you have a story."

"I don't want to ruin my father."

"You can share your story without ruining anyone."

*Tell her.*

Emerald smiled. "If you can extend your visit past Sunday I think going to church with us is a good place to begin."

∞

A month later Cowboy Church filled with people and Emerald watched her husband on the podium with his guitar.

An older man who never attended church rushed in. He pushed past the congregation, his face red, out of breath. "Emerald!"

She turned around, startled. The voices around her quieted as the man approached her with a large grin on his face. "There's been a woman looking all over town for you."

"What?"

Jack joined her. "Buck, what's going on?"

"Her name is Anna. . . ."

"Anna Lockingdale?"

The man nodded. "She said she interviewed you and now you're all over the headlines."

She and Jack exchanged looks.

"We already know that, Buck."

"Yes," Buck grinned wider, "but did you know they want to interview Emerald on *O'Reilly*? Even Oprah is interested in talking to her."

Emerald gasped, and Jack grabbed her and placed a big kiss on her lips.

Caleb laughed softly. "It's happening, Emerald. God is going to use you to minister to millions of people."

She looked from Caleb to her husband in disbelief.

God was opening the doors. He had chosen her to bring light to a dark and hungry world. To lead a diseased population to a God who healed. He had chosen her to reach out to millions of people. She closed her eyes at the powerful revelation. A chance to share her story, her life, and her Creator with the world. This really was quite exciting!

Jack touched her face. "The calling on your life is most powerful."

∞

Bradford sat in his office, staring blankly at the documents. He'd heard the news earlier; his daughter would be interviewed on national television to share what she called her testimony.

With a light tap on his door, Sidney entered. "It's unbelievable, Sir. It just shows how far the media will go to expose the McGintay family and name." He shook his head.

"Sidney, have you ever believed in God?"

For a moment Sidney gawked, unsure he'd heard correctly. Then he laughed. "Bradford, you can't be serious."

Bradford heard the cold judgmental attitude in his younger colleague's voice. "It's a simple question. Yes or no, without any scientific explanation behind your answer."

"No, of course not."

Bradford slipped his reading glasses back on and returned his attention to the documents before him. He lost awareness of Sidney as he re-read the letter, the sadness deepening within him. He didn't feel like sharing his mood after Sidney's rebuff. Why waste words he'd never spoken in his life?

At some point Sidney left the office, closing the door with a snap.

*Bradford, the Lord has shown me that we will have a daughter, and she will have a powerful calling. When you are unsure of answers, you must stop what you're doing, sit in the quiet, and let Him speak to you, so you can understand what is happening to her.*

*Please forgive my choosing to be here, with the Lord. I will see you again in Heaven,*

*Love, Alexandra*

He thought of all his daughter had said in that brief and painful visit a month ago. She'd glowed with every word. The story of the old prophet factually agreed with what he'd learned twenty-two years ago after sending an investigator to Guatemala to inquire about Alexandra's death. According to the report, villagers said the Holy Spirit had anointed Emerald. At the time, it sounded like some kind of witchcraft. He didn't want any spirit at all touching her.

His heart pounded as he remembered the look on Emerald's face when she'd repeated the story to him—this time with details he'd never heard before.

A chill racked his body until he was trembling again. At least this time it was behind closed doors, without the humiliation of Emerald touching his shaky hand on the windowsill. Her hand had been hot, and had sent an electrical charge through his body.

Feeling as if he was not alone, Bradford checked to see if Sidney had returned. He looked at his wife's letter, and then lifted it to his nose, hoping to once more catch the subtlest hint of her perfume. He'd always done that with her notes and grocery lists. There it was. A trace of the scent, even now. To be sure he wasn't dreaming, he opened his eyes. He felt Alexandra so strongly he could scarcely breathe.

He whispered, "Forgive me, so we can be together."

Focusing on her presence he closed his eyes again, and a revelation struck him. It wasn't Alexandra or her perfume. It was the aura that had been with her the last few years of her life.

Emerald's plea to stop resisting the truth overcame him again. He gritted his teeth in the silence and for the first time tried to let go. His mind quieted, and he let it wash over him: the conviction that God wanted to be with him and loved him as he sat there alone, closed off from the rest of world.

Finally, he picked up his pen and below his wife's words wrote:

> *I forgive you. I'm so sorry, Alexandra. I miss you every moment of every day. But most of all, I miss the feeling of peace and small hope of freedom I had those last few years when you were here. But it wasn't you, was it? I feel it now. If you and Emerald were ever mad, then I must also be. For I, too, feel a presence I cannot explain.*

# Epilogue

SIDNEY STARTLED AWAKE FROM A DEEP sleep. A shriek pierced through the darkness and his cell phone lit on his nightstand. He groaned as he glanced at the clock. Three A.M.

"Greg, what's going on?"

"I know who it was."

It took Sidney a moment to make sense of the statement. "Who took the disk?"

"It was the only other woman who came upstairs that night."

"Who?"

"The woman said she was blond. I was wearing the same color jacket as you that night. I hadn't been wearing a jacket for the last hour—I'd taken it off downstairs."

"What?"

"She thought it was my jacket, Sidney."

"I don't understand."

"It was Anna."

Sidney sat up straight, stunned by Greg's answer. "What are you going to do?"

"Whatever I need to."

"Maybe you can talk to her."

"My entire family and career is at risk here. She could ruin all of us. If my father finds out. . . ."

"Greg, I can't afford to get my hands dirty on this one."

"We never get our hands dirty, my friend. That's what others are paid for."

THE END

## Acknowledgements

A special thanks to my editor, Lisa Wysocky, for all the long hours and valuable input, and to Cool Titles, Cindy and Neville Johnson, for believing in me.

To my agent, David Dunham; to Rita Cosby, who introduced me to David; and to Keith Jeffords for his expert advice.

To my family, who has always encouraged me to be my best. And to my husband Billy, for everything.

## Author Information

Brittany Glynn is a passionate mother who lives with her husband and two young boys in the South. Although family is first, she has a wide range of responsibilities, including writing weekly articles as Nashville's examiner for working moms, being on the Board of Women of Christian Media in Nashville, and serving as the director of public relations for GAP (Girls Against Pornography). She speaks regularly to couples, youth, and parents, and appears on radio across the country.

Learn more at www.brittanyglynn.com or contact Brittany for a speaking engagement at brittany@brittanyglynn.com.

## For Information

on Brittany Glynn's next book,
*Unblemished*, or for information on other
very cool books, please go to:
www.CoolTitles.com.